By the Time You Are Married

Vol. II

Second Generation Americans

1933 - 1944

Susan Linden Emde

Copyright © 2021 Susan Linden Emde

All rights reserved. All names, places, characters,
organizations, and incidents are either products
of the author's imagination or used fictitiously.
ISBN: 9798723777576

DEDICATION

To my parents and grandparents,
and to the thousands of Swedish families who emigrated to
America in the late 19th and early 20th centuries
to find prosperity and live the American dream.

.

ACKNOWLEDGMENTS

Thank you, as always, to my husband and children for their patience and support and to my parents and grandparents, who told me so many fascinating stories about their lives,
about leaving the old country and emigrating from Sweden to America to find a better life.
Special thanks to my Aunt Ramona, now in her nineties, who continues to tell me stories about growing up in Brooklyn during the Great Depression and World War II. This book was inspired by those stories but is, nonetheless, a work of fiction.

PROLOGUE
Background from
By the Time You Are Married, Vol. 1

Mimi Pamelia Antoinette Lindín has come a long way since her courageous trip to America from Sweden in 1911, seventeen years old, alone and with only a few words of English. She learned those basic expressions on the ship with the help of Sven, a likable young fellow immigrant. At Ellis Island, the two young friends were separated, and Sven was sent back to Sweden. To Mimi's great surprise, he would turn up again many years later to play an important role in her life.

She has accomplished what she set out to do. She brought five of her six younger siblings, Lambert, Walter, Svea, Johan Bernhard, and Hans to the United States and helped them get settled in their new country. One sister, Saga, stayed in Sweden to care for their parents, but the other, Svea, took the big leap and started out doing the kind of work in the household of a wealthy New York family that was the norm for female immigrants, just as Mimi herself had done in Rochester. Svea soon left that work, however, to marry another fellow immigrant, August, who was wholeheartedly welcomed into the family.

Quite amazingly, all of the brothers – who had done very different work in Sweden, anything from lumberyard or factory labor to working for the local blacksmith – followed Mimi's suggestions and trained as hairdressers so that she soon was able to establish a salon in Brooklyn with them. There had been some surprising twists along the way, but the biggest obstacle for success in the hair salon was the unexpected financial downturn of the Great Depression and the ongoing recession.

The Björkman family is now well established in their house in Brooklyn's Park Slope. Bertha and Frank have successfully weathered the first third of the 20th Century: WWI, the 1918 Spanish Flu Pandemic, and Prohibition Times. As a capable engineer and carpenter with a reliable job at American Machine and Foundry (later known as AMF, Inc.), Frank did not need to join the military when the war started. Nor, when the Depression began, did he think of returning to vaudeville or burlesque to make extra money the way he had before he married Bertha. Nonetheless, being a man of many talents and great ingenuity, he found a way to supplement his income and get through the Prohibition era profitably, by brewing his own brand of liquor and peddling it from the kitchen of the house on Park Place. (That undertaking was so successful that he was able to invest and build a little summer house in Connecticut.)

Bertha protested and put an end to that business, however, when a late addition to the family arrived – the twins were already sixteen years old and Helen was a year older. She insisted it was too dangerous with a baby in the house.

Everyone had heard radio reports of the mafia bosses shooting each other in the streets. The three older daughters, Helen, Signe, and Anna have grown up and are working office jobs in the city at the time when we pick up the story again. After the two Swedish immigrant families, the Björkmans and the Lindíns (who have changed their names to Bjorkman and Linden since accent marks only caused complications in the United States) got to know each other in the Swedish Club, one of the twins, Anna, and Mimi's brother Johan, now using his middle name Bernhard, became sweethearts. Their relationship deepened when Bernhard came back from a trip to the old country.

The youngest of the Björkman girls, the late addition to the family, is Ramona, Mona for short, who will soon start going to school.

1

Brooklyn, New York

Ramona

One hot and muggy Friday afternoon in mid-August of the year 1934, Mona. who was six years old now, had been sitting in the hall at the bottom of the stairs for what seemed to her a terribly long time, waiting for something, anything, to happen. She was bored. She had thick, curly, light blond hair and her father's round blue eyes. She was a pretty child and the family doted on her. Nevertheless, it was perfectly natural that she was not always completely contented with her young life, not always happy. This afternoon, for instance, she was not. None of her friends were home and no one in her family wanted to play jacks or go for a walk with her and Prince. She had been wanting to take Prince, the Bjorkmans' dog, for a walk by herself for a long time. They, the people in the grown-up world she lived in, told her she was too young, too little. Lately she had protested, "But I'm already starting school, next month!" Even that did not work.

Sometimes she wondered if it was worth the bother, having three sisters who all had at least a sixteen-year head start on her in life. (They did give her nice presents though, especially Signe. But, when it came down to it, she would much rather they were her age, and she could play with them.) She had serious doubts that she would ever catch up with them and asked her father, who had just come home from work, if she would be as big as her sisters in sixteen years. He told her, "Yes, probably earlier than that. And you may be even bigger, taller than they are. They say children are getting bigger with every new generation!"

Sometimes she wondered if it was worth the bother, having three sisters who all had at least a sixteen-year head start on her in life. (They did give her nice presents though, especially Signe. But, when it came down to it, she would much rather they were her age, and she could play with them.) She had serious doubts that she would ever catch up with them and asked her father, who had just come home from work, if she would be as big as her sisters in sixteen years. He told her, "Yes, probably earlier than that. And you may be even bigger, taller than they are. They say children are getting bigger with every new generation!"

He was surprised to see that that did not please her. She did not want to be bigger. Just the same size and equally as grown up. "Don't you know how big I will be?" she asked, astonished, her blue eyes, already like saucers, widening.

"No. We'll just have to wait and see."

He knew everything else, why didn't he know that? She did not bother asking him if she could take Prince, their big German shepherd, out alone. She already knew the answer to that question.

Mona followed her father glumly down the stairs to the kitchen where – compared with the rest of the house – it was pleasantly cool this time of year. The family was assembled there, everyone, that is, except Helen. Helen had eloped and caused a lot of commotion in January. Mona had not been told much about what had happened back then, but now she had her suspicions that her other sisters might be doing the same thing someday, maybe soon.

The conversation that her mother and sisters had been having ceased abruptly when Mona and her father reached the bottom of the stairs.

Frank asked, "Can I get a cup of coffee here?"

"Of course, Dear. How was your day?" Bertha asked as she stood up and got the percolator from the stove. As she took another cup from the cupboard, she looked over to her youngest daughter and said, "Mona, do you want a glass of milk?"

Mona shook her head.

"Well then, go upstairs now and play for a while. We have something we have to talk about here. It's not meant for your ears."

Mona stomped a bit as she climbed the stairs. How could they drink hot coffee on a day like this? In the hall, lying on the carpet between the stairs and the front door, was Prince, half asleep, his head resting between his paws. He barely opened one eye for a second and shut it again. This was not someone who could take him out for a walk. Mona sat down next to him, putting her arm around him, and wishing he could understand what she was unhappy about. She was feeling lonely, especially since her cousin Elsie, Faster Emma's granddaughter, was away on a trip and would not be back for a long time. Mona desperately needed someone to play with.

Then, a harmless idea popped into her head when she noticed the leash hanging on the hook next to the door. She would just attach it to Prince's collar and pretend they were going for a walk, maybe up the stairs to her room and back down again. But when she connected the leash, Prince jumped up in surprised anticipation, wagging his tail and then pulling toward the door. He was convinced he would be going out with Mona after all.

"Well, why not?" Mona thought to herself, "I've led Prince before, many times. I'll just have to prove to them that I can do it by myself!"

Quietly she slipped out the front door. Prince immediately bolted down the stairs ahead of her. Luckily, she was not surprised by this – he always raced down the steps toward the gate – and wisely let go of the leash, knowing that he could not get any farther than the gate. This was the first test of her dog-walking ability and she was proud of herself. She had not let him pull her stumbling down the steep steps, had she? When she reached the bottom step, she scolded him in a whisper, picked up the leash, and gripped it tightly as they went out the gate. The gate creaked wearily, a result of long years of service as a makeshift plaything for all of the Bjorkman daughters. She managed to close it without being heard and decided she would not go far, just to the corner and back. No one would even notice that she was gone until she got back and rang the bell. Then they would surely be impressed, she thought, proudly anticipating her triumphant return.

In the kitchen, Frank was stirring the sugar in his second cup of coffee. "I can't say I'm surprised," he said. "Not that it matters. What could it matter if the baby is coming a little earlier than we expected? She's married, isn't she?

"No, of course that doesn't matter. I just wish the father was someone else. He's not a good husband and he won't be a good father either."

"Maybe he'll shape up when the baby comes. A lot of men do. I certainly felt different about my responsibilities when I learned that Helen was on her way."

Bertha looked at her husband, raising one eyebrow slightly. Signe and Anna did not notice this exchange. They were both experiencing a confusion of emotions, looking forward to having a niece or nephew, but neither one enthusiastic about their sister's choice of husband. In fact, they were worried about her, knowing more than their parents about their brother-in-law's behavior toward his young wife.

"So, are you going over to stay with Helen, or is she coming here? Where does she plan to have her baby?"

"She hasn't even been to see a doctor yet, Frank! I want her to come here as soon as possible and see my doctor at Shore Road Hospital. But she says that won't be good for her marriage…"

Frank interrupted saying, "Well, tell her she's welcome here. The rest is all women's talk…And you'll do what you want anyway." He had finished his coffee and was getting up from the table when they heard a dog barking outside.

"That sounds like Prince," said Signe." She stood up and went to the kitchen door. "That *is* Prince. What's he doing outside?" Through the small window in the door, she could just make out their dog, who was standing and barking at the gate, "How did he get out?" She knew her father was not a careless person; he would never have let the dog out when he came in. There was only one other person who could have done it.

Anna, thinking the same thing, went out into the hall and called up the stairs, "Mona! Did you let Prince out?... Mona!"

Anna went up the stairs, immediately followed by her mother, both calling out as they climbed the steps. Frank joined Signe, who had unlocked the kitchen door with the key that was always left in the lock. They went out together and up the four or five steps that led to the gate. There they let Prince, who was panting, wagging his tail, and trailing his leash behind him, into the front yard. Then Bertha came to the front door and said in an alarmed voice, "She's not in the house!

Anna confirmed this and all four went out the gate, looking up and down the street both ways. There was no sign of Mona. Now Frank was getting worried as well and, loosening his tie and wishing he had a short-sleeved shirt on instead of the one he had worn to the office, he set off along the hot pavement in the direction he always went when he and Mona took Prince out, toward Prospect Park. He did not have to go far, however, before he saw Mona come trudging around the corner and up Park Place, hanging her head, and looking utterly dejected. As she came closer, he noticed both of her knees were scraped and bleeding. When she finally reached the house, he could see tears as well. He decided not to scold her yet, he simply asked in his sternest voice, "Is there any explanation for this?"

Mona just shook her head and mumbled, "I'm sorry." After a moment, however, she defended herself, saying, "I would have done fine with Prince if that other dog hadn't turned up! I only wanted to go to the corner, but..."

"No excuses, Mona," Frank said. "Now you know why we don't want you to walk him alone, right? That's what happens when little girls don't listen to their parents."
"Come with me, Ramona, I want to have a look at your knees," said Bertha, taking her by the hand and leading her into the house. Bertha didn't scold at all either, instead she soothingly applied the old panacea, *"Det går bort, det går bort när du ska gifta sig..."* (That will go away, it will be gone by the time you are married...") as they went up the steps. She had no doubt that the iodine would make a lasting impression on her daughter without her having to reprimand her as well.

Little Ronny

One month later, Mona did not want to go to school in the morning. She had been looking forward to school for so long and enjoyed her first week so much that no one could understand her change of attitude. She was upstairs in her room, refusing to come down to breakfast.

"I know she likes her teacher," said Bertha, "That can't be the reason."

"She just has to go to school and that's that!" Frank would have liked to apply more stringent measures, but he had left the disciplining and general upbringing of his daughters to his wife all these years and didn't want to start playing the role of a strict father with his fourth. He shrugged, "You, all of you, are spoiling her, so it's no wonder."

"I don't spoil her," Bertha threw back at him, "But the twins do, I have to admit. And they're always giving her presents."

Anna answered, "It's not my fault. Signe gives her all those presents, too many."

"I guess I can give her all the presents I want. It's my money I'm spending, isn't it?" Signe was indignant. When had generosity become a sin?

The twins stood up; it was getting late. They had to catch the subway to Manhattan and go to work.

"I'll go upstairs and see if I can persuade Mona to get ready for school. I want to check and see if Ronny is still asleep, too," said Helen, who was sitting at the table. Her long blond hair tied back severely in a low bun, she was thin, almost skinny, and looked more than a year older than her twin sisters. She had had her baby, a little boy, and was staying with her parents for the first month or two. There were so many things she needed for the baby that she and her husband just could not afford yet. Bertha and Faster Emma were knitting little sweaters, booties and bonnets and sewing baby bed clothes and diapers on one of Uncle David's sewing machines. Bertha wished she had not gotten rid of all of Mona's baby clothes only four years before, when her youngest child turned two, but that was what she had done. Superstition might have played a substantial role in that decision. In any case, she had wanted it very clear that she wasn't having any more babies and had, since then, given away everything as soon as Mona had outgrown it.

A few minutes later, Bertha had sent Frank off to work with the promise that she would "of course" get Mona to school on time. She would have to hurry. She left the breakfast dishes in the sink – she or Helen could do them later – and climbed the stairs to Mona's room. She thought to herself, "I wish Frank had been just as determined to give the twins a good education." The story of how their schooling had been cut short still needled her. "Why didn't I insist that they finish school instead of just wanting to avoid arguments with Frank? Why was I such a coward?" It was too late for that now, but at least Mona would finish school. There was no doubt about that.

When Bertha opened the door to Mona's room, her youngest daughter was not there. Her pajamas were lying on the bed, so at least she must be dressed. Then Bertha started up the next flight of stairs to the room that Helen and her baby were staying in, the room Bertha had not rented out for the past six months and which now, luckily, was vacant for Helen to take "refuge" in. As far as she was concerned, Helen and the baby could stay as long as they wanted. In fact, she wished Helen would never go back to her husband but was wise enough to leave that decision to her daughter. Halfway up, she could hear Helen talking in a gently soothing voice to Mona. As she reached the top of the stairs, she heard Helen say, "Don't worry. We're not leaving here for a while yet. ...Of course, we will still be here when you get back from school. You know what? When you get home you can help me change him, okay? But you do have to go to school today."

Mona came running out of Helen's room, blue eyes aglow, almost colliding with her mother. She shouted, "Mamma, I'm going to change Ronny's diapers when I get home from school. We have to hurry now."

"Shhh! You'll wake Ronny," said Bertha, shaking and nodding her head at the same time and thinking, "Of course. I should have known that's why she didn't want to go to school today. Now she'll want to hurry to school so she can hurry home again. How is she going to pay attention to the teacher?" As they hurried down the stairs, they could hear little Ronny begin to whimper and then break into his desperately hungry newborn's wail.

2

A few months later, in early December, Helen had just packed her belongings, taken her little son, and gone back to her husband that morning. In the quiet that seemed to take over the house immediately, her mother Bertha wondered how she could get a feeling for Christmas going now that Helen and Ronny were gone, leaving a big gaping void not only on the third floor. With Mona going to school every day and the rest of her family going to work, she was almost surprised that she did not feel relieved to have more time to get her own housework done. No, instead she wondered if life in the big house on Park Place could become too quiet. She went to the pantry to look for her traditional *Jul* candlesticks, and other Christmas knickknacks. Each year she took out the carved wooden candlesticks, colorfully painted with funny Swedish *jultomtar* (Christmas gnomes), that she and Frank had brought back from their trip to Sweden years before and displayed them in the hall and the front parlor. As she put the biggest and most elaborate, five-branched candlestick on the table in front of the parlor window, she thought about the last Christmas and the year that had passed so quickly. She sat down in the chair next to the window for a moment to think back.

A full year had now passed since Bernhard first came back from his trip to Sweden. He and Anna had been happily reunited in time for Christmas, their first Christmas together. He had brought back a set of little silver souvenir spoons with "Jönköping", the name of his hometown in Småland, and a Swedish flag enameled onto the bowl of each spoon and a colorful traditional Swedish folklore scarf that he gave her as Christmas presents. Anna accepted these somewhat impersonal little gifts graciously as proof that he had not forgotten her while he was gone and stowed them away carefully in her cedar hope chest. Since then, their lives had continued much the same, on a dependably happy but not especially exciting level, both working hard during the week and spending most of their free time together. They met on weekends, often out in the Bjorkmans' summer house in Connecticut, where Anna's family spent as much time as possible. That Anna and Bernhard were a couple was taken for granted by all. Their relationship had become very stable, neither one went out with anyone else and everyone was expecting them to get officially engaged and be married, presumably sometime soon. But, since everyone seemed happy enough as it was, Bernhard did not feel the need to change anything. Anna would, of course, never bring up the subject that was in the back of her mind half of the time. Bertha and Frank were glad the way things were. They did not want the rest of their daughters hurrying into marriage the way Helen had done, especially since the prospects for Helen's happiness still looked quite bleak.

Throughout the spring and the summer, Signe's boyfriend Richard helped Frank with house improvements while Bernhard was very willing to help with more "agricultural" projects. He took a hoe to the vegetable patch regularly, picked strawberries and tomatoes, harvested fruit from the trees and dug up potatoes, all according to season, much to Frank's satisfaction and often causing Anna embarrassment. When she complained that Bernhard, and just about everyone else who came to visit, was being used as an unpaid workforce, Bernhard just laughed, saying he needed some kind of work to balance out the hours when he stood in one spot doing ladies' hair, or sitting in the shop kitchen waiting for clients. The exercise in the gym once a week was not enough for him. Besides, he loved being away from the city, out in the country and the fresh air.

This past year there were more summer gatherings than ever before at the Bjorkmans' place on Moose Hill. Now that they had been spending more time in Connecticut, they had good friends in Guilford, some of whom joined in the gatherings. Especially often a part of the group were the Seagrens, also immigrants from Sweden, whom they had met at the Swedish Club. When they too bought a house in Guilford, the wife, Gunhill, had become a close friend of Bertha's. In fact, Bertha had named her youngest daughter Ramona Gunhill after the heroine of the novel "Ramona" and her friend.

Bernhard often brought along a friend named John Gare. He was the musician who, although not a Swede, had caught Frank's attention the year before when playing with the band at the Swedish Club. Frank had hopes that John might teach him to play the banjo or the mandolin, as if he did not have enough interests, skills, and talents already. A photograph of John sitting playing his banjo in the sun, a big white handkerchief knotted at the corners and draped over his head, his friendly dark eyes smiling, made its way into the family album along with others of Frank with his accordion and many of the long table of guests under the trees. On those occasions the music added greatly to the group's enjoyment, so that no one wanted the weekend get-togethers to end. When evening came there was often talk of what a shame it was that the summer daylight hours did not last as long in Connecticut as they did in Sweden, where in *midsommar* it only got dark for a few hours each night. So,

Frank put lanterns on the table and the Bjorkmans and their friends sat together late into the night. For some reason or other, Frank never did learn to play more than a few chords on the banjo, although he later in life taught himself to play the organ. Eventually, he bought a small electric organ that he kept and played at home until the end of his life.

The summer cemented Bernhard's relationship with Anna's family as well as with Anna. Only Signe knew that Anna had been disappointed when the tiny birthday present she received from Bernhard in July turned out to be a small golden pin and not what she had expected. Bernhard never even noticed that she spent a couple of days after her birthday trying to be slightly aloof toward him. Then she forgot about it, disliking her own pettiness, and realizing that there had been no intention to affront her on Bernhard's part. It was, after all, a very pretty pin. But in that short phase of negative feelings, she did declare she was no longer going to the gym, saying she did not have time, although the truth of the matter was that she had just never felt like it was something she was meant to do. She was glad for any excuse – at least to herself – to stop participating. Bernhard may have been disappointed but had already begun to accept the fact that his girlfriend was not in any way interested in sports. So, Anna became an enthusiastic and avid spectator and enjoyed the social events that the gym club offered. In all other respects, the Bjorkmans' life went on pretty much as usual.

Meanwhile, as the financial depression dragged on, bigger changes had been taking place in the Linden family. Business in the shop had not been forced to close and was slowly, very slowly, re-establishing itself. Everyone was thankful for that, but there had been differences of opinion concerning the way in which the shop should be run.

Indirectly, as a result of these differences, Lambert, who, strangely enough, had never liked the idea of marriage, was happily married and living in back of the beauty parlor with Agnes. Walter had opted out of the family business, found new employment, and after marrying Ingrid, moved with her to Providence, Rhode Island, close to where Svea and August lived with their new baby girl. Bernhard had moved into Mimi's basement apartment with Hans when Mimi moved out. Of all these changes, by far the biggest and most unexpected had taken place in Mimi's life. Anna would soon find out why.

.

3

Bernhard, Anna, and Mona were standing in the tiny front garden of the house on Park Place at the bottom of the steps that led up to the front door, laughing and fooling around, stomping the snow from their shoes, and trying to brush off the stubborn traces of a snowball fight from their overcoats. Mona's coat was thoroughly caked with snow on the back after making the imprints of half a dozen angels on the hill. They had just come back from walking Prince in the park, where he had made them laugh as he tore up and down the snow-covered slopes, inspiring them to their own antics. Christmas was only a week away and the snow had arrived just in time. That had not kept Mona from saying for the third time in the last five minutes how she would love a pair of roller skates for Christmas "because the snow will melt away again soon."

Inside the house, when they had all shed their coats, Mona went up to her room, declaring indignantly that of course she was able to take care of herself without Anna's help. She promised to change into drier clothes while Anna and Bernhard went downstairs to the kitchen, looking for Bertha and some cups of hot coffee from the pot that, as always, was standing on the back burner of the stove. There was no one in the steamy warm kitchen, so Bertha was probably upstairs somewhere or had gone out shopping.

As they sat down at the table, cradling the hot cups in their cold hands, Bernhard thought Anna looked as if she might have gained some weight. She looked more rounded out than she had even last week, almost plump. He liked her rosy cheeks and bright blue eyes. She was thinking he had completely lost every trace of the country bumpkin he had seemed to her to be at times when they first met. Thank God he could not read her mind! Now he looked absolutely handsome, in her opinion – what did they say was the ideal most women were attracted to? Tall, dark, and handsome? Yes, most definitely, the description fit. She smiled dreamily at him over her cup. He smiled back.

After a few moments of silence, she asked him, "Have you heard from Mimi? How is she?"

"She's okay," he answered.

"You know, Bernhard, you haven't really told me what happened to make her go away so suddenly. I didn't even have a chance to say goodbye!"

He did not answer immediately. Then, reluctantly he said, "She likes Rochester and never really got used to the city. And, of course, there were some things we couldn't agree on about the shop. For one thing, it was not doing well enough to support all of us."

Anna did not want to pry, but she did not think the shop was the real reason for Mimi's quick disappearance. She waited to see if he wanted to tell her more.

"One morning Hans said he wanted to do something entirely different. Said he didn't know how he had ended up hairdressing. And that got us all started. We didn't want to criticize Mimi, but it became clear to us all that it wasn't what we ever had had any real inclination to do. It was her project, not ours. It didn't even help matters when Lambert and I both tried to reassure her that we were perfectly happy being hairdressers, but that we just might never have thought of it on our own. Mimi was depressed anyway, what with Sven disappointing her and all that."

"But what about Sven? I thought they were a perfect couple. What happened? Do you know where he is?"

"Yes, I do. He's gone back to Sweden. He has a sister in Stockholm."

"How could that happen?"

Anna shuddered, feeling a real chill, although it was warm and cozy in the kitchen.

"I don't mean our family, Anna, she didn't leave to get away from us. Mimi would have stayed and helped us clear any problems with the shop. It was Sven's fault. She left to get away from him."

"But why?"

Bernhard looked at Anna in disbelief.

"You must have noticed that Sven had a drinking problem."

"Of course, I know that. But a lot of men we know have a hard time turning down a drink. He was trying to stop, wasn't he?"

Bernhard was wondering how to change the subject. He did not want to talk about it. He liked Sven too, and was not completely convinced that Mimi had made the right decision. But his loyalty to Mimi would never allow him to criticize her.

"You don't know that while we were in Hemlock Hedges last year with the gym club, he went on a binge – isn't that what they call it? – and made a mess of their apartment. Lambert and Walter tried to help him cover up, but somehow Mimi found out. The window in the door was broken and they couldn't replace it before she got back. Anyway, to make a long story short, Mimi made him swear that he would never touch alcohol again."

Anna looked up from examining the traces of coffee grounds at the bottom of her cup. She had been trying to decide if she saw a lop-sided heart or a rather plump small-headed chicken. She waited again for Bernhard to go on but when he did not, she asked, "And did he?"

"Did he what?"

"Did he start drinking again? I've never seen him take a drink."

"Do you remember that weekend when he and Mimi were supposed to come out to your parents' house in Connecticut and didn't show up?"

"That was in the summer, the middle of the summer."

"Well, it seems someone gave Sven a bottle of wine for doing such a good job fixing some old generator and he didn't want to be ungrateful... He never made it home with that bottle. Stopped off somewhere and didn't turn up until two days later. Mimi was beside herself with worry. And that turned into fury when he finally did show up."

"But he managed to keep off it for about ten months then. Surely with a little help he could get off the habit completely, don't you think so?"

"He begged and pleaded with Mimi, but when she makes up her mind about something, there's no influencing her. Honestly, we all tried."

It was getting warm in the kitchen. Bernhard pulled his turtleneck sweater off over his head and watched Anna as she took off a cardigan. He noticed that there was another one under that.

"Anna,... don't think badly of Mimi. She had an awful experience with a drinker many years ago in Sweden and I guess you could say she's allergic to them."

"Don't worry, you know how much I admire your sister and what she did for all of you. I think she's amazing, such a strong woman. It just seemed strange, because they seemed the perfect couple and the story of how they finally found each other...You know, it was really romantic!"

Just then Bertha came bustling in the door and into the kitchen. She had been shopping and had two big paper bags of groceries that Bernhard hurried to take out of her hands. "*Tack ska du ha*, Bernhard!" (Thanks, Bernhard!) she said smiling, "*Det är riktigt kallt idag!*" (It is really cold today!) and went back upstairs to take off her coat and hat.

When she came back into the kitchen, Bernhard was watching Anna take off another sweater. When he saw that there was still another underneath, he burst out laughing and said, "How many layers of clothes have you got on, Anna?"

Bertha laughed, too, saying, "You don't have to worry about Anna keeping herself warm, Bernhard! She won't risk catching a cold just to look pretty."

"That was the last one I'm taking off, Bernhard. And I wasn't any too warm on our walk either!" Anna explained, as her cheeks slowly got even redder than they had been when they first came in from their walk.

"Well, I'm glad of that," Bernhard said. "I was worried there would be nothing left of you. And just a few minutes ago I thought you were getting fat! No, I didn't really think that... And…," He cleared his throat, "You couldn't look prettier, anyway!" The look in his eye made this remark very convincing.

Even more embarrassed but pleased and laughing, Anna got up from the table. She left them saying, "I'll see if Mona has changed into dry clothes," and escaped up the stairs. Bertha put the groceries away and then turned to look at Bernhard.

"*Pår tår*, Bernhard?" ("More coffee?") Bertha asked before she poured herself a cup.

"*Nej tack*, Mrs. Björkman," ("No, thanks.") "I've had two cups and that's enough for me."

Still smiling, Bertha sat down at the table with her cup. She wondered why Bernhard never called her Fru Björkman. Nothing was said for a moment.

Then, more or less just to break the silence, Bernhard asked a question for which Bertha immediately felt she had the proper answer. In Swedish he said that he had not yet bought a Christmas present for Anna. He wanted to know if she had any suggestions.

Bertha trusted her instincts and said, without more than

a moment's hesitation, "For goodness sakes! Get the girl a ring, Bernhard!"

At first Bernhard was astonished by her candid answer and did not know what to say. He searched the bottom of his empty cup like Anna had a few minutes before. Then, suddenly he looked up, smiled broadly, and said, as if it would never have occurred to him, "What a good idea! Of course!" It was as if the entire burden of the decision and its consequences had been taken off his shoulders, he was completely happy and confident that it was right although he could not really understand it himself. He felt immensely grateful to Anna's mother and said, "Thank you, Mrs. Björkman!" Both were laughing again as Anna came back down the stairs and into the kitchen. When she asked what they were laughing about, they exchanged a conspiratorial smile and left her in suspense.

That evening there was a lot of laughter in the kitchen. Frank and Bernhard made *glögg* (mulled wine) together while Anna and Signe made *spritz* cookies with Mona. Bertha sat and watched her kitchen being turned into a disaster zone. She did not mind. The *glögg* had to be tasted again and again to see if there was enough cinnamon or too much cardamom, or vice versa. The remaining almonds were counted and found to be sufficient for another bottle of wine. It would be needed since the repeated tasting had already cut the first supply by half. Between the tears of laughter, unnoticed by the others, real tears came to Anna's eyes when she thought of Sven for a moment and how it would have been for him. He would not even have been able to enjoy taking part in their carefree evening. She decided she must nevertheless try to understand Mimi's situation.

4

Connecticut, June 1935

Five months later, it was a warm Saturday afternoon. Anna had escaped to the gazebo with a book while. Signe and Mona were playing checkers at the table under the trees, where the sunlight broke through in patches that came and went with each passing cloud. Prince was lying on the ground next to them, his tail, twitching to ward off flies, sent up little smoke signals of dust. Anna was glad for some time alone; she did not mind that only two could play checkers at once. All three sisters had their bathing suits on under their summer clothes and were waiting for Bernhard to arrive. They were going to Sachem's Head, their favorite beach.

Anna's book, a volume of poems by Robert Frost, was lying on the table in front of her. She had just reread her favorite poem and was thinking she should try to memorize it. But she could not concentrate. Maybe it would be easier if the woods around her had been full of snow, but they were not. On the contrary, it was a very warm day.

She looked down at the ring on her finger, still amazed at

the size of the diamond. It was not what could be called a rock, but it certainly was bigger than she would have expected. She did not know that Bernhard would be paying it off in installments for the rest of the year. She had to laugh when she thought about Christmas Eve again and the way he had wrapped her package. He had used that old trick of putting the ring in its tiny blue velvet-covered case from the jewelry store into a big carton stuffed with newspaper. And she had fallen for it! At first she had braced herself for a disappointment, as she was meant to do, and then she had, of course, been surprised and thrilled. She did laughingly threaten to hit Bernhard over the head with the big empty cardboard box for a moment, but then, unable to take her eyes off the ring once it was on her finger, dropped the box and decided to go on being the sweet, demure blond he was more used to. Maybe it was not the most romantic way for him to ask for her hand in marriage, but that did not matter to her anymore. She was already learning that life did not always proceed along the expected paths. If it did, it would probably be boring, she told herself.

Years later Anna would not only know life better, but also her husband and the Linden family. For one thing, she would find out how they loved surprises. Like her engagement ring hidden in deceptive packaging, they took every opportunity to spring unannounced out of each other's closets – with the help of a cooperative family member – or at least knock unexpectedly at the front door when they were supposed to be at the other end of the world somewhere. Laughing and slapping each other on the back, they acted like a gang of little boys who had vowed to go through thick and thin together. Despite frequent and even fierce "discussions" about every possible topic, in which each brother defended his respective opinion vigorously and stubbornly, they knew they could depend on each other's affection and loyalty to the death.

By the Time You Are Married

When Bernhard arrived, Bertha came out of the house with a basket of sandwiches. Sometimes she went with them to the beach but today she had decided to stay at home. She would be making *blåbäskräm* (blueberry pudding) with the wild berries she had picked with her daughters in the woods that morning. She watched as they climbed into Bernhard's car, an old Chevrolet, with towels, blankets, and the sandwiches. Then, shouting, "*Venta et ögenblick!*" (Wait a moment!) she ran back into the house for the thermos of coffee and the bottle of apple juice that she had forgotten to put in the basket. As the car drove off down the dirt road, Mona waved goodbye to her mother through the small back window of the car. Bertha stood waving back to her and watched as the car turned onto Moose Hill Road. From there they would drive down to Sachem's Head Road and then on to Vineyard Point. The trip to the beach did not take more than twenty minutes.

At the coast, a pleasant breeze was blowing in from the Sound. They found a nice spot on the beach where there were not too many people. Signe and Anna spread the blankets and stretched out in the sun, both ready to fall asleep. Next to them, Mona sat in the warm sand, digging with her hands, and letting handfuls of sand run through her fingers to form mounds and valleys and wondering if her sisters were going to sleep all afternoon. They were ignoring her pleas to go into the water with her.

Bernhard, who had not lost any time getting into the water, was suddenly standing dripping wet next to the sisters. "Come on, girls! Anna, the water is wonderful! It's not cold at all. Maybe a little too warm even. This time you have to go in, you can't just lie there all afternoon like you did the last couple of times when we've been here. No excuses!"

"I'll go in with you, Bernhard," said Mona.

"Okay, but Anna has to go in, too."

Anna mumbled half asleep, "I'll come in a little later. It's so nice here in the sun, let me just lie here for a while. I'll come in to cool off later."

"All right, but I'll hold you to your word!"

A few minutes later Mona had had enough and came back to grab a towel and dry off. "Bernhard is waiting for you in the water, Anna," she told her sister.

Signe was fast asleep and snoring softly. Groaning, Anna pulled herself up and saw Bernhard standing there smiling at her from the edge of the water. "He really wants me to do this," she thought to herself. "I might as well get it over with. Maybe the water really is warm today." She wondered if the black knit bathing suit would look as nice wet as it did dry; she had never been in the water with it before. In fact, Bernhard had never seen her wet before. Until now she had always managed to avoid going into the water. Not just because she did not want to get wet, but because she was embarrassed that she did not know how to swim! Why didn't she? Signe had learned years ago, why hadn't she?

Then Anna stands up and walks somewhat reluctantly down to the water, but with Bernhard smiling at her so encouragingly, she cannot refuse him. There are no waves, just a gentle roll that mirrors the light from above dazzlingly.

She gets her feet wet, testing the temperature. Then Bernhard takes her by the hand and leads her into the shallow first few yards. She is thinking, "Thank goodness it isn't as cold as I expected and at least there aren't any waves." Nonetheless she shivers as the water rises up her legs and begins to wet her bathing suit. They continue walking slowly but steadily straight out toward the deeper water. When it reaches her waistline, she sucks in her tummy and tries hesitatingly to pull back. She feels it is time for Bernhard to let go of her hand, but he is holding it so firmly and gently, and she does not want to tear it away.

"Bernhard," she says in a soft voice, "Bernhard, I

can't..."

He goes on smiling and calmly leading her as the water reaches the top of her bathing suit and finally laps over her shoulders. Then, their eyes still locked, Anna's big as saucers, he lets go of her hand and says, "And now we swim."

And, for the first time in her life, Anna swam. She held her head up high, leaned forward into the water, stretched her arms forward and felt her toes leave the sandy ground. She was amazed to find herself so buoyant as she instinctively paddled with her arms and tread with her feet. She went in a small half-circle and turned back toward shore, wondering if Bernhard had hypnotized her. When her feet reached down to find the ground again, she stood and looked back at Bernhard astonished.

He laughed saying, "Anyone can swim! I know you thought you couldn't but now you know you can. We'll have to work on your style though," he laughed a bit harder at that but then became serious. "And you have to learn to float. Come on, let's give it a try. Floating is easier than swimming. You just have to relax."

Anna let him pick her up in his arms and support her on the gently undulating surface of the water. Under the circumstances, she found it not unpleasant and certainly not very difficult to float. In fact, it seemed ridiculously easy. The salt water boosted her legs and body up as soon as she followed Bernhard's instructions to put her head back and stick her chin up into the air. She wished just for a moment that she did not have to get her hair wet and wondered again at Bernhard's ability to get her to do things she had no desire to do. Whatever the reason, it had something to do with the intense look in his eyes and some kind of magic, or was it really hypnotism? Bernhard for his part was wrestling with mental pictures that had him carrying Anna off to a secluded place behind the sand dunes.

After a few more minutes of successful paddling and floating, they left the water and walked, dripping wet and hand in hand over to Signe and Mona, who were sitting on the smooth flat rocks by the water's edge, basking in the sun. Bernhard told Anna they did not need to dry off, that the salt water was good for her.

Signe grinned, and Mona, who had been watching Anna and Bernhard, frowned, and said, "I thought you didn't know how to swim, Anna!".

Then she looked at Bernhard, shrugging and shaking her very blond curls in disbelief, and said, apologetically, "I really didn't think she could. I have never seen her swim before!"

Bernhard raised a finger to his lips and smiled at Mona.

5

Brooklyn, 1936
Wedding Dresses and Leopard Skins

Faster Emma and Bertha were sitting at the kitchen table, downstairs in the Bjorkmans' house on Park Place, drinking their afternoon coffee. On the table, there was a pile of Simplicity dress patterns between them, that they had been studying.

"*Var snäll och säga tacksomycket til* Uncle David. (Please say thank you to Uncle David.) It was very nice of him to get these for us, but I don't think we need them, at least not yet. They haven't even set the date, neither one of them. Anyway, both girls say they want to buy their wedding dresses. They've been earning pretty good money and been saving, so they probably won't be sewing their dresses themselves." Bertha was well aware that the idea behind the dress patterns could not have come from Uncle David. They were definitely Faster Emma's doing even if he had ordered them for her through his business. She had probably been after him to get them for so long that he had finally given in, and then probably reluctantly.

"Well, he said to tell you he would help with the sewing, too. It's not that easy to sew on those materials, you know, satin, taffeta or silk."

"I'm sure it isn't. I certainly wouldn't even want to try." Bertha paused and then said, "These dresses are beautiful, especially this one." She held up one of the patterns. "But all the buttons! Each one probably has to be covered with the dress material, too."

As they went through the illustrations of the different dresses again in silence, Bertha wondered how long Uncle David could go on with his work. His eyes were failing him, and everyone knew that a tailor needed good eyesight. But everyone needed money these days, too. Her uncle had just recently mentioned President Roosevelt's Social Security Act, telling her it was a good thing and that it worked in Germany since being introduced by Bismarck before the turn of the century. Then he had laughed and said that he might be in time to pay into it but did not think he would ever get a payment. She would not think of bringing up that subject now though.

Then Faster Emma said, "I don't believe in long engagements, you know. A bride has to be fresh with anticipation, not worn out with waiting! It's been over a year since Bernhard gave Anna her ring, and there's still no mention of setting a date, is there?"

Bertha took a deep breath and looked at her aunt. "No, not that I know of. But I'm not meddling with their plans. They're engaged and that is enough. Bernhard doesn't want to marry until he can support her. Not until he is able to pay the rent and all their expenses from his own pay, if Anna can't go on working, you know. There will be children to take care of, probably. That's planning ahead. That's good sense!" The thought going through Bertha's head now was that her aunt Emma was not aware Bertha herself had done a tiny bit of prodding about the ring last Christmas. She would rather not turn herself into the meddling mother-in-law before they were even married.

"And what about Signe? She has her ring now, too. Wouldn't a double wedding be nice? After all, they are twins. That would be..."

With relief, Bertha heard Mona coming down the stairs. She wandered into the kitchen, trying to look nonchalant and holding out something that looked like one of her stuffed animals without the stuffing.

Bertha examined the ragged piece of fur and started to laugh. Faster Emma leaned toward her to get a better look but could not tell what it was that Bertha had spread out on her lap.

"Is it a bathing suit, Mamma? It's a funny one if it is!"

"Where did you find this, Mona? Have you been in the attic?"

"You never said I couldn't go in there. I've done all my homework and none of my friends have time to play. I'm tired of roller skating by myself. Elsie had to go home. I'm bored, Mamma!"

Mona could tell that her mother was not going to scold. She was not like some of her friends' mothers, who were – if what her friends said was true – always slapping them or threatening to tell their fathers about their bad behavior when they came home.

"It was in an old trunk," she said, "a big black one with all kinds of stickers on it."

"I thought that was locked," said Bertha, as she put the patterns in a neat pile and set them aside. Then she got up from the table with the leopard skin costume in her hands. "Do you feel like climbing four flights of stairs, Faster Emma? If you do, I'll show you something. Frank's old trunk from when he was doing the vaudeville circuit. That was before I met him you know."

As Mona scurried on ahead up the stairs, her mother followed more slowly. Faster Emma was now in her seventies and although quite fit for her age, she was not used to more than one flight of stairs at a time and had to stop on each landing to catch her breath. By the time she reached the attic, Mona had opened the trunk and was showing Bertha some old photographs that she had found inside. "Is that Pappa? Really?"

"Yes, Mona, your father has done some crazy things in his life." Turning to her aunt she said, "You know about Frank's years on the stage, but have you ever seen these pictures?" She passed a couple of photographs to Faster Emma, who carried them over to the little window under the roof to look at them in a better light.

"*Herre Gud!*" ("Lord God!") Frank could have played Tarzan in the film we saw just a few weeks ago!" Emma laughed heartily. "He looks more authentic than the German actor, what was his name? And look at this one of him standing on the other man's shoulders, that's him on the top, isn't it? *Jag har altid sagt att hon var tokig...* (I've always said he was crazy...) what with the burlesque and wearing those costumes and all."

Bertha gave Faster Emma a serious look, gesturing just slightly with her head toward Mona, who was digging in the trunk with her back to them, but as usual listening to whatever they said. Faster Emma then tried to make amends, saying in English, "He's just a little crazy, just enough to make him interesting… And a man must stay interesting for a woman…"

That of course made matters worse, but it was too late for Bertha's look of exasperation to silence her aunt because now Mona turned around, holding up a pair of high button-up leather boots. "Look at these!" She put them down next to a battered old top hat and asked curiously, "What is burlesque? Do you think Pappa is crazy, Mamma, just a little bit?"

"No, of course not. That's nonsense. Burlesque is just another kind of vaudeville, a show on stage. Faster Emma is only joking."

Bertha put everything back into the trunk and closed it, thinking, "Maybe we're all a little crazy. Maybe it's better that way." Then she laughed, too, and, pointing to the different stickers on the trunk, she said to Mona, "Look at all the places your father was on stage. In Boston at the Old Howard, in New York, New Jersey, even in Chicago, I think, but some of these stickers are getting hard to read. The trunk has been up here in the attic for a long time." Where have the years gone, she wondered.

"Let's go back downstairs," she sighed. "I have to start making supper soon. But I guess we have time for another cup of coffee, haven't we?"

"*Nej tack*," said Faster Emma, "David will be wondering where I am if I don't get home." She thought it might be best to go now and let her embarrassing little *faux pas* be forgotten as quickly as possible. As they went down the stairs she asked Bertha, "Have you heard from Helen? Is she coming to visit soon? How is the new baby?"

"I had a long talk with her on the telephone a few days ago. Yes, she and her boys are coming to visit, and this time I'm going to try to make her stay here for good. Honestly, I hope she never goes back to him."

Faster Emma bit her lip and thought to herself, "Good for you, Bertha. I only met the man once two years ago, but I told you he was no good and that he would drink away anything he earned. It's about time you put your foot down. What a shame that you weren't able to protect Helen from this experience and now she has two little boys to bring up!" All she said to Bertha, however, was, "Tell Helen if she wants to come back and get a job, I'll help you take care of her boys. I think you said Gunhill Seagren has said she would help, too. We women stick together!"

With that she was out the door, leaving Bertha standing in the hall, surprised by what she had just heard her aunt say but relieved and confident that she could count on Faster Emma's support in something she herself had decided needed to be done.

6

Another year had passed. It was evening and the date on the newspaper Frank had just folded and slapped onto the kitchen table read April 28, 1937. "I told you the Germans were up to no good when they left the League of Nations. I know that was years ago, but can you believe it? Those were German airplanes that bombed that city in Spain!"

Uncle David was sitting across from him, holding his chin in his hand, and resting his elbow on the table. "Guernica? That's a civil war, Frank. And it's been going on for quite a while now. The Germans didn't get that country into the mess it's in. But you're right. I don't like what we've been hearing about Germany lately any more than you do. Something awful is happening there."

"My Anna's young man, Bernhard, went on a short motorcycle trip to Germany while he was in Sweden just about four years ago." Frank went on, "Last week I asked him what it was like when he was there. He said there was a lot of unemployment and real poverty. He and his friend thought the people were great, the food was okay but mainly potatoes and sauerkraut. When I asked him if he'd heard anything about Hitler and the Nazis, he said there was one incident he wouldn't forget. They had been talking to a couple of young fellows one night in what he I think he called a *kneipe* (bar) in Hamburg. One of them said Hitler was going to save Germany, two or three others laughed at him. Within seconds the whole bar went silent, the friendly atmosphere changed completely, and Bernhard and his friend decided to leave and try some place else."

After a moment, David said thoughtfully, "I've always admired the Germans and their culture. Philosophers, composers, scientists...I hope at least some of what they've been reporting about how they are treating the Jews is just rumor. How can it be true? Weren't a lot of their greatest men Jewish? I think it might be better to just plain do away with religion. What's the good of it?" He shakes his head in disbelief.

"I don't agree with you there. We all need something to believe in," Frank protested.

David did not want another debate about religion. They had had enough discussions on that topic, and he could not understand that Frank was still considering becoming a member of the Adventist Church. So, after a short silence he picked up the more neutral topic of German science instead.

"Now look at that zeppelin, the Hindenburg, traveling across the ocean in only three days. They say it's the most comfortable way to travel, costs a pretty penny, too, I suppose. I hear it's going to land at Lakehurst Naval again next week for the first time this year. I guess they couldn't fly in the winter. Too cold or too much wind!"

"It's an amazing aircraft, but you know I've heard the passengers are allowed to smoke on board. Imagine that! With all that hydrogen gas just above their heads. Sounds pretty risky to me, especially since I read somewhere that the ship was designed to be fueled with helium, not hydrogen. Hydrogen is highly inflammable! But so is helium, I guess. Anyway, I'm sure they've got it all thought through, they know what they're doing."

"Of course, they do. That's what they're known for, isn't

it, thoroughness? But I don't think we can say that much for their politics. If Hitler doesn't stop causing trouble, Europe might be in for some bad times."

Frank agreed but then added, "Not just Europe. What about us? FDR may say we won't get involved, but that's what they said last time. With the Germans, the Italians, the Japanese and maybe the Spanish all getting awfully friendly toward each other and aggressive toward anyone along their borders. That spells big trouble."

He stood up and said, "And my girls are getting all excited about getting married. Anna's wedding will be in October, and Signe and Rich are planning to marry next year, I guess you know that... Hope they have more luck than poor Helen!"

He stood next to the table, suddenly looking thoughtful and shaking his head. "*Fan ocksa!* (Damn!) I sure hope their young men don't end up as cannon fodder! Come on, let's go over to O'Hara's and have a beer. Thank God at least that's not illegal anymore."

7

A week later, the world was shocked by the news of the Hindenburg's disastrous arrival in New Jersey. A newsreel that was presented along with the main features in movie theaters all over the country showed the enormous zeppelin bursting into flames as it was about to land. Audiences watched the horrible incident taking place while they listened to the hysterical voice of a news reporter, overcome by shock and emotion.

Anna refused to go with Bernhard to the picture show. She wanted to see a film titled "A Star is Born" but would not go until she was sure they were no longer showing the newsreel. When Bernhard could not understand why she did not want to see it, she said, "Mamma brought me up to not go and gawk at an accident on the street. How can we go and watch people burn to death while we are sitting in a movie theater? That's even worse!"

She did not want to talk about such things. This was to be a wonderful year, leading up to her wedding in October. She would rather discuss their plans for the wedding or, another date coming up next month, a big hairstyling contest. Hairdressers would be coming from all over the United States to compete in New York City. Bernhard's brothers were not interested in taking part, but he was looking forward to it. He had already practiced doing Anna's hair a couple of times and had decided how he would style it for the contest. He would give her a low part on the right side and flatten her blond curls into sleek waves all the way over to her left cheek and curling forward at the chin line. She was to wear something elegant and off the shoulder. Although they had been successful in smaller contests before, Anna was nervous. Bernhard, however, was confident that they had a good chance of winning.

For the big event, Mimi was coming down from Rochester – something she did not do very often –and was bringing her new husband Harry and his sister Mae along with her – something she had never done before. She and Harry had married and were living in his little house, out in the country just a few miles northwest of where the Curtises lived. James and Esther Curtis were Mimi's oldest and dearest friends in America. She had spent her first months as an unexpected guest in their house and practically become a member of their family. They had been very surprised, but above all very happy to welcome her back to Rochester.

For the big event, Mimi was coming down from Rochester – something she did not do often –and was bringing her husband Harry and his sister along with her – something she had never done before. She and Harry, her old beau, had married and were living in his little house, out in the country just a few miles northwest of where the Curtises lived. James and Esther Curtis were Mimi's oldest and dearest friends in America. She had spent her first months as an unexpected guest in their house and practically become a member of their family. They had been very surprised, but above all very happy to welcome her back to Rochester.

Mimi had told Bernhard on the telephone that she would not miss this hairstyling contest for the world and that she had asked Lambert to reserve a table at their favorite restaurant for that evening. When Bernhard remarked, "You seem to forget I might not win!" she had answered, "then we will still go out for dinner and celebrate. It's an honor to be even admitted to this competition, Bernhard!"

8

The Isle of Manhattan, 1937
A Celebration

"Here he is! Fill the glasses!" Mimi exclaimed as she jumped up from the long table, pride written all over her face, and, while corks popped in the background, she rushed forward to greet Bernhard, who had just come in through the front entrance. Grinning his biggest ear-to-ear grin and leading a smiling Anna by the hand, he followed Mimi into the separate back room of the restaurant. He did not accept the glass of champagne Mimi offered him from the tray Lambert brought immediately but first, with an amused but triumphant gleam in his eye, held up the prize "loving cup" he had just won and placed it on the table. Next he helped Anna out of her light coat, and, after handing it and his hat to a waiter, turned back to Mimi. Then, with some of the friends and family standing up and others twisting around in their seats smiling and watching him, he took the glass, but while Mimi turned back to get her own, he passed it to Anna. When Mimi discovered that he still had no glass, she was, for a fraction of a moment, perplexed. Seeing the glass in Anna's hands, she gave him hers with a laugh and got another for herself.

Obviously impatient and literally bursting with pride, Mimi finally could raise her glass for a toast. and, beaming at the guests around the table, put her arm around Bernhard's shoulders and asked, "Does everyone have a glass? Yes?" Then turning to her brother, she said, "You did it, Bernhard! I knew you would! *Skål pa dig!*"

He answered with a wink, "We did it! Look at Anna, how could I lose?" and raised his glass first to Mimi, then to Anna, to whom he gave a fond and proud kiss on the cheek. Everyone else at the table clapped their hands, raised their glasses, and said, "*Skål!*"

Now Mimi smiled at Anna, raised her glass to her, and then went around Bernhard to give her a little hug. "Yes," she said, "You do look lovely. The dress is perfect. I told him you would be a good model."

Then there was a slight commotion as chairs were moved to make room for Anna next to Bernhard, who, of course, had been designated a seat on Mimi's right. On her left sat Harry and his sister Mae, a big heavy woman, almost as tall as Harry, with a friendly smile and hearty laugh that, along with the jangling of the many bracelets she wore on her well-rounded arms, would be heard frequently all evening.

Although a few of the people at the table, Hans, Lambert, and his wife Agnes, had been to the Sheraton Hotel earlier in the evening with Bernhard and Anna and had managed to get a glimpse of some of the other contestants and their models waiting in the hotel lobby, they had been unable to acquire tickets to enter the banquet hall and had gone on to meet Mimi and the others at the restaurant. The decisions would not be made known by the judges until after the gala dinner when the awards were to be presented. So, no one knew the results until Bernhard and Anna arrived. The suspense had been building up all evening and spilled over now in laughter and discussions, as the big, heavy silver cup was passed along the table.

Hans and Lambert both had been certain that the competition would be tough and had voiced that opinion while they sat around having their dinner and waiting for Bernhard and Anna to come to the restaurant.

"You've never seen such elegance!" Lambert had said several times. Hans had been more impressed by the many photographers crowded into the lobby along with the contestants and the enormous black limousines that kept stopping at the curb in front of the hotel to drop off the elite guests. His comment had made everyone at the table laugh when he said, "Everyone looked really – what do they call it? – snazzy!"

Mimi, who had not gone to the hotel, had remained optimistic as it got later and later. She insisted, "The fact that they are taking so long to get here – the dinner must have been over hours ago – is a very positive sign." And she had been right. She proudly watched Bernhard and listened to his report of the evening.

One of the first things he said was, "*Det är synd om maten* (It's a shame about the food) neither one of us could eat much. We were both too nervous, too excited. Is the kitchen still open here? Do you think we could get a bite to eat?" A wave of laughter went down the table as his words were reported to those who had not heard him. "We could have been here much earlier, but then the photographers were let loose on us and wouldn't let us leave. They must have taken dozens of pictures of Anna from every conceivable angle." He looked at Anna, who was trying not to blush.

She said, rolling her eyes, "He's exaggerating."

Bernhard shook his head and went on, "And some very interesting people came up to talk to us. I have offers to work for some of the finest salons in New York and even in Chicago!"

He took some slips of paper from his inside jacket pocket. "Look! A couple of them gave me their telephone numbers and business cards."

Mimi listened intently as Bernhard read out the names of two or three men who had come up to talk to him. He told her he was also especially impressed by a glamorous looking woman who came over to congratulate him. Unfortunately, he had forgotten her name. Anna came to his assistance, saying, "Her name was Elizabeth something."

Mimi said, "That might be Elizabeth Arden. She's a big name in cosmetics. We used some of her nail polish, remember? Her support would be very valuable for the shop."

Bernhard shook his head, "I don't think so. She has her own salon in New York and more or less offered me a job there. But I can't do that. I couldn't abandon our shop. Not now when we are finally getting back on our feet."

"Well, we don't want to worry about that now, do we?" Mimi said. Then she pushed back her chair and got up, "Come, Bernhard, we have to at least tell Lambert and Hans about this." Their brothers were sitting at the other end of the table. So, Bernhard got up, too, and left Anna sitting alone. But not for long. A moment later Mimi's sister-in-law, Mae, heaved herself up from her chair to come over and chat with Anna.

She lowered herself carefully into Bernhard's chair and asked Anna, "Why haven't you come up to Rochester to visit us yet? I've been looking forward to meeting you since I met Bernhard. You should have come to the wedding last year."

Anna didn't think it would be appropriate to tell her she wasn't invited until it was too late so she said, "I was working and couldn't get the day off. It was easy for Bernhard. He just canceled his appointments for the day."

"I suppose it was short notice and of course it was a quiet wedding. It wasn't a big celebration, like yours will be, Anna. That's in October, isn't it? You must be getting excited." When Anna nodded smiling, Mae said sincerely, "You make a lovely couple."

"Thank you, that is nice of you to say so. I hope you can

come down with Mimi and Harry in October. How long are you here for now?"

"We'll be here until the weekend, staying with Lambert, sleeping on some foldable beds. I hope they can hold us. Harry and I are big people for foldable beds," Mae laughed good-naturedly.

Before Anna could think of any possible polite remark in reply, the waiter came with two bowls of minestrone and a basket of bread, which was all the kitchen could give them at such a late hour. Leaning on her heavily beringed hands and rattling her bracelets, Mae got back up again with a smile and a groan. Then, motioning to Bernhard, she called out, "Your soup is here, Bernhard. You'd better come and eat before it gets cold. It's a mystery to me how anyone can survive until tomorrow on a portion like that though. They didn't give you much bread either."

.

9

Three days after the celebration, it was late afternoon, and Mimi and Mae were sitting in the kitchen drinking coffee and resting their swollen feet after a day walking around in stores in the city. They were waiting for Harry, who had spent the day on his own, not in the least interested in what Manhattan's shops had to offer. They planned to go to a movie that evening after a Chinese takeaway dinner with the brothers. The last client had left the shop and Bernhard had taken the afternoon off. Lambert and Hans were closing up for the day. Mimi could hear how the broom knocked against the woodwork as Hans swept away the last bit of hair trimmings and curling papers. The cash register had just rung out for the last time that day as Lambert put the day's intake back into back drawer of the register, duly counted and recorded in the book.

"Why didn't you tell Bernhard to bring Anna along tonight?" Mae asked. "Then he would have come, too. I don't think you can complain of his being disloyal, Mim."

"I guess that's what I should have done, but I don't know. There just isn't enough room here for so many people, Mae. We can't eat Chinese food on our laps, can we? And I didn't feel like putting up card tables again. Besides, walking over to the movie theater we would be like a procession. Anyway, it doesn't matter."

Mimi got up and opened a drawer in the cabinet next to the sink. She took out a long narrow pair of scissors that the kitchen had inherited from the shop. Then she picked up the newspaper that was opened to a press report on the hairdressers' convention that showed the prizewinners of the competition. There was a lovely picture of Anna that she looked at for a moment thoughtfully before she started cutting the article out for her scrap book.

"You know what? I'll give them a call. Maybe they can still come. We've got the Bjorkmans' number somewhere I'm sure."

Before she finished what she was doing, they heard someone come into the shop. The little bell on the shop door rang with a sudden jerk.

"That's an unexpected customer, isn't it?" Mae commented.

"Some of these women think they can come whenever they please. Lambert should put an end to that. But he doesn't listen to good advice."

"That sounds like a man to me. In fact, I can hear two men. Do they do men's haircuts, too?"

"Once in a blue moon," Mimi answered. She started going toward the door that led to the shop, but Mae stopped her.

"Wait a minute, Mim."

"I just want to call Bernhard. I'll tell him to bring Anna along."

"Be quiet a minute. I don't think those men are late customers." There was an urgency in Mae's voice that stopped Mimi in her tracks. Both women listened as they heard the voices getting louder. When a chair was knocked over, Mae asked in a whisper, "Where can we hide?"

Wide-eyed with shock, Mimi motioned toward the bathroom. They tip-toed out to the hall. Mae probably had not moved as quickly and lightly in twenty years. Mimi, on the other hand, was still reluctant. Mae had to coax her to go inside and then locked the door.

"Now we can't even hear what's going on," Mimi complained, obviously suffering.

"Do you really think we could make a difference?" Mae asked. "If we could have called the police, yes, but the telephone is in the shop."

"Right, but we can't just do nothing!"

"I can!" Mae looked at the rings on her fingers.

Three or four minutes later, they could just barely hear the voices in the shop. Mimi could not take the suspense any longer. She said to Mae, "I'm going out there. I'll talk to those men. I can be pretty persuasive when I want to be. Don't forget I grew up with four younger brothers!"

"Sure, but I don't think they'll listen to you, Mim. Don't do it." Mae gripped Mimi's arm and tried to hold her back.

But Mimi had made up her mind and there was no stopping her. She tore her arm loose, giving Mae a look of impatient irritation and turned the key in the lock. Then she slipped out the door, whispering to Mae to lock herself in again, and entered the kitchen just as one of the men came through the swinging door that separated the shop from the living quarters. Mimi wiped her hands on her skirt, stood very tall, tried unsuccessfully first to smile and then to look indignant and asked, "Who are you? You're not supposed to come in here, it's private."

The man Mimi later described to the police as of average height, average weight, with brown hair but "remarkably well dressed for a thief" took a quick appraising look at Mimi, ignored her impertinent questions and ordered her to sit down in the only armchair in the living-room. "Is there anyone else here?" he wanted to know, looking toward the hall.

"No," she lied valiantly, protecting her sister-in-law, and went on to say, "But my husband and brother will be here, and some friends, any minute, so you had better...."

"Shut up, lady. Follow instructions. No one's getting

hurt if everyone cooperates nicely. Just stay where you are."

Mimi cleared her throat, which was incredibly dry for someone who had drunk a cup of coffee no more than ten minutes ago. "You know," she said shakily, "If you just go home now and leave us alone, we won't even tell the police. I'm sure you have money problems. A lot of people have financial worries these days. We can talk about that." She drew a deep breath, trying to build up her courage and regain her calm. The man looked at her, amazed, as she continued, "You don't want to go to prison, do you? But you have to promise..."

With a brusque laugh the man cut her off saying, "Listen lady, you're wasting my time. You can give me that ring on your finger now and I see you're wearing a nice watch. You can give me that, too. Just put it on the table."

Reluctantly, Mimi twisted her wedding ring off her finger, turning her engagement ring to hide the diamond that was her pride and joy. Then she unclasped her watch and laid it on the table with the ring.

"Both rings, lady. And what about those earrings? Almost overlooked them. They're real nice." Mimi looked at the man in disgust and dismay as she unwound the tiny clasps of her earrings. She placed them along with her engagement ring on the coffee table next to her watch and her ring.

"That's a good girl. Good taste you got, too! My compliments!"

He scooped the items up and dropped them into his left jacket pocket. Mimi could not help noticing that his right pocket bulged suspiciously. When he took a big roll of masking tape out of it, the pocket still bulged. Mimi sat dumbfounded, trying not to look at the pocket and imagine its contents. The man proceeded to wrap the masking tape around her, fixing her to the back of the chair. She could not think of anything else to say before it was too late, and her mouth was taped shut. As her heart pounded in her ears she thought to herself, "What have they done to my brothers?" She would never forgive herself for bringing them to America if...At least they have not shot anybody. I haven't heard any shots." She shuddered, as tears of anger welled up in her eyes.

Another man came through the swinging door that separated the shop from the living quarters. He was dressed in a dark suit like the other man, but it looked sleazy, shiny and unpressed. He was not wearing a tie. More important, he was holding a gun in one hand and a small box that she recognized as one that the bottles of peroxide were delivered in in the other. It was probably filled with the contents of the cash register.

"Aha!" he said in a jeering voice, "Who's this? Have you got enough tape?"

"Yeah, sure, come on. She ain't going nowhere. You finished in there? She said they were expecting company."

"Yeah, what we took out of that cash register ain't worth getting caught for. Get a move on." The man laughed, "They were expecting company, were they? I bet they weren't expecting us!"

"How much we got?"

"Not much. This wasn't their busy day, I guess."

The two men went back into the shop, swinging the door so it slammed back and forth on its hinges, and then out through the shop door. Before they left, Mimi heard the man she had tried to talk out of robbing them say, "You shoulda heard this dame. You really missed something. She was gonna let us go," he sneered, "and not even tell the police! Wasn't that nice of her! Can you believe it?" he hooted. "Come on, let's get outta here."

Mae had been listening at the bathroom door and managed to hear the shop doorbell ring crazily as the men went out and then heard their steps as they went down the stairs. Confident that they had left, she emerged from the bathroom and went into the living room. She was shocked to see what they had done to Mimi, but when she removed the tape from her sister-in-law's mouth, using the scissors that she found still lying on the kitchen table, Mimi burst out, "Go see how Lambert and Hans are for God sakes!"

Mae found the two brothers unhurt but suffering from acute fury and frustration. As soon as she had removed the towels that the robbers had draped over their heads so that they could not see what was happening and pulled the tape from their mouths, Lambert burst out in Swedish cussing she couldn't understand. But she could imagine what he was saying without a translation. Hans just shook his head while he brushed himself off. Worst of all was probably the embarrassment of finding themselves taped to the chairs that their clients sat on when, on a normal day, they had their hair done. The drawer of the cash register had been left open and was, of course, empty. Aside from a chair that had been knocked over next to the desk, and some bottles of peroxide lying on the floor, everything else looked untouched.

10

"By the time I got there, they were sitting in the kitchen drinking coffee. The police had already come and gone." It was the next day and Bernhard was telling Anna about the robbery at the shop. "I wish I had been there. I would have thought of something to prevent them from making off with our earnings."

Anna shook her head, "No, Bernhard. There are some ruthless people out there. They had guns! I'm glad you weren't there. Thank God no one got hurt!"

"Harry got there a few minutes after I did," he went on. "I really admire that guy. He didn't say a word when Mimi told him about her jewelry. He didn't get upset until Mae told him he had a brave wife! Then Mimi started crying. I don't think I've ever seen her cry, you know that? Well, she did and after a few minutes she told us the whole story. I can't believe what she did...."

Bernhard told Anna what had happened, how Mimi had left the relative safety of the bathroom while Mae stayed in there. How she had been so furious with herself for being such a fool, how she said she was not brave at all, just foolish and that Mae had shown better sense.

"Poor Mimi, what an awful experience!" said Anna.

"She's a brave woman. She believes in the good in anybody and thought she could influence them, I guess."

"I don't know about that, maybe you're right, but Mae certainly did show better sense. She was right there! Who knows what could have happened! It was just a shame we weren't all there when they came in. They wouldn't have tried to take on five men. Anyway, Hans told Mimi she overestimated her ability to make people do what she wanted. That wasn't very nice of him, was it? After what she had gone through!"

"It was a bit harsh. But he had just had a scare, too, or he would never have said that. He's as loyal as the rest of you," Anna remarked.

"I've never seen him like that. He doesn't get upset easily. He even said something about it being a good thing for her to finally find out about herself."

Bernhard seemed thoughtful. Anna was surprised. With eyebrows raised, she remained silent. She did not know what to say. She could hardly imagine any of Mimi's brothers criticizing their sister. She waited for Bernhard to finish his story.

"Mae was so thankful that she had saved all her own jewelry and felt so sorry for Mimi that she gave her one of her own rings. I'm sure you noticed that her hands are covered with them. All those rings and bracelets. Mimi didn't want to accept it. But when Harry said they would have to wait a while before he could afford a new wedding ring, Mae insisted. She gave her one from her little finger, the others were all too big. Anyway, Mimi is really embarrassed and wants to go home to Rochester the day after tomorrow. She says she never wants to come to the city again."

"But she'll have to come back soon for our wedding! She wouldn't want to miss that, would she?" Anna looked astonished. "I've even invited Mae and she said she would love to come. Surely your own sister will..."

"Of course, she will. She was so upset that she didn't

know what she was saying."

"I guess they never got to the movie theater. They were planning to go out, weren't they? Do they still want to go?"

"That was the last thing on anybody's mind, Anna."

"Well, of course, but I thought maybe we should ask them to go with us tomorrow night. It would be good to get Mimi's mind off what happened. What's showing?"

"There's a good western with John Wayne that I'd really like to see. I was going to suggest it for us this weekend. I don't know the name of the movie, but I hear he's riding a stagecoach that is attacked by outlaws. He finishes them off and a couple of Indians as well single-handed. That's what I call a good film. A lot of action. In fact, that's the kind of life I'd like to lead."

With eyebrows again raised, Anna looked at Bernhard in disbelief. "Do you really think that would be such a good idea?"

"Why not? I came over to this country looking for a little adventure, you know."

"No, I mean should we take Mimi to see that movie?"

"Oh. Why not?" Bernhard said again. He obviously still had no idea what she meant.

"With all the shooting and killing after what happened yesterday?" Anna laughed, shaking her head at him in disbelief.

11

An October Wedding

It was a beautiful but cool fall day. Everyone later agreed it had been a lovely wedding. Anna looked stunning as she walked down the aisle in her exquisite, white silk taffeta dress. It had tight fitting sleeves that were puffed at the shoulder and buttoned below the elbow where they met the tops of her long gloves. The boxy neckline came to a wide v and had flattened ribbon ruffles. It was high in the back and buttoned with 30 tiny buttons that reached down to the small of her back. She was carrying a bouquet of pink and white rosebuds that would later be caught appropriately by her maid of honor, her twin Signe, who, tiny as she was, managed to catch it by leaping higher than the taller girls from the Gym club. Anna's dress had a short train that was held both carefully and proudly by Ramona as Anna entered the church smiling serenely on Frank's arm and then left it almost an hour later equally serenely on Bernhard's. The rice and good wishes in English and Swedish rained down in abundance as the couple left the church and headed for the limousine that had been hired in accordance with the day's glory to take them to the reception.

Weeks later when a colleague at the Metropolitan asked Anna if the ceremony had been held in Swedish or English in the Swedish Lutheran Church, she was surprised to find that she could hardly remember and almost had to ask her sisters. She confessed she thought that she had been in some kind of dream state from beginning to end and hadn't woken up until being bombarded with rice on the steps of the church.

Of course, Mimi had come to the wedding along with her husband Harry and sister-in-law Mae. That afternoon at the reception, when Anna and Mimi were standing together for a few minutes alone, Anna told Mimi how glad she was that she had come and said that she had been honestly worried that she might not appear after what had happened in the beauty shop just a short time before, Mimi laughed at Anna as if the thought were ridiculous.

"You don't really believe I would have missed my brother's wedding, do you? It was a shock of course, but I was well over it by the time we were back in Rochester. I wouldn't have missed this for the world." She gave Anna an approving glance up and down, and a quick but hearty hug.

Anna recalled hearing from Bernhard that Mimi had said the same thing about the hairdressers' competition. She also remembered feeling distinctly uncomfortable in Mimi's company that evening. With all her heart and in the secure feeling of happiness that she had been experiencing all day, she decided to make a real effort to get her relationship with Mimi onto a positive course once and for all.

Looking at Mimi intently and with her warmest smile, Anna said, "You know I have three sisters already." She paused for a moment as Mimi nodded with a quizzical expression, then went on, "But I'm so very proud and happy that we are now sisters, too, Mimi!" She wanted to get closer to Mimi, whom her husband thought the world of, and she was determined to show her how sincere her feelings were. No sooner had she spoken these words, than she immediately began to wonder if the idea was a good one after all.

"Well, then," Mimi responded slowly, "You have two other new sisters besides me." She had an expression of mild amusement on her face as she looked into the younger woman's eyes. "There's Svea... Had you met her before now?"

"No, I spoke with her just yesterday for the first time." Anna looked over to where Svea was standing talking with her husband August and Hans, thinking to herself, "Svea is so sweet and gentle, she will be easy to be sisters with." She did not allow the vague thought to take shape – or was it a feeling going through her mind about Mimi, whom she admired tremendously but who always seemed to make her feel inadequate or unsure of herself?

"And you have another new sister in Sweden: Saga," Mimi went on.

"Yes! I can't wait to meet her... someday, I guess. She stayed back to take care of your father I understand."

"That was the reason at first. But my father took a new wife years ago, who could have taken care of him very well without her help. Of course, Natalia's getting older now, too." Mimi shook her head, saying, "Saga prefers life in Sweden. She has her husband and little boy. They could still come over here, but I imagine it is too late now. Her husband, just like my father, is too stubborn to leave the old country. But if Saga had really wanted to come, he might have been persuaded as well."

For a moment Anna could sense that Mimi had regrets about the situation, that she felt she had failed somehow and split up her family. All of a sudden, she realized Mimi might be suffering from a tremendous feeling of responsibility for each and every member of her family. She had convinced almost all of them that America was the land of golden opportunity and that there was no future for them in Sweden. She had managed to assemble most of her family around her and get them settled here, but some had been left behind and prosperity had not turned out to be easily attainable for those who had come across the ocean either. On the contrary, setting up a new business in America in the depression years had been as hard as it probably would have been in Sweden. Anna saw Mimi showing a weaker, perhaps even endearing side of her character and felt she was beginning to understand Mimi for the first time.

"And what about all your new brothers? Does that not impress you? That is really new for you, isn't it?"

"What? Oh, yes," said Anna, who had been listening to her own thoughts and hoped she hadn't missed anything else Mimi had been saying. "Brothers! I've never had one before and now I have three," she said enthusiastically. "I do have a big family now, haven't I!"

She turned and looked at the merry crowd standing around with glasses of champagne, talking and laughing, Lindens and Bjorkmans and friends. She was beginning to grasp that she honestly and truly now was married. She had reached that anecdotal state of being that she had heard about as a child where all little problems would be over for a woman. For the time being at least, she was almost convinced that could be true.

Bertha, who was talking to Bernhard on the other side of the room, looked over and caught Anna's glance. She motioned to her to come. It was time to cut the cake.

Two hours later Anna was sitting at one of the small tables with her twin sister and her mother. She had slipped off her high-heeled sandals under her long skirt with a sigh of relief and was resting her feet on the cool wooden floor, while wondering how she was going to be able to dance the opening dance with Bernhard. The little three-man band was already setting up their microphones and the drums, so she knew she did not have long to recuperate. A waiter was carrying a tray of coffee cups around but unfortunately the champagne had run out long ago. She was wishing for another glass, alcohol deadened pain, didn't it? The dance was obviously going to be painful. She looked at her mother, who was talking to Signe about someone in Connecticut that Anna did not know. Could she ask her or Signe to check in the kitchen to see if there were perhaps a last forgotten bottle of champagne put away to keep cold? Or should she herself ask the waiter for a cognac? She laughed softly to herself and looked again at Bertha. A memory had just crossed her mind. Once when Anna was going to her first cocktail party years earlier, her mother had told her to "stand close to a potted plant, Dear, you don't really have to drink everything they give you if you feel tipsy."

Bertha noticed that Anna was not listening to her and Signe and that she seemed to have something on her mind. "It's a big step, Dear," she said, "Is there anything you want to ask me about?"

Anna blushed and answered quickly, "Yes, Mamma, there is. How am I going to survive this dance? My feet are killing me! I should have gotten my feet used to these shoes."

Signe laughed, saying, "If that's all that's bothering you, take them off! No one can see your feet and you can dance barefoot, can't you?"

So that was exactly what Anna did. Bernhard thought his bride looked lovelier than ever and also somehow tinier than before. She danced on a cloud, holding the end of her dress's train in her right hand until her silk stockings snagged on one of the floorboards and she had to reveal her secret to Bernhard. He laughed, delighted at his new wife's lovely looks and funny little ways, and bent down to whisper, "You'll have to put them back on for the next dance though."

"Why, Bernhard? I don't know if I can, my feet hurt terribly."

"Just for a few minutes, Honey." Bernhard was still

whispering softly into her ear, causing little shivers to run down her spine. "It's time for our getaway and you have to run with me to the car. Lambert parked it around the corner for me. If we wait any longer, they'll do all kinds of things to it, but I think I've out tricked them here. Your father gave him all of your bags, mine were already in the car. If we get off now, we can make it all the way to Washington, D.C. by dark. They won't even notice that we've gone."

But it was Bernhard who did not notice how his brothers all disappeared from the restaurant during the next dance, after getting a wink from Frank. When Bernhard and Anna reached the car, Lambert, Walter, and Hans were standing nearby, hiding in a doorway, and jumped out to see them off. The rest of the family and guests streamed around the corner, cheering and waving goodbye, while Hans finished smearing "JUST MARRIED" onto the back window of the car with white paint. When the young couple drove off, Lambert and Walter had a good laugh, admiring their own fancy work as the firecrackers that they had stuffed into the exhaust pipe went off in a series of loud blasts and the long trail of tin cans tied to the back bumper with a rope clattered down the otherwise quiet afternoon Brooklyn street.

12

Postcards from Florida

Two weeks later, Bertha and Frank were sitting in their kitchen. It was late afternoon and already getting dark. It had been a chilly day and rain was now pelting down against the window of the kitchen door, making Frank glad that he had made it home before it started. On the table, next to their empty coffee cups, were the newspaper Frank had brought home with him and two postcards that had arrived that morning while he was at work.

"Well, now we know that they have reached Florida safely at least," said Frank in a matter-of-fact voice.

Bertha picked up one of the postcards and looked at it again. "*Det är en rolig tre!* (That's a funny tree!) It's like a whole family of tree trunks stuck together. Have you ever seen anything like it before?" She handed it to Frank for him to take another look.

"That isn't the trunk, actually. I think it must be inside there, hidden behind those air roots that grow back into the ground. Tropical trees have roots like that to pick up the moisture from the air, I believe. And those aren't leaves.

Look what it says here on the card, under Anna's note. 'Banyan tree hung with Spanish moss. St Augustine, Florida'. Anna writes that they're having nice warm weather. But I think it must be very humid in Florida in the summer."

Frank did not remind Bertha that the fall was the time of year for those terrible hurricanes, but asked, "How much farther south did they want to go?"

"All the way to Miami, I think. Anna said it had something to do with how long their money lasted though." She sighed and said, "She told me Bernhard wanted to get as far away from New York as possible."

"Why would that be?"

"Well, he isn't a city boy, is he? You came here from Göteborg, that's a city. He was born and grew up in Småland, where there's nothing but forests and lakes!... He does get that awful cough in the winter too, and I think he really will want to move somewhere out in the country someday. Of course, he came to America looking for adventure, too. You know that. His brothers are always teasing him about it. It wasn't just a joke about the wild west."

After a moment, she laughed softly, "So they've turned their honeymoon into a bit of an adventure, I guess."

No one else in either of their families had ever been as far south before. In fact, no one had gone farther south than Atlantic City, New Jersey — Walter had been there just recently — and that was not much more than a hundred and fifty miles south of New York. Their own explorations had been limited to trips farther north, to upstate New York or Connecticut.

Bertha picked up the other postcard. It showed an old waterfront fortress. With a sigh, she passed it on to Frank, who examined it again and looked at what was printed on the back. "'Saint Augustine Fortress. 1695.' This must be one of the oldest buildings in the United States, if I'm not mistaken."

Frank glanced at his wife and thought she looked

preoccupied. "They can take care of themselves, Bertha. Don't worry about them."

"I'm not worried about them on this trip, Frank, I know they're sensible. But look at this newspaper you've just brought home with you."

The paper was folded in two so that only the headline in bold capital letters was to be seen: EUROPE PLAYS PRE-WAR GAME. "What does it mean, Frank? Are we heading for another war? I'm telling you, I always wanted a son and I know you did too, but now I am glad we don't have one! I'm worried about Bernhard!"

"He's applying for United States citizenship when they get back, isn't he?"

"Will he be safe then? What if we go to war?"

Frank burst out laughing. "Don't worry, this country isn't going to get into any European war again. Roosevelt will see to that. He has enough on his hands here. And as for Bernhard, if we did go to war, which I really do not think possible, by the time he has US citizenship he'll be too old to be drafted. Why, he's thirty years old already!"

In the brilliant sun of an empty beach on the eastern Florida coast, somewhere between Palm Beach and the little town of Lake Worth, Anna would soon be watching Bernhard, barefoot and bare chested in his bathing suit, as he climbed up the leaning trunk of a palm tree. The tree was bent over at an angle that could only have been the result of many years of prevailing winds or a good number of hurricanes. At the top, which would have been much higher up if the tree were not leaning over as far, hung the coconuts that would entice Bernhard to make the climb.

Anna was wearing a wide-brimmed straw hat and one of Bernhard's long-sleeved white shirts over her bathing suit. With one hand she held the hat that threatened to fall off as she gazed up at her husband. In the other she held their camera, waiting for him to stop at some point so she could take his picture.

"I certainly don't have to tell him to smile and say cheese," she thought to herself. "He hasn't stopped smiling since we crossed the border to Florida. And I've never seen him looking so healthy. I wish I could get a golden tan like that." She reached up and picked off another bit of the skin that was peeling off her nose for the second time that week. At least her arms and legs seemed to be getting used to the sun now and tanning slightly despite the terrible sunburn she had had after her first day in the sun. The woman they rented their little cottage from had told her with an air of finality that she should stay out of the sun, limit her visits to the beach to early morning and late afternoon and that she should reconcile herself to the fact that she would never get a tan. She had then unceremoniously presented Anna with a bottle of vinegar and a small white linen towel to use to bathe and cool her burnt skin.

"A new and unique scent, the ideal perfume for the modern young bride on her honeymoon!" had been Bernhard's teasing comment. So, she had bought herself a big sunhat and accepted bleakly when Bernhard offered her one of his cool white cotton shirts.

"You look lovely in my shirt, Honey," he had said, bending over to roll up the sleeves for her that hung down below her knees. His eyes twinkled, defying the serious face he had put on, as he looked up and said, "It suits you somehow."

Anna had made no comment but just raised one eyebrow at him and told herself it would not do to sulk. Then she had set off collecting seashells, abundant on the sand at low tide, while Bernhard enjoyed – to the utmost – a solitary swim in the long waves of a gentle surf. She had stopped to look back and watch him dive into a wave just as the frothy white crest folded over him. When Anna returned, she found Bernhard lying in the sand next to their beach basket, looking up at the coconuts.

"No one will believe this," he said. "We are in paradise

and we didn't have to die to get here."

After a moment, he got up, studying the palm tree and the coconuts. Before Anna could stop him, he started climbing up the tree, saying, "Those are our coconuts up there and I'm going to claim them."

Anna wondered if it was too dangerous, but the sand looked soft enough. Even if he fell, he might not get hurt. Besides, she knew he would not listen to her. So, instead, she smiled and took the camera out of the basket. "Did you say they wouldn't believe us? They will if I take pictures of you climbing palm trees like a monkey!"

13

The Cozy Copper-Covered Cottages

Mrs. Lewis

When Bernhard and Anna got back to the little cottage they were staying in – further south on the other side of the lake in an area on Dixie Highway with just a few small wooden houses that made a stark contrast with Palm Beach, its hotels, and luxury estates – their landlady, Mrs. Lewis, was standing in the middle of the driveway that led to four cottages and her own two-story wooden house. She was wearing one of her formless cotton dresses, that had obviously been washed and hung out in the sun to dry so many times that the pattern and the colors were like a faded memory from another century. On her head was an enormous, ragged straw hat, tied under her chin with a frayed ribbon. She was carrying the long-handled secateurs that she seemed never to put down whenever she was outside of her house. She made way for them to pass through the driveway and then followed them slowly up the short dirt track to their cottage.

"How's yer sunburn, Annie?" she asked. She had stopped saying "Mizzz Linden" to Anna the day before, the second day they were there.

"I hope ya ain't been out in that there sun agin! I been thinking I shoulda told ya no time is the right time fer you to be in the sun! Not even early mornin or late afternoon! Just plain no sun is right for the likes a you!"

Then she started to laugh when she saw what Anna was wearing as she reluctantly climbed out of the car, in Bernhard's shirt and slightly embarrassed that she had not bothered to put her long slacks over her bathing suit. "That's a good idea, Hon! I shoulda thought a that myself. And you got yer hat on, too."

"Hello, Mrs. Lewis. You can see that I've taken your advice. This shirt was Bernhard's idea. It's nice and cool, and pretty much covers me."

"Look here, Mrs. Lewis," Bernhard said as he presented the three fat coconuts that had been sitting between him and Anna on the seat coming back from the beach. "I picked a couple of coconuts off one of the trees over by the ocean. It was a big palm, Are they ripe? And how do I get them open?"

"Well," Mrs. Lewis drawled, "They look ripe all right." She took one of them out of Bernhard's hands and shook it. "Sounds good," she said. "Plenty a milk in this 'un. As for opening it, there's more than one way t'skin a cat, ya know. And more than one way t'open a coconut. You kin take a hatchet to it, or a hammer, or just a big stone. Now I don't do nothin like that. I just take 'em up the stairs in back'a my house and drop 'em on the pavement. That does it every time. Only problem, ya got to run back down to pick 'em up fast before the milk all runs out. That is if ya set any store in the milk. Lots of folks don't like it an don't care 'bout that."

Bernhard was not sure he had understood everything she said but he asked if he could use her hatchet or a hammer.

She looked at him for a minute perplexed and then

asked, "Why don'tcha use m' stairs? I know I got a hammer somewhere, but I don't know 'xactly where. Now, the stairs? I know where they're at. And I reckon you do, too!"

So, they set off together toward Mrs. Lewis' house. Bernhard slightly puzzled, Anna just amused. She was not having as hard a time understanding their landlady as Bernhard was. On the contrary, she was enjoying the older woman's drawl.

"Tell me, Mrs. Lewis," she said as they walked down the sandy path, "Some of those coconut palms over at the beach are bent almost all the way to the ground. Is that normal for them to grow that way?"

"No, Hon. A course not! The hurricanes done that! We had two real bad ones 'bout ten years ago. Wrecked half the houses 'round here. Even those big classy houses in Palm Beach had damages. We was lucky. A lot a folks weren't. The first one blew one of the cottages we had t' bits, the second just took the roof off the one you're stayin' in now. That's why it's got sech a nice shiny copper roof. We put that one on in 1928. We rebuilt the one that came down an put a copper roof on that one too. That was when me an' ma husban still had some money in the bank up in Georgia. Since then it ain't been easy."

The two women stood watching as Bernhard climbed the wooden stairs with his arms full of coconuts.

"Where do I drop them? Is this okay here?" he called down from the little veranda.

"Sure. Just make sure to hit the pavement over on that side!" She pointed to the area directly under Bernhard.

"Now,… those storms were killers. More than half the palms round here got blown over. The beach plain disappeared in some places and it grown twice as wide in others. And the palms that survived the storms are the ones that look like they're try'n t'lie down and take a nap." She stopped and called up to Bernhard, "Hold on there, Bernie, wait up, I'll be right back."

Mrs. Lewis left Anna standing there and went through

the banging screen door under the veranda that led to her kitchen. She came back out again a minute later, with a big battered white enamel bowl to catch the coconut milk in.

"You kin go ahead now. We're ready."

Bernhard dropped one coconut after the other and Anna went to pick each one up. She brought them back to Mrs. Lewis, who showed her how to rip off the thick outer husk and hold the actual nut hidden inside – if it was cracked too – expertly over the bowl and let the thin watery liquid dribble into it. If the nut was not cracked, she brought it back up to Bernhard so he could drop it again.

When they were finished, Anna gave Bernhard the bowl to have a drink. He claimed it might be "better than cow's milk, if it was kept in the icebox." Anna tried it, nodded, and smiled politely at Bernhard and their landlady.

Later, alone in their cottage, she told Bernhard she did not like the taste of it, calling it insipid.

"Now, what does that mean?" Bernhard wanted to know. "I've never heard you use that word before."

"I don't use it very often, it means tasteless. I was just thinking you need to learn some more vocabulary and I can hardly think of any new words. But we can start working on that now that we have time... Or on the drive back up north," she said as she saw Bernhard roll his eyes.

.

14

Dinner with Mrs. Lewis

Ten days later Anna and Bernhard were sitting at the dinner table on the screened in porch of Mrs. Lewis' house. It was Sunday evening, and they would be starting on their way back up north the next morning.

They had stayed longer than planned, reluctant to give up the trips to the beach on the pair of old bicycles their landlady rounded up for them the week before. They would miss their long walks along the shore. They had admired the big homes in Palm Beach – they had laughed when they heard that the owners called their expansive mansions "cottages" – and had seen new and even bigger ones being built behind the dunes along the beach. They had sat in a little coffee shop on Worth Avenue and listened to stories told by the woman who served them coffee and slices of banana cake. She talked about the early years of the town and the role played by famed magnate Henry Morrison Flagler in creating this unique resort. They heard about his railroad and the grand and enormous Royal Poinciana Hotel, how it had burned down and been rebuilt more than once, only to have been torn down just a year before their visit. Another of his hotels, the Breakers, directly on the oceanfront, had also been destroyed twice by fire but now, with an architecture inspired by the Villa Medici in Rome, it had been solidly rebuilt to endure.

Bernhard and Anna had strolled along the beach one evening to get a closer look at the Breakers from the ocean side. The double towered mansion had loomed over the dunes, its high windows ablaze with lights, shining out onto the beach. Black-clad waiters could be seen scurrying from table to table in the dining hall carrying trays of food like flickering shadow figures in a magic lantern that had come to life. Opposite, the moon was full against the night and reflected softly on the choppy surface of the dark ocean. A refreshing breeze was blowing, and the surf pounded rhythmically on the sand, chased back and forth by the tiny sandpipers called sanderlings that never seemed to rest.

Wanting to get a closer look, Anna and Bernhard had sat and ordered iced tea on the hotel terrace, listening quietly to the blasé laughter of a group of elegantly attired people whom they imagined to be either terribly wealthy or celebrities but whom they did not recognize. The long, subtropical coastal island had already become a favorite winter vacation site for the world's well to do and famous.

Sitting on Mrs. Lewis' porch that served as a guest dining room, Anna looked at her husband in the soft light of the hurricane lamp dangling haphazardly from the ceiling over them. It was the only lighting on the porch although there were electric lights in the rest of the house. Moths and mosquitoes were swarming at the screens on the outside. The dumb and futile flattering of the moths' wings made her slightly uneasy, but seeing again how tan Bernhard had become, how rested and relaxed he looked, Anna decided she was glad they had come to Florida for their honeymoon. City life was not for her husband, she knew that very well. Still, she could not understand how he could imagine living here in Florida. Every time he burst out in praise of the climate, the sun, and the sea – and that was several times each day – she simply agreed with him, thinking he would have to come back to his senses soon enough when they got back home to Brooklyn again.

If it had not been for the mosquitoes, his enthusiasm knew no bounds, it seemed to Anna. He admitted that there was that one negative thing. There were a lot of mosquitoes and they seemed to love him as much as he loved Florida. He had pinned a handkerchief over a hole in the screen of their bedroom window, but there were always one or two that kept him from going to sleep until he had found and destroyed them with the fly swatter that was part of the cottage's standard equipment. Still, he woke up every morning with a new crop of itchy bumps.

Mrs. Lewis came back out onto the porch carrying another basket of fresh hush puppies and a platter of steamed swordfish and fried chicken, "I'm gonna be sad to see you two go t'morra, but I know you'll be back." Her eyes twinkled knowingly as she looked at Bernhard. "Just make sure not t'empty your shoes before you go. If there's sand in 'em when you get home, you're sure to come back."

"The only thing that could keep my husband from coming back here are the mosquitoes, Mrs. Lewis." Anna looked at her plate, wondering how she could eat another portion of fish, succotash, and hush puppies, even if it was delicious.

"This was a bad year for skeeters, but the season's over now, ain't I told you that? Now on the west coast it's a differnt story. They always got em. Every summer, every fall. We jes get'em when the wind's from the west."

"They don't seem to bother me," Anna said.

"As long as yer husband's around, they won't tech ya. They don like ya, Hon!" Mrs.Lewis remarked drily.

Anna thought to herself, "And the sun doesn't like me either, so I guess that means Florida doesn't like me!"

"I guess I don't mind a couple of mosquito bites," Bernhard commented. "This place is the place I'd like to live my life. America's the land of opportunity, as they say, and Florida just might be the best place to find it. Palm Beach is really beautiful. Worth Avenue looks to me like it could be somewhere in Spain. I've never been there, but…The architecture, you know? I hear it's Spanish style. New York City is amazing, sure, but I wouldn't call it beautiful. And I'm glad we stayed a week longer than we planned. I'm going to miss our walks on the beach. If I lived here, I'd go for a walk and a swim every single day!"

"We have to be realistic, Bernhard. You might be able to work as a hairdresser in Palm Beach in the winter with all the wealthy women, but what would you do in the summer? Mrs. Lewis told me that everyone over there goes back up north because it gets too hot."

Anna knew that her husband was very impressed by the visible signs of extreme wealth in Palm Beach. She wondered if he thought it would be easy to get rich working there. She did not think so, at least not as a hairdresser.

Mrs. Lewis nodded and heaped butter onto another hush puppy before dunking it in the little cup of honey and popping it into her mouth. "Ya'd have t' do like they do, go back and forth with the snowbirds."

"Yes, I guess I do have to be realistic."

The disappointment in Bernhard's voice and his ironic smile made Anna regret she had said anything.

"A man has to have a job to support his family and I guess I'm dreaming. But it sure would be wonderful."

"Who knows? Maybe someday," Mrs. Lewis replied. "Lots a people are movin down here from the cold North. Not just for the season. But you should'a come here years ago. The way you like to walk the beach, you could'a bin another 'barefoot mailman'."

Then Bernhard and Anna listened as she went on to tell them the story of the man who delivered the mail along the coast of Florida all the way down to Miami before the railway was built. She told them about her husband who was "out in the sticks" hunting with his brother somewhere in

Georgia. He had been gone all month and she did not know when he was coming back. She did not seem upset about that at all, more like she enjoyed being on her own. "He's not much help when he's here" was her brief comment before she started telling them how the hush puppies got their name and recounting other tales of the South.

They sat there late into the night, until Bernhard stood up, saying they needed to get an early start the next morning. They planned to go as far as possible in the first stretch, especially since there was not much money left to finance overnight stays further north. He and Anna thanked profusely for the meal, promising to come back to the 'Cozy Copper-Covered Cottages' if they ever made it back to Florida. Then they headed back to their cottage for a short night. Bernhard made a dash for it, swatting at the swarm of mosquitoes that seemed to have been waiting for him outside the porch door. Anna walked along after him, looking at the moon and the way it reflected on the white oleander blossoms on the bushes that lined the pathway. This was what she liked best about Florida, the lush verdant trees and shrubbery, and the fragrance of exotic flowers. The climbing bougainvillea ranging in color from pale pink and apricot to deep red and purple, the bushes bursting with red, pink, and yellow hibiscus, the voluptuous blue plumbago, the strange sea grape trees with their low, twisted branches and round leaves at the beach. If they were to come back to Florida, she would want to come in the spring or early summer when the purple jacarandas, the blue wisteria, the bright red royal poincianas and the wild orchid trees that Mrs. Lewis had told her about were in bloom.

15

September 1940

Citizenship

Anna bent over and placed the two big brown paper bags full of groceries, one of which was beginning to tear with the milk bottle leaning precariously at the top, carefully onto the second step of the stairs that led up to the next floor, thankful once again that she didn't live on the fourth floor at the top of the building. Two flights of stairs were enough to climb with bundles. She fished around in the bottom of her shoulder bag to find the keys to the apartment door. As usual, they were not easy to retrieve, especially if she was in a hurry like she was today, and, as her fingers dug into first the one and then the other corner of her bag, she eyed the dumbwaiter leering wide open in the wall right next to her door. If she had gone down to the cellar with her bags, she could have tried sending them up on the tiny service lift – there was no access to the dumbwaiter on the ground floor. That door had been locked for some reason. She had thought about this numerous times, but, now again, it did not look especially clean in there. No wonder since the only thing the other tenants seemed to use it for regularly was to transport their garbage down to the cellar. She pictured her bags of groceries falling over on the way up, milk bottles breaking, eggs, fresh vegetables and fruit all spilling over and down the shaft.

Then she sighed, there were her keys at last, somehow wrapped into her clean handkerchief, in a way that she could not have achieved if she had tried, not that she would have wanted to do that. She shook out the dainty little piece of white batiste cotton cloth embroidered with tiny blue flowers, that her grandmother in Sweden had sent her at her confirmation, folded it and put it back into her bag. Then she inserted the key into the lock.

As Anna opened the door, a draught threatened to slam it shut again. She bent down to pull the heavy wooden horse that always stood next to the entrance to the apartment into place on the threshold where it would prevent the door from shutting. She took the groceries into the kitchen, placed the bags on the table, and, smiling, put the milk and the butter in the refrigerator that they still called an icebox. Then she went back to move the colorfully painted carved horse to where it belonged and close the door. She looked at the orange and blue "*Dala häst*", painted in the traditional folkloristic style of the Swedish province of Dalarna, thinking that it was probably her favorite wedding present. She wondered when she and Bernhard would ever take the trip to Sweden they had talked about so often. It would be a luxury, considering their financial situation, and now there was a war going on in Europe! But she swiftly dismissed those thoughts from her mind. There were too many fears associated with thinking about the war.

She still appreciated the enjoyment she was experiencing in decorating this new apartment on 87th Street. Bernhard had left it up to her to choose the colorful little couch that the advertisement called a love seat and the two green armchairs they had placed on either side. She had picked out the green curtains and the patterned reddish carpet after much deliberation and was pleased with the results. But her proudest acquisition had been the brand-new refrigerator in the tiny kitchen. It was not big, but it worked perfectly, unlike the one they had previously shared with other tenants on their floor in the apartment building on Gelston Avenue, and she still had to smile every time she looked at it. After all, the Depression was over, electric refrigerators had become more affordable, and everyone, including Anna, wanted to have one.

They had moved in just a few months before. Their first tiny apartment had been a cozy newlyweds' nest, but, it had been rented completely furnished, never felt like her own and after three years, it had also become too cramped to be comfortable. They had been pleased to find and move into this reasonably priced new two-bedroom accommodation in Bay Ridge, Brooklyn. Neither Anna nor Bernhard mentioned the fact that there now would be room for the family to grow, but that was what was foremost in Anna's mind. Bernhard was in no hurry to have children. In fact, although he had never actually said so, he did not really want children of his own. Their families were big enough already. He was glad they were both earning and able to afford to buy most of the things they needed or wanted.

Tonight, they had something to celebrate. Anna looked at her watch and wondered where to start. She had already prepared the sweet-pickled cucumbers and the *köttbullar* (meatballs). She knew the cucumbers would be better for being done the day before, but she was not so sure about the Swedish meatballs. Even if she had got off work an hour early from the office, she knew she simply would not have had time to mix, shape with a spoon individually and then fry fifty tiny meatballs. So, she had done them the night before while Bernhard was at the gym. They were now hiding in the back of the fridge and would be served cold. She had decided that would have to do. She started peeling potatoes, which, along with cleaning and cutting the fresh green beans was enough to keep her busy for some time. She hoped Bernhard would not get home early and that at least some of their guests would arrive before he did, to yell "Surprise!" as he came in the door. She knew that was something he, like all of his siblings, always appreciated. She had told those guests who owned cars to please park around the block or he might recognize the cars and suspect what was about to happen.

Half an hour later, when Anna was still busy dipping pieces of veal in flour, stuffing them with chopped parsley and pinning them together with toothpicks to pop them into the frying pan and make the last few "veal birds", the doorbell rang. She wiped her hands on her apron and went to press the buzzer for the downstairs entrance, but when she peered through the peep hole in the door, she saw that Margret was already standing there. Her sister-in-law, just recently married to Bernhard's younger brother Hans, was waiting with her arms full of packages.

"I got everything on your list, Anna, even the fresh *limpa*, all three loaves. No one else will be able to get any this evening!" she laughed, as she burst in. "They'll have to eat *knäckebröd*. (hardtack)" She put the packages on the kitchen table, took off her coat, and walked back out of the kitchen into the hall, shaking her thick curly red hair out of her cloche hat when she got there.

"Thanks so much, Margret. I couldn't possibly swing this without your help. There was no way I could have gone to the Scandinavian deli on my way home. I did get off early, but still, I couldn't even have carried everything by myself. And it wouldn't be a proper *smörgasbord* without these things..." She gave Margret a quick handless hug, who smiled back broadly, stretching her freckles. She and Anna had hit it off immediately when they met a little over a year before.

"So, where's the document? Shouldn't you frame it and hang it on the wall? That's what I'm going to do when Hans gets his."

Bernhard had taken his oath of allegiance as a naturalized United States citizen a few days before.

"He wouldn't want me to make a fuss, that's why this has to be a surprise. But after all that work, teaching him English! The spelling! I never realized how illogical our spelling is until I tried to teach him. He didn't have to learn perfect English, of course not. He's just such a perfectionist. A perfectionist with absolutely no talent for memorizing spelling rules that have more exceptions than regularities. He wanted to know the rules! I don't know more than 'i before e...' myself. The hours he spent learning about the Constitution, the Amendments, the Declaration of Independence, basic American history! He knows more about all that than I ever learned in school. Anyway, it wasn't easy and now I feel like there has to be some kind of celebration."

"Of course! Okay, now tell me what I can do to help. Can I set the table?"

"I thought I'd just put the plates and silverware, glasses and all at the end of the table, do the usual buffet."

"Right. It wouldn't be a *smörgasbord* otherwise, would it? I didn't mean to set places."

Anna looked at Margret apologetically. "Sorry, I guess I'm a little nervous. Of course, *smörgasbord* is no mystery to you either." Margret's parents were from Sweden too, and she had had the same upbringing as a Brooklyn Swedish-American as Anna had. "Come help me put up the card table. I have a nice long cloth that will cover both tables if we shove them together."

"I can do that, Anna. Just give me the tablecloth, I know where the card table is. And if you're almost finished in the kitchen – show me what goes in which serving dish. Then you can go get changed and be ready to welcome anyone who gets here early. Don't forget to wash the flour off your nose!"

"Good grief! I forgot the state I'm in. You are an angel!"

She turned, glancing at her watch, and pointing to some dishware on the table. "Look at these nice platters and the casserole. I borrowed them from my upstairs neighbor. They're a nice young couple. I think he's from Denmark. Moved in last month... Um, I thought I'd put the mashed potatoes in the big casserole, do whatever you think with the rest, okay?"

She pulled the tablecloth out of a drawer, handed it to Margret and then dashed out of the kitchen, pulling off her apron as she went.

16

A Celebration

"So that's why no one had time to go have a drink with me! They were all coming here!" The surprise was a complete success. Bernhard was amazed to find half of his and Anna's family and most of their friends assembled in his livingroom, cheering, and congratulating him as he came in the door. He had come home on the subway, puzzling over the fact that everyone had turned him down when he asked if they wanted to go for a beer. He had even called John Gare, who was always telling him to stop working so hard, saying it could not be all work and no play. Bernhard had for the past few years consistently made excuses when John had suggested going for a few drinks in a bar in the evening the way they had done regularly before both had married. John had called Bernhard a stick-in-the-mud and a teetotaler just a few weeks before.

Here he was among the first to give Bernhard a bearhug, laughing and clapping him on the back. Bernhard gave everyone his biggest smile, shaking his head in amused and pleased disbelief.

When Hans finished filling a few mouthfuls of champagne into every glass in the house – it was a weird assortment of juice glasses, tumblers, wine glasses and other unidentifiable glasses of all shapes and sizes – he signaled to Anna, who then called out enthusiastically, "Everyone please take a glass. Sorry we don't have proper champagne glasses, but at least the champagne is real, thanks to Mimi. I had no idea how hard it is to get this these days and couldn't find anything I could pay for downtown. The owner of the shop on 4th Avenue said something about having a hard time importing champagne and wine from France. Mim brought this from Rochester and wouldn't tell me how much she and Harry paid for it or who they had to bribe."

Everyone laughed, got themselves a glass and called out "*Skål!*" to Bernhard, who now stood next to Anna with his arm around her waist. She smiled proudly up at him, he gave her a quick kiss on the cheek, and both lifted their glasses answering "*Skål!*"

After a few personal toasts to Bernhard, one by his father-in-law Frank, who was taking a public speaking course and happy for an opportunity to practice, most of the guests stood talking in small groups, holding their plates, their glasses standing on the windowsills and every other surface area available. Anna's parents and Mimi and Harry had been offered the only comfortable seats on the couch and were balancing their plates on their knees. Dagmar, one of Anna's best friends, was highly pregnant awaiting the first baby in their circle of couples from the gym and had settled onto one of the four straight-backed chairs from the dining-room table. Her husband Fritz stood behind her chair holding both of their glasses. The rest of the chairs stood vacant like the last three *kötbullar* on a serving dish that everyone was too polite to take and place on his plate. So, Anna went around offering the last little bits of food, saying she would be insulted if anything was left over. As she made the rounds from guest to guest with each platter, she heard Mimi explain to Bertha that she and Harry always had champagne on reserve for unexpected special occasions.

Anna wondered if she would ever become as efficient as her sister-in-law. She laughed to herself at the absurdity of that as she offered Hans some more cucumbers. He smiled at her, saying, "*Nej, tack!* I have already eaten more than my share!"

She reflected on how happy he and Margret seemed since they had been married and thought, "Yes, the Linden brothers really do make good husbands!" She was feeling pleased that the party seemed to be a success. Gradually, however, she noticed that the main topic of conversation going on was one she did not wish to talk about at all, certainly not that evening. She heard the word "*Blitz*" in two corners of the room. First it was her new neighbors from upstairs chatting with her neighbors from downstairs who had loaned her the dishware. Then Dagmar's husband Fritz was talking to one of their friends from the gym, saying, "The *Blitz* just might be the end of the British. I wouldn't want to be living in London's fair city right now." Anna had heard of the German all-night bombing raids on London that had been in the headlines of all newspapers for almost two weeks.

She had heard her father telling her mother it was nonsense to worry about the United States being involved in the war. But he did not sound that convinced himself anymore. Everyone knew that the US was already producing arms in such quantities that made joining in the war seem almost probable. What were they preparing for if not war?

When she heard Bernhard's brothers joking with him that it was maybe not the best time to get American citizenship, she stood still at the door to the kitchen, listening. Lambert was saying, "I'm serious about the draft. Do you know what Mrs. Cohn said this morning? She's the one whose husband works on Wall Street. Somehow he must have survived when everyone else was jumping out of windows. You know who I mean. She came in real early, before you came to the shop today. She has straight very dark hair with lots of grey but doesn't want it colored... I'm sure you've done her hair, too, Bernhard, before she decided she preferred my styling." The brothers loved to tease each other and never missed an opportunity to do so.

Just when Anna was about to give up, thinking she had not heard Lambert right, and go on into the kitchen with the heavy empty platters she was carrying, he finally got to the point. "Anyway, she told me she knows for a fact that a law will soon be passed to reestablish the draft. That means, little brother, all men between the ages of 21 and 35 will have to register with their local draft board."

Just when Anna was about to give up, thinking she had not heard Lambert right, and go on into the kitchen with the heavy empty platters she was carrying, he finally got to the point. "Anyway, she told me she knows for a fact that a law will soon be passed to reestablish the draft. That means, little brother, all men between the ages of 21 and 35 will have to register with their local draft board."

"Have you been reading the papers lately, Mr. Bjorkman? I think you will see a change in opinion."

"Of course, I read the newspapers, young man. I don't think this country wants to be involved in another war, that's all. It's all right to help by producing weapons for the right side, that's getting our economy back on its feet. That's what we're doing at my company. But as for going to war, I can't believe that."

Lambert did not know whether to be pleased to be considered a young man or worried that he had spoken to Frank in a disrespectful manner, something he had not intended. For a moment, the room seemed to go silent. Everyone turned to listen. It was as if the word "war" possessed a piercing quality that caused it to reach people's ears through the hubbub of voices and trivial conversation. Then, suddenly, everyone was talking at the same time again.

Hans was explaining to Mimi that he was in the kind of industry that would keep him off the draft, making precision instruments that they were selling to the arms industries. He would be given what was called "security clearance" because of the classified data he had access to. For the first time Mimi was glad he had stopped working at the shop with his brothers. Being the youngest of her brothers at twenty-seven, he would have been "eligible material". Margret and Dagmar were listening to Fritz, who was saying that he had heard about the draft, but that it would apply to young men from 18 to 30 years of age. Someone else said, "If there's a war, they'll take every man under sixty!" Another voice was saying the United States wouldn't have to worry about the "*Blitz*" at least, since airplanes could not fly that far without landing.

Anna went into the kitchen, managed to put the platters into the sink without breaking them and wondered if she was going to faint as her ears started ringing loudly in her head. She dropped onto the little three-legged stool that she kept under the table, putting her head down between her knees and thinking she would like to send Bernhard on the next boat to Sweden. Her father, who had followed her into the kitchen, patted her clumsily on the back and said gruffly, "Don't worry, we're not even in the war yet. And I don't think we ever will be."

"I'll get Mamma," her father said.

"No, I'm all right." She sat up and looked at him. "Are you looking for some coffee? It's ready and I'll have it on the table along with Mamma's coffee bread in a minute. Please go back and sit down." She reminded herself that she had other guests as well and got up slowly from where she was sitting, attentive to any signs of dizziness. She had a drink of water from the tap and decided she was all right.

Out in the living-room the voices had died down. Anna could hear John Gare tuning up his guitar. She would put on a bright face, but inside she knew she would be thinking of the terrible irony that might make her Bernhard eligible for the draft just in time. He was 33 years old.

.

17

November

"Take a look in the cellar, Anna!"
Signe was down to visit for the weekend from Connecticut where she and Richard were living since they had married. Anna had come over to their parents' house on Park Place for the afternoon and the twins were getting ready to have coffee with their mother in Bertha's kitchen..

"Why? What's new in the cellar, Signe? Have you been exploring? Don't tell me Pappa is brewing up something special again!" Anna got up from the table sniffing and saying, "But I don't smell anything suspicious."

Bertha watched embarrassed but resigned as her twins went over to the cellar. "Signe doesn't miss a trick!" she thought to herself.

"Good grief! I've been here almost every weekend and I never noticed this. You never told me about this, Mamma. It can't all be beans, can it?" Anna came back into the kitchen with amazement written all over her face. "Has Pappa gone mad?"

"Don't talk that way about your father, Anna. He's

thinking ahead. At least we won't starve if there's a war."

Signe laughed saying, "I didn't go exploring, Anna. I just went looking for a can of condensed milk for our coffee this morning and discovered all the new shelves. Brand new and already sagging with provisions for the rest of the century! Of all things, beans! I wonder if there is such a thing as bean poisoning?"

Bertha shrugged helplessly, "What can I do? You know your father."

"So, he has changed his mind about America going to war, has he?" Anna was not laughing, and Signe closed the cupboard door without taking out the three coffee cups she had gone to fetch when she heard the serious tone of Anna's voice. She turned and both young women looked at their mother.

"*Jag vit inte!* (I don't know!) He read something in the paper about beans being the ideal food, full of proteins and vitamins or something and he thought it was a good idea to stock up. There was a special offer somewhere that he read about in the next day's paper. They haven't been there long. He didn't ask me first, I don't even like beans. They don't agree with me. You know what I mean."

Signe thought of the joke she had heard, about how in Boston people ate baked beans and the Long Islanders lived on the Sound. But it did not sound that funny to her at the moment. Richard was a year younger than she was and she was afraid to think of what that could mean.

Bertha went on, "He bought them two weeks ago. Right after election day."

Roosevelt had just been reelected for an unprecedented third term as president. His landslide victory had taken place only six weeks after he had not hesitated to confirm the "Burke-Wadsworth Act" establishing the draft for the American armed forces. That too was unprecedented. Never before had the United States introduced conscription in peacetime. All men between 21 and 35 had had to register and would be selected by means of a lottery. Both Richard and Bernhard had had to register with the draft board, Bernhard in Brooklyn and Richard in Guilford, Connecticut. Neither one of them thought it would come to war though. At least that was what they had told their wives.

Anna's colleagues at work at the Metropolitan Insurance Company were of divided opinion, but no one could ignore the fact that there were decidedly more life insurance policies being taken out by young married men lately. Anna had noticed that Bernhard had stopped bringing the newspaper home from the shop and had developed a habit of turning off the radio whenever the news came on. They had talked about it a few times, but it was simply too depressing for Anna.

The three women sat in silence for a few minutes. Then Bertha stood up from the table and got the cups and saucers. She poured the coffee, thinking to herself, "And now Frank wants to join the Adventist Church. That's why he has stopped drinking alcohol. It all fits together. He might really think there's a danger that the government could draft older men if war breaks out. Maybe he wants to save his soul before they send him to Europe. Hadn't Faster Emma said something about registering men up to age 65 just a few weeks ago? Then the beans are for us, poor women left at home. '*Nej! Det är tokig!* (No! That's crazy!) I'll have to talk to Frank about this tonight when we're alone."

Signe and Anna, each deep in thought, looked up when they heard their mother mutter "*Nej!*" and laugh strangely under her breath. All she said as she took the condensed milk from the icebox, was, however, "*Grubbla inte över det!* (Don't worry about it!) Let's not be pessimistic! Maybe it won't happen and none of our, I mean neither of your husbands," she hurried to correct herself, "will ever have to become a soldier. Now, have some of my fresh *kaffeebröd* (coffee cake). I made this for you, Signe." For a moment Anna thought she had detected an undertone in what her mother had said but dismissed it as a result of her own worries about Bernhard. Then those worries reclaimed her thoughts and feelings. Signe, too, looked preoccupied as she dunked her coffee cake into her coffee. She was thinking about the little house Richard was building for them on Moose Hill just down the road from her parents' summer cottage.

That evening Frank came home late. It was unusual for him to work on a Saturday anyway, but he did not get home until after nine o'clock. He had told Bertha before he left in the morning that he had an important meeting with the board of directors at his company. As it got later and later, she sat in the kitchen, wondering what the meeting was about. Anna had gone home, and Signe and Mona had already eaten. They were upstairs when he finally came in the front door and down into the kitchen.

Frank sat silently at the table reading the newspaper that he had brought home with him while Bertha heated up their dinner. When the food was on the table, she could wait no longer.

"What was the meeting about, Frank?"

"What? Oh, just the usual time schedules and supply problems." He kept his eyes on his plate.

"*Nej, du! Det tror jag inte!* (No! I don't believe that!) You've never had meetings this late, and on a Saturday, too! What is going on?"

Frank hesitated a moment, then took a deep breath and said, "I had expected it for a while, but now I know that AMF will soon be officially involved in wartime production, uh… for the military. The company already is to a certain extent, actually, but that will be raised to our main line of production."

"But you make machinery for the tobacco industry! And you said something a few weeks ago about sports equipment."

"We also make blast valves. I'm not sure, but the

foundry may have been supplying parts for ships and airplanes for years now. I have nothing to do with the sales department. We had to discuss different changes in schedule to accommodate a change in pace in case it becomes necessary. There are a lot of rumors going around."

"Blast valves? Rumors? Does that mean...?"

"That we are going to war? I don't know. But I'm beginning to think the government is just waiting for the right opportunity."

"*Kära God*, Frank. Then I guess it's true. That's terrible," she sighed. With a shaking voice she went on, "But at least they won't be sending you anywhere if you're in an important position here, will they?"

"Me? For God's sake, woman! What would they want with me on a battlefield? I'm an old man, I'm 52 years old! Have you been worrying about that? Besides, I'm worth much more here. If we're not making a lot of parts for the war industry now, we will be soon. I may be old, but I can do my part by doing my job."

"You're only old on paper, Dear," she said, knowing he did not really consider himself old either. Then, putting her fork down, she reached over to touch his hand and smile strangely at him.

Frank looked at his wife and wondered why she still looked downtrodden.

She shook her head slowly, "So if the war doesn't cross the ocean and reach us here, I'm glad that we at least are safe."

Frank nodded and went on eating.

Anxiously, she then asked, "But what will our girls do if their husbands are all sent off to Europe to fight a war? They may never come back. *Det är förskräckligt!*" (That is terrible!) She paused, sighing, and then went on sadly, "It might be all three of them, Frank, now that Helen might be getting married again soon, too. She's getting serious about this Bob."

By the Time You Are Married

Mona had come down the stairs to say goodnight before she went to bed. She heard her parents talking seriously. Her mother sounded unhappy, worried. Mona listened to hear what they were talking about. She only caught the very last bit and came into the kitchen, wondering how such a good piece of news could make her mother sad. And why should good news be kept secret? She did not want to admit to having eavesdropped but could not contain her excitement and burst out, "That's wonderful news!"

Her parents looked at her, wondering what she could possibly mean.

"Another wedding!" she said, happily. "Who's getting married? When will it be? ...Can I be the flower girl again?"

.

18

Brooklyn, 1941

A year passed. Life did not change for Anna and Bernhard. There were the newspapers full of bad news from Europe but that did not directly affect them. In fact, Anna wondered if they were getting used to and slightly immune to the horror. Bernhard was not called up. He won a number of hairdressing competitions with his wife as his model. Everyone told them they were an unbeatable pair. Bernhard's brothers made fun of his new, big, 16-inch-tall loving cup for "finger waving", won in a contest in which the only hairdressing tools that could be used were a comb, setting lotion and the hairdresser's own fingers. Walter especially enjoyed saying he could wave his fingers as well if not better than Bernhard..

Anna was proud of Bernhard and his success and would have been living a life of marital bliss, had she not been waiting in vain for signs of pregnancy. She had talked to her mother about it a few months before and was told they should be glad to have some time for themselves, the babies would come and then her life would be different. She would have to give up her job and they would miss her earnings.

"Look at poor Helen," Bertha had said, "Now that she has remarried there's another baby arriving very soon and she has enough with, ...with the first two!" Bertha had awkwardly cut that discussion short, causing Anna to assume such topics were still simply too embarrassing for her mother, ever since she had had to contend with a late, unexpected pregnancy of her own. At that time Bertha's sixteen- and seventeen-year-old daughters had been unable to recognize why their mother was losing her waistline until it was undeniably clear even to them.

But Anna was not aware, nor was Signe, or even Frank, for that matter, that Helen had had a serious crisis just two years before. The problem had been "solved" but at great risk in a somewhat dubious doctor's office, leaving Bertha and Foster Emma terribly worried about her but promising, hand on heart, never to tell what had happened. Now those two women were worried about Helen again.

They, on the other hand, had no idea that Anna and Signe had also been sworn in to keep a secret for Helen. A different one. Although the story would come to Bertha's ears eventually, she did not yet know the complicated details about Helen's more recent predicament. Her new husband Bob, a kind and friendly man the entire family liked immediately, had been engaged to another woman. Helen was not aware of this woman's existence or her legitimate claims until the engagement ring was dramatically returned while she and Bob were sitting on a bench in Guilford Square. When Bob offered the ring to Helen she furiously refused to accept it and, as the story goes, threw it at him. Bob later gave it to his mother and got a new ring for Helen.

Nonetheless, after a month of despair, Helen was married again and happy now at last. She and Bob were the proud parents of a baby girl. So much for her mother's reasoning. Babies did make women happy. Anna knew that for a fact.

The only one still about to despair was Anna. When she went to her doctor with the one complaint and feeling otherwise perfectly healthy, he advised her to stop working if she wanted to get pregnant. She could not raise that topic with Bernhard, not yet at least, so her life went on unchanged, leaving her with a constant feeling of vague disappointment.

When change came, it was profound and upended not only Anna's and Bernhard's life but that of everyone they knew. It shocked all of America out of a kind of illusionary semi-slumber. It came suddenly and unexpectedly, because it came from the opposite direction while America had its eyes trained on Europe and what was happening there.

Everyone knew that Roosevelt wanted to fight Hitler and that preparations were obviously under way – United States industry was producing weapons and military supplies at a rapid pace – but the Japanese attack on Pearl Harbor on December 7th, 1941, came as a surprise to most civilians and even, obviously, the military. It turned the general antiwar sentiment around almost overnight. Many young men enlisted voluntarily, not wanting to wait for the draft board to pick them. Anna argued daily with Bernhard, who felt indebted to his new country and was developing a bad conscience with his hands in his pockets, or "holding a curling iron instead of a gun", as he put it. He felt that he should join up. Anna kept reminding him that he was older than most of the volunteers and that he was just beginning to make a name for himself. Mimi, too, argued with him on the telephone from Rochester that it would be pointless to volunteer one year before he would become ineligible. But those arguments would soon fall flat. Two weeks after the attack by the Japanese and the United States' declaration of war against Japan, which had immediately been followed by the declaration of war by Germany and Italy against the US, Anna came home hours late from work. Bernhard was already home waiting for her and getting worried.

"What's wrong, Anne? What happened?" Bernhard had started calling his wife Anne sometimes, as if he felt more American doing so.

She was already looking despondent, but when she tried to answer she burst into tears.

"It's Margie's husband," she said. "Her mother called her at the office to tell her Jim has been declared missing. His ship was at Pearl Harbor!"

Anna sobbed as Bernhard helped her out of her coat.

"I felt so terrible. I had to accompany her home. She was so upset, she wasn't even going to put on her coat, just wanted to get home."

"He's missing, maybe he wasn't killed!"

"But if his ship went down? They'll declare everyone missing, won't they? And we saw the pictures, nobody could survive that!"

"Don't be so pessimistic, he might be all right," Bernhard spoke soothingly while Anna blew her nose into the handkerchief he had pulled out of his pants pocket and handed to her.

"She had been saying all week that she was sure his ship wasn't at Pearl Harbor, but the way she kept talking about it I knew she wasn't really sure."

"Come on, sit down," Bernhard led her into the living-room where she collapsed onto the couch.

"I felt so terrible, Bernhard. Remember how he had joked about joining the navy to see the world? I'm sure I told you how he had said he might even make it to Hawaii! He'd always wanted to go there, you know, hula skirts, ukuleles and all that. Margie was being so brave, not crying and I was fighting back the tears all the way to her house on the subway."

"She didn't even cry when she opened the door to her apartment and her mother came towards us with the baby on her arm. Little Jimmy came running up saying he wanted to show her something he made. I managed to take the baby and asked Jimmy to show me what it was that he made and went with him into the nursery. Margie went into the kitchen with her mother and I thought they would never come back out. They were telephoning with relatives and....anyway it was a good thing I was there, I guess."

Anna sat looking down at the handkerchief and, taking a deep shaky breath, said again, "I felt so terrible, so awful and do you know why?"

Bernhard shook his head, "No."

"I've been envying Margie for years now, Bernhard."

"Why?"

She looked up at Bernhard sadly, almost pathetically, and said so softly that he could just barely hear her, "She didn't have to ask twice for her babies, and I can't even get pregnant. I'm so ashamed I ever envied her and now she might have to bring the boys up on her own, what will she do? Thank God her mother is still fit and willing to take care of them while she's at work!"

Bernhard knew that Anna desperately wanted to have a child, but he thought they had plenty of time. He was aware of how too many children could keep a family poor, having been brought up where money was scarce but the house full of mouths to feed. He had an almost symptomatic habit of wolfing his food at meals that he had developed as a survival tool. As the next to the youngest child of a big family he might not have got enough if he had not been able to eat fast. Anna was always noticing that, after she dished out their dinner, took the pots to the kitchen and came back to pick up her own fork and knife, he was already half finished. She had given up trying to break him of the habit. At least he did not do that when they were eating with other people or on the still rare occasions when they ate out in a restaurant.

They sat together on the couch, talking about the state of the world for a while, agreeing that it seemed ironic that they had more or less gotten over the depression only to now enter into another world war. Was it a good time to have children? That was a question people had asked themselves throughout history. At the end of their discussion Anna expressed the hope that Bernhard would be sensible, as she put it, and not put himself in harm's way unnecessarily by volunteering to serve at his age. He did not comment, but changed the subject, suggesting they should go out for supper. It was late and Anna had not had time to shop for food. So, they went to their favorite little Chinese restaurant downtown, a dark, narrow place that extended deep into the building and gave Anna the impression of being on a train without windows and where the soft-spoken, impeccably polite waiters padded about silently, serving them their *chow mein* with many bows and smiles and pouring their tea into little cups without handles.

A few days later Bernhard came home in the evening to say that, after talking to Walter on the phone, they both had enlisted and that he would be getting a letter in the mail telling him where to go and what to do. The only explanation he gave Anna when he told her – gently but very firmly – what he had done, was, "Either I'm an American or I'm not an American, Anne."

She accepted it, amazed at herself, realizing he could not have stood by and watched any longer. She thought about what a good shot he was and remembered dolefully how he had told her several times that he had come to America looking for adventure. Now he might get more than he bargained for. She managed not to cry that evening but hardly slept all night.

A short time later a new selective service act extended the draft lottery to include men from 18 to 45. Even those aged 46 to 65 had to register. It was established that the term of service in the armed forces was to continue until six months after the war ended, whenever that would be.

.

19

Summer, 1942

The letter that Anna dreaded receiving came but not until early summer. Bernhard said wryly that maybe they didn't need hairdressers, only barbers, and since they hadn't asked him if he could shoot a gun, they weren't aware of his skill with a rifle. His father-in-law Frank told him they would not take married men of Bernhard's age that quickly as long as there were plenty of younger men to do the job.

Secretly, Anna had hoped his documents had somehow gotten lost. But then Walter, who was older than Bernhard and also a hairdresser, was called up. A few days later the notice arrived telling Bernhard to report for a medical checkup at a recruitment center in downtown Brooklyn. The doctor who examined him found him to be in excellent health and in fact told him he was in a better state than most of the younger men he had seen in the past year. He did not know Bernhard's lungs looked fine in the summer even if he had coughed throughout half of the winter. Then he handed him a letter confirming his full eligibility and instructing him to report to Fort Dix in New Jersey the following week.

Anna asked Bernhard to please wait a few days before telling Mimi the news. Bernhard was fine with that and said he did not want two women fussing over him before he had to leave. Anna was relieved. She did not feel like sharing him with anyone else.

A few days later, Anna was asking her boss for overtime work. Anything was better than sitting alone in the apartment for longer than necessary.

At Fort Dix, Bernhard thought he looked pretty good in his uniform with his cap set just slightly jauntily to one side when he tried it on before going to an introduction in the mess hall in the evening. He could not see much of himself in the wavy metal shaving mirror over the sinks in the barrack's bathroom, but he was satisfied. He wondered somewhat vainly how Anna would react when she saw him, if she would find him especially attractive. He had heard that women liked men in uniform, but judging from her opinion about the war, she might not conform with that rumor. He was aware that his coloring was not especially good in the pale, greenish beige material, but he knew that would soon change after getting a glimpse of the men already further into their training. They were all tanned from the physical fitness exercises and drills conducted on the open field next to the barracks. To be honest, he was looking forward to testing his fitness and agility on the various structures of the obstacle course he had seen men struggling over and under, as he had walked toward his designated camp address with his neat pile of army clothing under his left arm and his right hand gripping the small bag of belongings he had brought with him.

When he found his barracks and was wondering which bunk to claim as his own, a young boy who looked about 15 but who had to be 18 smiled at Bernhard and said hello.

"This lower bunk here is free. I've got the uh upper… uh unless you want the upper?"

Bernhard wondered if the boy had lied about his age to get into the army. He was not even sure he could be 15 at closer scrutiny. "I don't care, either one will do. Are all the others taken?"

"Not all the others but these are the next in line as far as I can see," said the boy.

Bernhard stretched out his hand and said, "My name is Bernhard. We're going to be spending a lot of time together so we might as well get to know each other, right?"

"I'm Gerhart," said the boy, blushing vividly.

Bernhard wondered why he was embarrassed for a moment. Then it occurred to him that Gerhart was a German name. Maybe that was the reason. He swung his satchel onto the bed and laid the clothes next to it.

"You're supposed to put your things into the trunk at the bottom end of the bed. I've got mine in the trunk here by the wall. But I was thinking maybe you want this trunk if you have the lower bunk. Then you can… yu yu yu, use it to put things you want to reach from your bed at night. I can take my stuff uh uh uh… out again," said Gerhart.

"Oh my God," thought Bernhard to himself, "This boy's a nervous wreck."

All right," he said, "That's really nice of you. It's a good idea. Thanks."

Gerhart opened the trunk and transferred his things quickly to the other one. "My mom told me I have to keep everything really neat. Nobody's going to tidy uh uh uh… up for me here."

If Bernhard had thought he could handle any kind of abusive treatment during basic training just by being prepared to do so, he was sorely mistaken. The hair stood up on the back of his neck and both of his hands were clenched fists as the sergeant went through his routine of making them all feel like scum.

"Schroder!" the sergeant yelled. Bernhard wondered for

a split second why he did not start at the beginning of the alphabet with his roll call.

"Me?" asked Gerhart.

"Of course, you nitwit! You should know if you're Schroder or not! And," he yelled, "It's YESSIR! When I call your name, you little fool!"

"Yessir."

"LOUDER!"

"Yessir!" slightly more audible.

"Do I have to kick you to help you find your vocal cords?"

"YESSIR!"

The other men all winced and stifled a laugh, but the sergeant ignored the absurdity of Gerhart's answer, not wanting any good-humored slack in the tension he had created.

"What kind of name is that? Gerhart, Scchhrrroder. That sounds German to me. Is it?"

"No sir."

"What do you mean, no sir? That's about as German as a name can be."

"My grandfather was German."

"Your grandfather was German, SIR!"

"Your grandfather, no, my grandfather was German, sir! The rest of my family was..."

"Don't answer questions you haven't been asked, Private! I'm gonna call you Lee, not Schroder. That's your middle name, I see. I'm gonna pretend you aren't a German, Lee!" the sergeant barked.

"Yessir!" Gerhart was shaking.

Bernhard stood ramrod straight, the way he had learned as a gymnast and bellowed his "Yessir" as loud as he could when he heard his name. The sergeant came up to him, looked him up and down, then studied his list.

"You're the old man of this platoon, John Linden. Show these kids how to behave!"

"Yessir!"

"Where are you from?"

"Sweden, sir. I mean New York, sir."

"You better know where you come from! You're a naturalized citizen, are you?"

"Yessir!"

"Did you serve in Sweden before you came here?"

"No, sir."

The sergeant looked him up and down for the second time and then called the next name on his list. Bernhard looked out of the corner of his eye to see how Gerhart was doing. The boy was standing a lot straighter than before, but tears were streaming down his flaming cheeks. While the sergeant was looking in the other direction, yelling at someone on the other side of the room, he quickly tried to wipe his face with the backs of his hands.

When the sergeant went back down the row of men a few minutes later, looking each one in the eye and explaining the "rules of the game" as he called them, he used each man as an example for some violation of those rules. Two had to report to the barber's that evening, several had to cut and clean their fingernails, others had to learn how to stand up straight. When he got back to Gerhart, Bernhard was surprised that he did not make a laughingstock of the boy as he expected. He could not help seeing the smeared trace of tears but went on talking about some conduct regulations. Bernhard was also spared intense scrutiny for some reason or other and stood listening in surprise as the sergeant passed him with merely a quick glance as he gave some last-minute instructions about their schedule before calling out, "At ease!" and leaving the barracks.

The men stood around in silence for a minute, digesting the initiation experience they had just gone through, before most of them started cussing under their breath in disgust. Bernhard, however, felt his anger die away and decided the sergeant might be okay. He was only doing his job. Maybe he was not such a bad guy after all. He was sure there were worse sergeants. He sensed that this man would somehow be fair. He might be someone who would give each soldier a chance to cope in his own way, as long as they were trying their best.

20 CHAPTER NAME

Dear Anne,
> How are you? I'm ok. I don't think I ever was so tired in my life, but I'm doing ok, in fact better than some of these kids. My training at the Swedish Gym Club sure is coming in handy. We won't get leave until basic training is over. Sorry about that. I know I told you I thought I would be coming home for a weekend sometime soon. Whoever told me that did not know what he was talking about. But you can come here and visit me after the fourthe week for an afternoon if you want. We can meet in town. I feel sorry for these young guys. Some of them have never been away from home (and their mothers!) before. They call me the grande old man. I miss you.

Your loving husband Bernhard

For ten days Anna had been checking the mailbox with crossed fingers every evening when she got home from work. Finally, this short letter penciled onto a sheet of lined paper arrived. She read it a half a dozen times, laughing at the extra e's, one of which Bernhard had imperfectly rubbed out on the end of the word "old". She imagined how he must have heard her voice saying, "Why should there be an e on the end of 'old'? That's the way they wrote hundreds of years ago, ye olde this and ye olde that, but not anymore!" She had said it to him so many times, but he had hung onto that e for all it was worth. Now, apparently, he had remembered.

Unfortunately, there was fourthe and grande to contend with.... "No," she chided herself. These little spelling mistakes were so endearing, she swore to herself that she would never correct him again, if she could just have him back home safe. That thought brought tears of frustration. How could they just take him away from her? What was going to happen to him? Then she remembered how she had longed for this letter and sat right down at the dining table to write him an answer that she could drop off at the post office the next morning on her way to work.

She wrote:

Dearest Bernhard,

> I was so glad to hear from you, I have
> been so worried...

No, that wasn't right. There was no reason to worry yet. She took out another piece of paper and started over again, determined to think ahead:

Dearest Bernhard,

> I was so glad to get your letter, I've missed
> you so much! It seems you've been gone
> such a long time. I can hardly believe it will

> only be two weeks on Monday since you left.
> Of course, I will come visit you if I may. Let
> me know as soon as you know when I
> should come so I can ask to get the day off.
> Or will it be the weekend?
>
> You wrote you are tired. Is that because
> you can't sleep at night, or is it the exercises
> they make you do? Is the food any good? I
> guess it can't be very good if they call it
> 'mess', but do you get enough at least?
>
> I went to the pictures with Margie last
> weekend. She is such a dear friend. Her
> wonderful mother suggested we go out and
> have some fun now that...

Anna was about to tell Bernhard about how much happier her friend was since being notified that her husband had survived the Pearl Harbor attack by a stroke of incredible luck. But she dropped the idea. She could not write to him about luck. She wrote:

> Margie's husband has, thank God turned up
> uninjured. So, we saw a good movie with
> Ingrid Bergman and Humphrey Bogart,
> "Casablanca". I think she is my favorite
> actress, but I don't really care for him. I
> much prefer Clark Gable and I'll never
> forget him in "Gone with the Wind". You
> know how he reminds me of you, his eyes
> and even his facial expressions, that look he
> has of a good-hearted rascal.

She hesitated and wondered if she should use that word "rascal", but, after a moment decided to leave it. "Being a rascal might even come in handy in a war," she thought, shuddering, and went on writing.

> I've been very busy at work. We have a new department head. Mr. Burns was called up. He must have been younger than we thought. The new boss is much older, a Mr. Avery. They put two of our departments together under him and I don't see how that is going to work. We thought one of us girls might have been made head. We certainly know our way around this department better than Mr. Avery, but that'll be the day! Anyway, that's boring.
>
> Mamma and Pappa haven't been back from Connecticut yet. Maybe next week. Pappa has more vegetables this summer than ever before. He calls our vegetable patch the Bjorkman Victory Garden. Mamma is making preserves. They are talking about selling the house on Park Place and staying out in the country all year round as soon as Mona is finished with high school. And of course, the war is over.
>
> Please write again soon. Tell me what a typical day is like for you so I can imagine where you are and what you are doing at different times of day. You know, when do

you get up and so on. Now that I have the address, I'll try to write every day.

I miss you very much.

Your loving Anna

Anna made good her promise and wrote a letter to Bernhard every day for the rest of his basic training, some longer, some shorter, but all written on fine pale blue stationery in her gracefully slanted hand. The envelopes she sent on Monday mornings were heavier and thicker and required twice as much postage since she had more time to write on Saturday and Sunday. The post office was of course closed on Sundays so she would put both long letters into one big envelope each Monday morning. Bernhard, who, to say the least, was not an enthusiastic writer of letters, received them with all the more enthusiasm. And he did his best, sending her one of his dynamically scrawled notes for every three letters he received.

His days were long and hard. Bugle call came at 5 am each morning and made him increasingly sure of one thing. He would never again complain about an early client, seeing as he had never had one earlier than 7 o'clock in the morning and most likely never would. It was soon clear to him that he had had enough of the athletic challenges basic training presented him with. He knew it was necessary preparation for what would come but, when it came down to it, he preferred working out in the gym club.

Anna's visit at Fort Dix was over with so quickly that she could hardly believe it had happened. She had taken an early train to Trenton that Sunday and from there a bus to a small town near the camp, feeling like she was going on a blind date. At least that was the way she had felt when she was picking out the clothes she wanted to wear days beforehand.

She got to the little luncheonette in North Hanover that Bernhard had named as their meeting place early and ordered a cup of coffee. She sat by the big window next to the door, watching the people going by, more and more soldiers in uniform. She wondered what Bernhard would look like in his uniform and came to the inevitable conclusion that he would look striking. He had written that the training was tough, but nothing he could not handle. That was because he was a trained athlete with good posture and not an ounce of fat on him. He would look very handsome; of that she was quite sure.

As she waited, she gave herself another good talking to: absolutely no tears even if she had to bite through her tongue! She was not going to embarrass him and, since it was obvious that this war had to be fought, she understood that he wanted to do his duty. If she had to be a war wife, she wanted to be a good one.

Lost in these thoughts, she did not even notice Bernhard come into the restaurant. Later she would not understand how that could have happened. But suddenly she felt his presence behind her chair and turned to jump up into his arms. The other people in the room hardly gave them any notice as they kissed. The town was used to these scenes.

"You look wonderful!" they said to each other in unison and then laughed delighted at the coincidence. Bernhard held Anna at arm's length and admired her suit and the pretty new hat she had bought to go with it while Anna nodded her head, smiling her approval at Bernhard's appearance in his uniform.

"Your hat has the same shape as mine," she said. "And you wear it at the same angle, it seems."

"Maybe we should switch for the afternoon?" Bernhard joked.

Anna laughed at the idea and then said, smiling pertly, "No, I don't think so."

"Why? Do you think they would dishonorably discharge me because it's against our dress code?"

"No. The colors don't go!" she answered impudently, and then, "On second thought, I've brought the camera, so we could do it for a picture. That would be a funny souvenir about this day." Setting her jaw firmly she went on striking the most positive note possible, "We'll look at this picture when we are old and grey."

"Okay, whatever you say, honey. Just let me have a cup of good coffee and we can go for a walk and take some pictures. The coffee at the camp is disgusting."

"This isn't very good either," Anna said, pointing at her empty cup, "But I'll have another to keep you company. It looks like they have some nice donuts at the counter, too."

They had coffee and donuts and then went for a walk. As they strolled down Main Street, Bernhard told Anna some of the things he had not written in his letters. He said, for example, that he had talked to the sergeant privately a couple of times. He did not want to boast, but the sergeant was impressed with his gymnastic skills. In fact, it was getting embarrassing that he was always asking him to show the other guys how to do things.

"Like what, for instance?" Anna asked.

"Well, stunts like swinging on a rope over a deep ditch to get to the other side. Some of the guys in the platoon just don't seem to get it, the hang of it, or should I say the 'swing' of it?" he joked. "Thank goodness the young kid in the bunk over me, the one I wrote to you about with the German name, thank goodness Gerhart's pretty good at this stuff. I wanted to punch the sergeant in the nose for the way he laid into him on the first day. He still calls the poor kid Lee, but otherwise he's all right with him. I was sitting having a coffee at my table after supper the other night when everyone else had left and Sergeant Bode – that's our sergeant – came up and sat down across from me. I guess he has a little more respect for me because of my age. I must be about the same age as he is. Anyway, he told me how he hates the Germans and the Japs. Of course, I said, we're at war with them. When he didn't go on, I felt I had to say something and I said I still had some good friends who were German descent and that I even had been to Germany just four or five years ago and that I had met some nice people there, too. He looked at me and said it was hard to instill the necessary fighting spirit in these young kids if you didn't make them hate the enemy."

"What did you say to that?" Anna asked when he stopped walking, stood still, and looked at her.

"I was afraid I had said too much already, but I couldn't help myself. I said I heard they were taking Japanese-Americans out of their homes and putting them in camps to prevent them from spying."

"Good grief, Bernhard! That wasn't very smart. I wish I hadn't written to you about that. I bet that got you peeling potatoes all night."

"No, it didn't. Believe it or not, he said he didn't agree with that either. He said he hated the Japs for what they had done in the Pacific, but he had had a Japanese American friend in high school out in California with a really nice family. Then he gulped down his coffee and got up, saying, 'But we gotta be tough to win this war!' I agreed with him there."

The rest of their afternoon together went by in a flash. They walked to the edge of town and back and had a bit of lunch together, talking non-stop about everything under the sun. Anna tried to avoid topics that would be depressing for both and gritted her teeth as the time came for parting. She told herself that it would not be as hard this time, since Bernhard would get a weekend off as soon as basic training was over in about two weeks. Anna was struggling, willing her eyes not to produce tears. She was afraid to ask what would happen after that, if he would be sent somewhere else, farther away, but Bernhard's kiss blanked that out of her mind.

Feeling silly, and with a big shaky smile, Anna saluted

Bernhard as she got on the bus that would take her to the train station.

21

Cheating Clocks

Sitting alone at the kitchen table in their apartment on 87th Street, Anna was wondering about the honesty of clocks. That was what she called it to herself. Could a clock lie? After waiting for two interminably and tediously long weeks, Bernhard's weekend at home had finally come, and like his first afternoon off, it seemed to have been over before it began. Anna had prepared his favorite meals ahead, so as not to waste any precious time shopping or cooking. They had visited with Bertha and Frank and then gone for a walk in Prospect Park, something they had not done for a long time. They had gone for an ice-cream soda at their favorite ice-cream parlor. She had clung to him at night like never before until he had actually complained that he could not sleep if she didn't let go. Trying to get a hold on time so they could enjoy their short two days together proved as futile and pointless as making the clock stop ticking by putting it under a pillow. Time marched on relentlessly and faster than usual if you wanted it to slow down. Of course, it did the opposite if you wanted it to go by. She had never been so conscious of that in her life before. She felt like time was cheating her and Bernhard.

Alone in the week since their weekend together, she had started reading the articles about the war in the papers, needing to know what was going on. She had always skipped over them before, finding them too upsetting and depressing. But now she had to know what Bernhard was getting himself into. She already knew from the little he had told her on the weekend that his platoon would be part of a division that was serving somewhere in Europe, he did not know where. He only knew they would have about one more month's special training before shipping out and another weekend off before that. He had laughed and said that it was ironic but after all that long distance marching they had been practicing, they had been told they would be driving tanks. That had pleased and comforted Anna since it meant he would not be walking around unprotected but traveling inside an armored vehicle.

There she sat with the New York Times spread out on the table in front of her, the plate that had held her scrambled egg sandwich pushed to the side, still thinking about the time factor in her life and how the time Bernhard would be spending in Europe was going to be disastrously endless, and much harder for her to bear. The thought she did not allow her mind to complete was that that waiting period must not come to a disastrous end. She shivered and refused to think any further in that direction. As she scanned the page of war news she had opened to, not knowing which article to read since they all would be awful, her eyes caught the caption over a shorter article toward the bottom of the page: "Treacherous Tank Traps".

Horrified, she read on: "If we once were confident that our soldiers were better protected fighting from the enclosure of the heavily armored and armed combat vehicles we call tanks, we now have learned that the enemy has developed the ability to not only destroy these tanks but the soldiers inside of them by adeptly tossing hand grenades into the tank through the hatch. The Nazis are training special troops to know how and when to attack and reports have been coming in for the past few weeks that this simple method is becoming especially effective. The number of tanks and soldiers......"

Anna stopped reading, furiously crumbled the whole newspaper into a ball and threw it on the floor. She cried helplessly for half an hour, then suddenly got up, put her coat on and ran out of the apartment, down the stairs and out of the house onto the street.

Still hurrying, Anna stumbled down the steps to the subway station on 4th Avenue and 86th Street. She noticed in surprise that there was no one else in the dimly lit subway station. She looked at her watch. It was 9 o'clock! Was her watch telling the truth? Was it fast? She held it to her ear and heard it ticking. What was the matter with her? Now that she thought of it, the streetlights had been on as she came around the corner of 4th and 87th Street and it was already dark. What was she doing taking the subway alone in the evening? She had not done that once since Bernhard had left for basic training more than seven weeks ago because she just did not feel safe. She wondered if she should go back home but felt she could not face the empty apartment that night.

Finally, she heard the rumbling engines of the approaching train and felt the thrust of hot air as the train came through the tunnel and entered the station. When it came to a halt, she looked for a car that was not completely empty, tugged at the door and chose a seat near a middle-aged couple, who were probably on their way downtown to go out for dinner or to a movie. Like she and Bernhard used to do, she thought to herself. She hung her head, feeling hopelessly depressed and looking down at the cream-colored plastic weave of the bench covering of the seat she was sitting on. She had noticed the new covers on the weekend when Bernhard was home and wondered how the city thought they could keep these light-colored seats clean.

She supposed they would hose them off. The subway was so dirty. Sighing deeply, she tried to look out through the grimy train windows, but of course it was dark in the tunnel, with just an occasional utility light to be seen between stations. Very few people got on the train or off it, mainly people who must have been working late, she assumed. Lost in thought she almost forgot to change trains.

By the time Anna got to Park Place and started walking down the street that she had grown up on, she had managed to calm herself. Lights shone through the windows of the long series of rowhouses, all built in the same style as her parents' house, with the long steps leading up to the front door. The street had been widened a few years earlier, so the front gardens were smaller than years ago. The tree that had been planted in their garden as a sapling in her childhood was now a tall and spreading shade tree that grew between the sidewalk and the street.

She knew a lot of the people who still lived in the houses and wondered about their children, especially some of the young boys she had known as a child. Where were the three O'Hara brothers, a few years older than her, and the rest of the other big Irish family that used to live in the house on the corner? They had moved out just after Black Monday although Anna remembered her parents saying the father had nothing to do with Wall Street. What were they doing now? And the Dagostinos' sons who had worked in the family restaurant amid all the mafia rumors, where were they? What would happen to them? The thought that they could all be soldiers or even worse, that they could all...It did not bear thinking about.

The streetlight across from her parents' house had gone out weeks ago and not yet been repaired. The trees cast a shadow from the light further on down the block, so Anna was already at the gate before she noticed that someone was sitting in the dark on the top step in front of the door. It took her a moment to recognize who it was.

"Mona? What are you doing out here?" she asked.

"Is that you, Anna?" Mona asked in surprise. "I'm not doing anything much, just waiting for Pappa to come home again so we can eat. I'm starved!" In a glum voice she complained, "We eat later and later every night. Soon we'll just skip the meal, I guess, and wait for breakfast!"

The door opened in back of Mona and Bertha stuck her head out. "Who are you talking to, Mona? Anna? Where did you come from?"

"I just wanted to stop by and see you." Choking up a bit, she went on, "It's getting awfully lonely in our place."

Bertha looked up the street to see if there was any sign of Frank, but she could not make anything out in the dark.

"Come inside, you two, it's getting cold out here."

She led the way down into the kitchen, saying, "I've got something on the stove that I'm trying to keep warm and not burn to a crisp. *Har du ätit, Anna? Vill du äta med os? Det fins nog.*" (Have you eaten, Anna? Do you want to eat with us? There's enough.) She laughed softly, "*Men vi har bruna bönor igen!*" (But we are having beans again!)

"Beans again!" Mona groaned.

"*Nej tack!* I had my supper at home. Besides I'm not hungry."

"What's the matter, Anna?" Bertha asked as she stirred the beans and scraped the bottom of the pot where they were beginning to stick. She watched Anna and Mona sit down at the table. "Any news from Bernhard? How is he, now that he's finished basic training?"

"Oh, Mamma!" Anna looked sadly at her mother. "He's been assigned to a tank battalion..."

"*Jag vit.* (I know.) You told me that on the phone. I thought you were glad about that."

"Yes, Mamma, but I just read something terrible in the newspaper...really terrible!" Anna broke out in tears and could hardly go on. Slowly, in bits and pieces, she managed to report what she had read that evening, while her mother and her little sister sat listening, horrified.

Without thinking, Bertha started to comfort Anna by saying, "*Det ga bort, när du...*" only to break off, realizing the pointlessness of their old customary litany. Mona, however, picked up the thread.

"When she gets married? That's silly, Mamma. She already is married! And," she went on cleverly, "She wouldn't have a problem with a husband if she wasn't married, would she?"

Bertha gave Mona a look that meant "Don't be so smart, young lady!" but could not think of anything helpful to say. Instead, she sighed as she put the wooden spoon down next to the pot and went over to put her arm around Anna.

"Why don't you stay the night here tonight, *lilla* Anna?" she urged softly. "If you don't feel up to it tomorrow, we'll call in to your office and tell them you aren't well."

"They need me at work, Mamma," Anna answered.

"This one day won't make any difference to them, but it might do you good!"

Anna nodded listlessly, "I sure don't feel like going to work. Maybe you're right. Just this once."

They heard the front door open upstairs. Mona jumped up and ran up the stairs. Anna smiled weakly at her mother as they heard Mona say, "You're home at last! Now we can eat. I'm so hungry even if it's beans again!" And as she led the way down the stairs, "Guess who's here! Look, Pappa.".

22

An Unexpected Telegram

Anna took her mother's advice and stayed at the house on Park Place all the next day. She called her office, saying she was ill, and then did not go home to her own apartment for a change of clothes but spent another night there as well. She passed the day helping her mother do a wash in the big tubs in the cellar and playing checkers with Mona when she came home from school in the afternoon. She washed and ironed the blouse she had been wearing and found some clean underwear in a drawer in her old room so she could go directly from her parents' house to work the next morning. All the while she was thinking. She could not feel happy about the turn her and Bernhard's life seemed to be taking, but, after a day with her mother and sister, she felt more resigned to accept it as inevitable and was now determined to make an effort to cope. Bernhard would be coming home on leave again in a few weeks and she was determined to make it the nicest weekend of his life.

Just before her lunch break at the office, Anna was still sitting at her desk, wading through the papers that had landed there and piled up in the past two days, when her new boss, Mr. Avery, came up with a telegram in his hands.

"For me?" she asked, confused. "Who could be sending me a telegram?"

Mr. Avery stood waiting, looking uneasy and trying to remember if Anna was married, if she had a husband in the service. He had not had time to get to know the members of his new department well enough and was afraid he had just handed one of his prettiest and sweetest employees some very bad news indeed. He had noticed the stamp on the envelope indicating that it was military correspondence, and he had a sinking feeling in his stomach. At the same time, he felt as if his bow tie was getting too tight and tried to loosen it inconspicuously with one finger. He was reluctant to leave her alone with the envelope but not sure he could handle her reaction if what he feared turned out to be true. The young woman seemed baffled but strangely unconcerned, however. He watched her tear open the envelope and read the message. What would he do if she fainted?

Anna read carefully for a moment and then, her eyes still on the telegram, stood up, pushing back her chair with a puzzled expression on her face. Without meaning to be rude, she ignored her boss, who stood there waiting, and turned to her colleague who was seated at the desk behind hers.

"Marge! What does this mean? Bernhard's sergeant has sent me a telegram to say he couldn't reach me? And a telephone number to call."

"Well, you weren't at home last night, were you? Didn't you say you stayed at your parents' house overnight?" Margie asked.

"Right. I was at my parents' the night before that, too. But why would he want to call me and even send a telegram? Anyway, I wonder if I can use my phone to call this number. If it's an emergency..."

"Go ahead, Mrs. Linden, of course you can," said a deep

voice behind her. Anna jumped. She had forgotten that Mr. Avery was still standing there.

"Oh yes, sir. Thank you very much," she turned, her face flushing in embarrassment.

"Or, why don't you use the telephone in my office?" he cleared his throat and suggested. "It will be more private. Is your husband serving in Europe or in the Pacific?"

"Not yet, sir. He's at Fort Dix in New Jersey. He's just completed basic training. He's waiting to be sent over to Europe sometime soon. If I could use my own phone, sir..."

"Of course, of course!" Mr. Avery assumed the worst had not happened. He was immediately relieved on the one hand that there wasn't going to be an emotional scene, but on the other hand he was – for just a fleeting moment – slightly disappointed that he would not be the one to comfort this young lady. He had had mental pictures of himself fanning her face with his handkerchief and handing her something to drink if she fainted while seated on a chair in the coffee corner of his office. He turned and went back to work, intending to follow whatever happened by watching through the glass partition that separated his office from the desks of the women working under him. Within minutes, however, he was busy again and forgot the matter almost entirely.

After Anna had made a few unsuccessful attempts to reach the number indicated in the telegram, a switchboard operator answered. She asked Anna if she wanted to be connected with administration. Anna said yes. The secretary she spoke with then could not find any special information on Private Linden and said to call again later. After an hour, Anna tried once more, using the Fort Dix administration office's number, only to learn that she could not talk to the same secretary, who had gone home for the day. Frustrated, she left her office telephone number with another secretary and asked if they would call her back. Yes, of course they would. As the afternoon went by, Anna became more and more worried. She did not go on her lunch break. Her call was not returned. She put the claims documents she had been working on between calls to Fort Dix into her "urgent" box for the next day or at least until she had spoken to Bernhard, feeling certain that she was unable to handle them properly, that she was too distracted. With her mind focused on her husband, she decided she would spend the rest of the day doing some routine filing and leave the more important matters for later.

Just before time to finish work and go home she called the telephone number on the telegram once again and was relieved to be told – when she gave her own name, "One moment please, Mrs. Linden. Sergeant Bode will want to speak to you himself. Hold the line. I'll have to find him. He's been trying to reach you."

A few minutes later a man's voice said, "Mrs. Linden?"

"Yes, I'm Mrs. Linden." "This is Sergeant Bode speaking."

"What's the matter, sergeant?"

"Does your husband always have this much trouble getting in touch with you when he's away?"

"We usually correspond by mail, sir! What is the matter? Is Bernhard okay?"

"Well, he's doing fine, but he's had a little accident. I'm sorry to say this, but if he wasn't such a good athlete it would never have happened. I guess I was a bit hard on him, but he'll tell you all about it."

"But what happened?"

"He broke his shoulder demonstrating a certain technique to some new recruits. He was exceptionally good at it. I never thought he could have any trouble carrying out that stunt, he was so good at it. But that's the way it goes sometimes. They operated on him yesterday and he's in the hospital. Nothing to be worried about, Mrs. Linden, they'll patch him up, but you might want to come and visit him sometime soon."

The conversation with the sergeant was over quickly.

Anna only asked him where the hospital was and got reassurance that Bernhard's condition was not serious. When she hung up the phone, she sat at her desk for a moment, both stunned and relieved. Then she realized that Margie, who had been trying unsuccessfully to put together what she could from Anna's half of the conversation, was standing there, waiting in her coat, concerned, but as always at this time of day in a hurry to rush home to her mother and children. Anna explained what had happened as well as she could without really understanding it herself. If Bernhard was "so good" at some special technique, how did he break his shoulder doing it?

Margie advised her to go to Fort Dix right away and not waste any time. She promised to finish off the claims in Anna's "urgent" box on her desk the next day if Anna was able to get the day off. Then she hugged her and hurried off.

Minutes later Anna was knocking at Mr. Avery's office door, trying to resist the urge to peek in through the blinds on the glass partition. She found him putting some papers in his briefcase and getting ready to go home, too.

"Mrs. Linden. Did you get through to your husband? Is everything all right?"

"I did, sir. Yes, he's all right, I mean, no, he isn't all right. He's in the hospital. He's had an accident."

"I'm sorry to hear that. Is it serious?"

"I'm not sure," Anna did not want to exaggerate, but did not want to minimize the situation either. That might ruin her chances of getting some time off.

Mr. Avery pulled on his jacket and picked up his briefcase. "I suppose you will want to visit him then."

"Yes, I would like to go there tonight or tomorrow morning and wondered if I could have the day off."

Mr. Avery decided not to offer Anna a ride home in his car, smiled at her and said, "Yes, of course you can have the day off. Let me see, it's Wednesday today. Why don't you take Friday off, too? I want you to be back on Monday, but you might want to spend the weekend with your husband."

"Oh, Mr. Avery! Thank you so much. That would be wonderful. You're so understanding!" Anna gave him an unexpected hug and an impulsive kiss on the cheek, shocking herself and her boss, who stood there looking embarrassed, watching her hurry back to her desk, pick up her coat and pocketbook and rush out of the office without looking back.

All Anna could think of on her way home on the subway was, "This means he won't be sent off to war for a long time after all. And if he isn't in a lot of pain, it's almost a good thing. Like Mamma says, '*det goda kommer med det onda*' (good comes along with the bad). It's true, at least for me."

Again and again, she wiped away unabashed tears that kept coming to her eyes as she experienced an emotion that she couldn't easily identify, a mixture of joy, embarrassed gratitude and tremendous relief, that could only have been concocted by her guardian angel.

23

Multiple Fractures

The next morning at nine o'clock, Anna was sitting, tired but wide awake, in the lobby of the small military hospital at Fort Dix. She had caught a night train connection and was waiting for visiting hours to begin at ten. She watched doctors and nurses in crisply starched white uniforms hurry by in all directions. A young soldier in a bathrobe and on crutches stood smoking a cigarette near the wide entrance, looking out at the street, while another one gathered up mop and bucket, having finished mopping the tiled floor of the lobby. The friendly grey-haired receptionist, who had informed Anna when she arrived at 7:45 that she would find Bernhard in room 207 on the second floor but would have to wait for visiting hours to begin at ten o'clock, was talking on the phone. She had told Anna where she could get a cup of coffee and smiled at her understandingly. Now, as more people entered the lobby, she was busy answering questions and operating the switchboard.

Anna spent another hour looking through the newspaper she had bought for Bernhard and already read that morning on the train. She watched the people, other visitors, who came into the lobby, wondering what fate had brought them there. Did they have husbands or sons who had had accidents in basic training too? Or were these the usual cases of appendicitis or pneumonia? The men here should all be in the best of health. No wonder it was not a big hospital. Had Bernhard's doctor been qualified for the kind of operation he had performed? She thought about the grim reports in the newspaper that morning. How different the conditions must be, how deplorable, for the injured soldiers and civilians who were being maimed in the war zones and ended up in field hospitals. She shuddered and shook her head, wondering how humans could do such things to each other.

Hoping and praying the war would never reach America's shores, she made herself think of other things. At the same time, she kept her eye on the clock that hung on the wall above the reception desk, ticking loudly but oh so slowly. She willed the hands to move more quickly. Was this an honest clock? She flipped through the pages of a ragged military magazine without seeing the pictures or reading any of the articles until she watched as the hands on the clock finally clicked into place at exactly ten o'clock. Then she stood up and went to look for the stairs to the upper floor.

The door to room 207 was slightly open although all the other doors Anna had passed were shut. She heard voices inside and was about to knock when it opened abruptly. An efficient looking doctor came briskly out, trailed by an equally efficient looking nurse who closed the door behind her. She was marking a patient's chart on a clipboard as she hurried along after the doctor.

"The x rays look okay," he said. "But it was a multiple fracture and when we discharge him, it's my guess the army will discharge him as well. Now what do we have in 206?"

Anna heard these words. She repeated them to herself a few times and tried to figure out if they could have been referring to her husband Bernhard's condition as the doctor and the nurse went on past her into the next room. Then she knocked on the door softly. When no one answered, she knocked again more firmly and heard two voices say "come in" in unison. She opened the door and saw three beds in a row. The first bed was occupied by a young man, one of whose legs was suspended from the ceiling in traction but whose smile broadened as he saw Anna. Another man was sleeping on his side in the second bed. In the third bed sat Bernhard with a newspaper spread out in front of him on the bed covers and his right shoulder and chest wrapped in broad bandages. The sun was shining on him through the window, making a stark contrast between the white bandages and what could still be seen of his tanned upper body. His hair, very dark for a Swede, hung boyishly over his forehead and his brilliant blue eyes caught Anna's as she came up to his bed, smiling her gentlest smile.

"Oh, Bernhard! How are you feeling?"

He smiled sheepishly back at Anna and said, "Hello, Honey. Much better today. They've patched me up."

"What happened?" She kissed him and could not help noticing how he winced when he tried to put his healthy left arm around her.

"Just don't make me laugh, Honey. That's what really hurts. I must have broken a rib, too. One of the nurses said I might, but when I asked them about it, they said they couldn't do another x ray and there's nothing they can do about broken ribs anyway. I can tell you this is really uncomfortable. At least I don't feel gruggy today."

"Gruggy? Groggy?"

"From the anesthetic."

Anna saw now that his right arm was tightly bound to his chest to prevent him from moving it. "But how did it happen? You still haven't told me. Good thing it's your right side since you're left-handed. Here's today's paper, Dear."

Bernhard gathered up the old paper clumsily with his left hand and gave it to her.

"Well, to make a long story short, I fell in that pit I told you about."

"The pit?"

"You know, the one where you run and grab a rope hanging over the pit, the ditch, or whatever you call it, to swing over it. I never had any trouble at all doing it. But, I must have done it a dozen times in a row and the last time I just sort of lost hold of the rope. I don't know what happened."

"Why did you have to do it so many times? Were you doing a demonstration again, or what?"

"Well…, *ja, fan ocksa!* (Yeah, damn it!)," he winced as he tried to sit up straighter. "Ja, for some new recruits. But I did it so many times before without any problem. I guess I was tired. I was up half the night trying to calm Gerhart down. His mamma came over to visit him on the weekend and all of a sudden he was scared to death to be sent to war. He was fine until then. Didn't seem worried at all, but now…I almost thought I should ask the sergeant to check his age, he can't be 18 yet. He's just a kid, still wet behind the ears, you know? And all these new recruits, half of them kids…A lot of them can't do these tricks. The only sports they have ever done is play baseball. They call me 'the grand old man', Anne!" Bernhard winced again as he tried to change position. "Some grand old man I am now!"

Anna helped him move the pillows behind his back and sat on the edge of the bed.

"The worst thing is that I told Gerhart and a couple of other guys not to worry, we'd be going over together in the same unit. Sort of like I would take care of them. Hah! Now I'm not so sure. It could take months before they send me over."

Anna was silent for a moment, then she asked Bernhard in a noncommittal, lowered voice, "What's the matter with the man in the first bed?"

"He's got a broken leg. He's been here for six weeks. He's going home soon." He called over to him, "You're glad to be going home, aren't you Jake?"

"Sure am!" answered the young man. "Best part, I don't have to report back for six months. They already told me that. War might be over by then."

After a moment Anna asked in a whisper, "And what about this man here?"

"He had pneumonia, but he's okay now. Guess he's still trying to get a little shut-eye before he goes back to his platoon after lunch."

Having wanted to ask this question since she came in the door, she asked softly, "Is it a multiple fracture you have, Bernhard?"

"What? A multiple fracture? Ja, that sounds like what the doctor told me just before you got here. Why? Is that worse?"

"I guess it makes it more complicated to heal, Dear," Anna could not conceal the jubilant tone that had crept into her voice.

Then she actually clapped her hands together and beamed at Bernhard, who asked, looking not a little perplexed, "Why should that make you so happy all of a sudden? I know I told you not to make me laugh, but..."

"Well, Dear, let's just say I'm glad they will let me keep you a little longer before they take you away again." She bent over, and lifting the hair off Bernhard's forehead, planted a kiss between his bushy eyebrows.

"Hmph! It's probably more painful too," he answered, wondering what was going on in Anna's head, as she continued to smile exuberantly at him.

Bernhard reconciled himself to the fact that he would never understand women. At the same time Anna said to herself that she would never be unhappy again and would even put up with not having children if it had to be that way. If she could only have her husband back.

.

24

A Letter from England

Six months later Anna had just come home from work. She found a letter for Bernhard in their mailbox in the entrance hall with an unfamiliar handwriting, no return address, and a foreign stamp that she scrutinized as she climbed the stairs to the apartment. It was hard to read. The envelope looked as if it might have been out in the rain somewhere, and the stamp had gotten wet, but she could make out the words: British American Ambulance Corps under a picture of a horseman fighting what looked like a dragon wearing swastika tattoos. The strange envelope had two censor stamps on it as well, one by the Royal Mail and the other by US Airforce.

When Bernhard got home, he went directly into the kitchen where Anna was cracking an egg into something she was mixing in a bowl. He gave her a kiss on the cheek and peeked over her shoulder. All he could see in the bowl was some chopped onion and breadcrumbs and the egg. Then he raised the lid on the pot that was just beginning to boil on the stove and discovered potatoes. He smiled contentedly and the smile got broader and brighter when he noticed the small paper package of ground beef half unwrapped and lying on the table next to a pile of fresh, green, string beans.

"Hello, Dear," Anna said and returned his quick kiss as she turned to pick up the meat to add to the mixture in the bowl. "You're a little early tonight for a Friday, aren't you?"

"No, not really, I don't think... Can I help, cut the ends off the beans or something?"

"If you like. I know you're hungry, but take your coat off first..." She was smiling to herself as he left the kitchen, and she called out, "Oh, and there's a letter for you. I put it on the table. Who do you know in England?"

"England?" Bernhard asked.

Ten minutes later, Anna came into the little dining corner of the living room with plates and silverware to set the table. Bernhard was sitting there in his shirt sleeves, his jacket hanging over the back of his chair, and reading the letter.

Another ten minutes later, Anna came in again with a serving dish, potatoes on one side and string beans on the other that she placed in the center of the table. Bernhard had hung up his jacket and rolled up his sleeves but was again seated and perusing the letter.

"Who's it from?" Anna asked, "I'm getting curious."

"A guy in my unit at Fort Dix. A really nice guy."

Anna went to the kitchen and came back with a frying pan full of meatballs, from which she took half and served them directly onto their plates. Once again in the kitchen, she put the remaining meatballs into a small bowl, cleaned out the pan drippings with a bit of water and cream, half of which went into a gravy pitcher and the rest over the meatballs in the bowl. That would go into the fridge and be the basis for the next day's supper. A tiny bit proud of herself, and her planning skills – they were going out

Saturday evening to see a movie and wanted to eat early – she took off her apron, got a jar of *lingon* (cranberry) jam from the fridge and brought that, and the gravy to the table. About to sit down, she noticed something was still missing. Back she went for salt and pepper.

"So, now Dear," she asked as she sat down, "tell me, who is this fellow?" She knew Bernhard would be having pangs of guilt about not doing what he called his share. He still talked about reenlisting, but the doctors had told him he no longer qualified, even if his shoulder had made a complete recovery. After a few weeks back at work in the shop he no longer had any problems using his right arm.

"His name is Joe," Bernhard said. "He's from Florida…"

As they helped themselves to potatoes and vegetables, Bernhard cleared his throat and said, "This looks good. How nice to have these beans. I like *bruna bönor* (brown beans), but I think we've had enough of them for a while."

They had been helping Anna's father make good use of his wartime investment in beans. But accomplishing that task was a feat his daughters feared might be impossible. Everyone was becoming reluctant to accept further supplies of that particular kind. Anna had told her mother that her kitchen was too small, her cupboard space too limited, especially since she and Bernhard had no storage options in the basement. "Thank God, for that," she had thought as she turned down the offer of another half dozen cans on the weekend.

"You know, the day may come when we will need them…," Bernhard said, "but…"

Anna laughed and interrupted him saying, "Tell me about Joe."

Bernhard was already eating at his usual breakneck speed and did not start telling her about his boot camp friend until there was only one meatball left on his plate and he reached with his fork for another potato from the serving dish. Then a remarkable thing happened, in Anna's opinion. He put the potato on his plate along with the fork and stopped eating.

She wondered where he was heading when he said, "You know before I came to this country I had never seen, not just never met, a colored person. And I haven't really got to know any other colored folks here in New York either. They keep to themselves, I guess, but I don't know if that is the way it should be."

Anna looked at him and said, "You're right, Bernhard, that's true. It isn't. But when you think of it, we live in a Swedish colony, too, more or less. The difference is that we get accepted a lot more easily."

"But they've been here a lot longer…"

"That's true too," Anna paused but then said, "That's just the way it is in this country, I guess. Someday it will change… I hope. Are you going to tell me about this Joe?"

"That's what I'm doing," Bernhard said. "There were three colored guys in my unit. Joe was one of them, …"

Bernhard mashed his potato up with the meatball and some gravy, ate it all in a blink of an eye and started telling Anna about Joe. One day at mess he had noticed this dark-skinned guy just taking a seat alone at the far end of the table for the third day in a row. Out of pure curiosity more than anything else, he went over with his tray and sat down across from him. The young fellow he had told her about with the German name, Gerhart, had gotten into the habit of tagging along with Bernhard and followed him there. They sat down and they all ate silently and with focus, if not enthusiasm, for a few minutes. Then Bernhard, who could probably eat faster than anyone else in the camp, pushed his empty plate back and said, "Well, that wasn't much good, but it filled the big hole in my stomach!"

Both of the other guys laughed, and Gerhart said, "It's not my momma's cooking. That's for sure. Don't even wanna think about that. If anything'll make me feel homesick it's thinking about momma's cooking."

Joe laughed again and agreed. The three shook hands, introduced themselves, and talked about the day's boot camp experiences for a little while before going back to their barracks. After that, the three of them sat together a couple of times and got to know each other better.

Bernhard said Joe talked like Mrs. Lewis, their landlord in Florida on their honeymoon, and that he had had trouble understanding him, just like he had with her.

So, he was not that surprised to learn that Joe had come from somewhere in Florida with his mother about four years before. They had been invited to come up to New York City by his uncle, who "rode the Silver Spur". It took a while to figure out what that meant. It turned out that that was a train that travels the East Coast from Florida to New York. His uncle worked on that train as a porter and had paid for their tickets. Joe said he and his mother were very happy to be able to leave Florida. But when Bernhard asked him why they would want to leave such a wonderful, warm, and sunny place, Joe said he did not want to talk about it.

Anna said she had heard rumors about the South that she did not want to believe. But she was afraid they could be true. Bernhard told her Mimi had talked about it and his brother-in-law, August, had told him things that he did not want to believe either, but August had it from the newspapers.

Anna got up from the table to clear away the dishes. She put them in the sink, but she left the dishwashing for later and came back to the table, where Bernhard was reading the letter again. He still was not used to American handwriting and was having trouble deciphering it.

"So, what does the letter say?" she asked.

"I'm not sure I read this right, but Joe writes he has been instructed not to insult the King or the Queen ..." Bernhard looked puzzled, "and wonders if he will get close enough to them to be able to do anything like that...Here, Anna, read for yourself, maybe you can make it out." He handed her the letter, saying, "He loves the English people, especially the young women."

Anna raised her eyebrows but smiled. After reading for

a minute or two she said, "That's funny about the King and Queen, but you got it right. That's what he wrote. All of the soldiers probably got a list of does and don'ts when they arrived, I suppose. He also says everyone he has met in England is brave despite the air raids and all the fires and destruction, despite all the dead and injured. He calls them heroes."

"What's that about their lip?"

"That's just an expression. The English are known for their 'stiff upper lip'. It means they have a reputation of being calm and courageous, you know, not being timid or emotional… And… he writes that they seem to treat him like everyone else."

Anna looked up from the letter, shaking her head, and said, "He's not used to that. That's what we were talking about. He means he was not treated well in Florida, or even here in New York, and that's because he's not white. But maybe it's not like that in England."

Bernhard was looking at Anna with his left elbow on the table and his head resting on his hand. He looked thoughtful but said nothing. She went on reading and then said, "He finds it hard to understand them. He says, 'they tell me they are speaking English and I am not, but it's hard to believe. I just keep smiling and do my best to figure out what they're saying.'

And then he says he's seen some funny things in England. A big sign said 'Eat More Herrings'. He didn't know what they were, so he tried one with his beer in a pub and says no wonder no one wants to eat them." Anna laughed.

"He says Gerhart gave him your address before he shipped out to somewhere in North Africa. He was going to write too but was afraid he might be too busy."

"Too busy?" Bernhard said in frustration. "Busy fighting and dying? I thought the unit was supposed to stay together! He wrote something about being put in a special unit. I don't understand that."

"I don't either," said Anna, frowning. She handed the letter back to Bernhard, who looked at the last line under Joe's signature telling him, "Gerhart says hello."

"I hope he'll be okay," Anna said gently, "and Gerhart. I'd like to meet them both."

"Pretty depressing, isn't it, while I'm here doing ladies' hair!" was Bernhard's comment as he got up from the table.

25

Another Letter

A few days later, Bernhard was already home when Anna arrived. She put the bag of groceries that she had bought on her way home from work on the kitchen table and was storing the perishables in the fridge when he came in smiling broadly.

"Look at this, Anna," he said, "I want to know if I've read this right," and handed her another letter. This one did not look anything like the one from Joe, it was handwritten too, but on cream colored stationery with an elegant golden HR monogram at the top of the page. The header, in gold print, said:

h e l e n a   r u b i n s t e i n
Spa, 715 Fifth Avenue, New York

It was addressed to Mr. Bernard, 315 87th Street, Brooklyn, New York and said that, after congratulating Bernhard on his recent success in a New York hairstyling competition, Madame Helena Rubinstein herself was inviting him to a personal interview for "a position at her salon" on Tuesday morning of the following week. "Please find time to accept my invitation," she wrote, "because my husband, Prince Gourielli, and I will be leaving on an extensive South American cruise in two weeks and may not return for several months. Bring your lovely model, I hear she is your wife, for a complimentary spa treatment if she would like that."

The short letter closed with "Looking forward to meeting you," and was signed with a flourish:
Helena Rubinstein
Helena Princess Gourielli

Anna read the letter a few times, then she looked at Bernhard and said, "Goodness! Including a spa treatment for me, but I'm afraid I can't get a day off for that... What don't you understand?"

"Well, I guess I understand everything although the handwriting is strange, but what do you think?"

"This might be just what you've been hoping for, it seems to me. That's one of the women Mimi talked about a while ago, isn't it? Her and that other woman in the beauty business. They make cosmetics. Elizabeth something... Elizabeth Arden. I think Mimi would have liked to do something like they did with your shop before she went back to Rochester."

"I'll have to talk to my brother about this," Bernhard said, "before I go to this interview. I can't just leave again. But it's not as if he couldn't handle the shop's business without me. He did fine without me when I was in training and all the time it took me to get back in shape. Even if I'm a lefty, I needed both my arms and that took a while."

Anna read the letter again.

"It's pretty clear. She's offering you a 'position'," she said. "What does that mean, I wonder."

"Well, I'm a hairdresser," Bernhard said, looking blankly at his wife. "What else would it be?"

"I don't know, she has a big international cosmetics business, but I'll talk to the girls at my office, they might know more than I do… Now I had better start getting supper on the table."

The next evening Anna had supper ready when Bernhard got home.

"Hello Dear, you're late and I was a little early, so the pork chops are already drying out in the pan," Anna said as she came to the door to greet him with a kiss. "Please go right to the table. I have so much to tell you."

"We had a busy day," Bernhard said, "we worked without a lunch break, and of all days! You know I wanted to talk to Lambert about that letter and maybe leaving the shop. I ate my sandwich in installments behind the door to the kitchen. After having such a long slow stretch! We could have kept Walter and Hans busy all day too today! How was I going to talk about leaving? There's a big wedding in the neighborhood tomorrow, we had the bridesmaids, the neighbors, and tomorrow morning the bride and her mother."

Anna put their plates already filled with the chops, mashed potatoes, and applesauce on the table.

Bernhard washed his hands in the kitchen sink and came smiling to the table. "Hmm! *Det luktar gott!* (That smells good!) Anyway, I almost put off talking about it until tomorrow, but when everyone was gone and Agnes was cleaning up in the shop, we sat down exhausted and had a beer in the kitchen. I told him about the fancy invitation to an interview and asked him what he thought about it. He said 'Don't hesitate! That could be your chance in a lifetime. A Fifth Avenue salon! Mimi would be thrilled. He started talking about how she had dreamt of a salon like that for us.

When I asked him how he would handle another day like the one we just had alone, he laughed at me. He said, '*Tveka inte!* (Don't hesitate!) *Är du tokig?* (Are you crazy?) and that he just wouldn't take anyone without a reservation. Then, as I was going out the door he said, laughing again, 'You haven't got that job yet, you know! But I won't hold this against you. You can come back.'"

While they sat and ate their food, Anna reported what she had heard at work. Margie had not heard much about Helena Rubinstein, but a couple of the other girls in the office had. They knew more about the other woman, Elizabeth Arden. Some of them passed her salon on the way to work. Everyone said Anna would be crazy not to take advantage of the spa treatment. They talked about the creams that were incredibly expensive and probably did not even work. One of the girls, Joan, had read about her recently and quoted her saying: "There are no ugly women, only lazy ones!"

To that Margie had laughed and said, "That's silly. Most of us don't have time to pamper ourselves. Are we lazy? Who can afford a little jar of cream for $20? Not me!"

Anna did not tell Bernhard that, as Margie then threw both arms up into the air to express her exasperation, Anna thought she could tell that Margie's dress was bulging again at the waist. Her husband had been home on leave for one short week a few months before.

Anna could not mention that to Bernhard, of course. Instead, she had bitten her lip and told him the rest of what Joan had said about Helena Rubinstein.

"She said it was a well-known fact that, if one of her products doesn't sell, she doubles the price and then it does sell! That's crazy isn't it? Arden does the same thing, and their prices are already ridiculous… But she said I definitely should take the spa offer!"

Anna went to get more applesauce from the kitchen and brought it back in the jar. She also brought some cinnamon to sprinkle on top. She gave herself a nice helping because the porkchop had seemed so dry. Bernhard let her put some on his plate too although he had already finished eating.

"I guess I should take advantage of the offer if I can get

time off," Anna said to Bernhard, "but I'm not even sure I want to… Anyway, I asked her if she knew if Helena Rubinstein really could call herself a princess. I told her that was how she signed the letter, Princess so-and-so. I couldn't remember the name.

Joan said she married a prince, much younger than her just before the war, 'to get the pretty title obviously'. And also, that she and Elizabeth Arden, who has beauty salons all over the world like the salon famous for its red door on Fifth Avenue, have been competing viciously for years… Joan, who reads all the gossip articles that I skip over if I read the newspaper, says there is a lot of spicy gossip."

After a moment Anna went on, "Isn't it amazing that two women can be such successful business owners and competitors in exactly the same field and at the same time!"

"Maybe the competition is good for them," Bernhard said, "it keeps them motivated."

Later in the evening, when Bernhard was settled down in the armchair reading the paper and Anna was sitting on the couch reading a big heavy novel, that someone in her office had bought and passed on to her. It was John Steinbeck's "The Grapes of Wrath", and her colleague had said, as she handed it to her, "This is a great book, but really depressing." Anna was inclined to agree with her but was determined to go on reading it. At least these were not war stories. News reports from Europe and North Africa about battles and bombings were horrific, but the worst were about the treatment of Jews in Germany. Anna had had to stop reading newspapers entirely.

Then Bernhard looked up from his paper and suggested they go into the city for a walk on the weekend. They could have a look at the building at 715 Fifth Avenue. "That's a good idea," Anna said, "we can do some Christmas shopping while we're there… Hmm,… if it's not too cold. The radio weather forecast said it could snow."

"Then we will dress for the weather and go somewhere for a coffee or a hot chocolate. I'd like to see what this place looks like before I go there on Tuesday morning."

26

Anna was glad she had worn her most comfortable walking shoes, wool slacks, and an extra sweater under her coat. In fact, she wished she could have worn her ski outfit, without the ski boots, of course, but the jacket, thick woolen pants, the scarf, cap, and mittens that had kept her warm enough on their last trip to the Poconos with Margaret and Hans. She had been happily surprised to discover that she enjoyed cross country skiing. Bernhard had been pleased as well. A cold wind was blowing as she and Bernhard came up out of the subway at Rockefeller Center. They turned and walked up Fifth Avenue the four blocks to 56th Street and then stood looking at the imposing building. She told Bernhard she must have seen the place before, passed by it many times but never paid it any attention. She was not that interested in cosmetics. There was a corner entrance and above the door was emblazoned the same golden HR insignia that appeared in the header of Bernhard's invitation to the interview. They agreed it was quite a classy place.

Anna had not yet decided if she should accept the spa invitation, she thought that it might put Bernhard in a less favorable negotiating position, that he might almost feel an obligation to take the job. She had heard that a couple of hours at the spa cost at least a hundred dollars, or even two hundred. But maybe Madame would be insulted if she did not accept the offer.

After looking at the building for a very few minutes – with the wind raging down the avenue and a snowstorm threatening – Bernhard suggested going for coffee and donuts. Anna said, "Good idea!" She had wanted to show him something one of the girls at the office called a "great bagel brunch place" on Madison near the MetLife building but that was "miles away" and walking anywhere would be a challenge. Now she just wanted to go inside somewhere out of the cold without another trip on the subway.

They found a little bakery coffee shop a few blocks away and went in. Sitting there in the warmth and delicious odors of freshly baked cakes, they had coffee and pastries. Happy to have found shelter, they watched through the steamy shop window as snow flurries soon swirled and gyrated in the blustery wind.

When they were ready to venture back out into the cold, they had discussed the changes they thought the new job might bring and both looked thoughtful. Bernhard would of course go to the interview, without Anna, although he had made it clear that whether she went along or not would not influence his opinion of what he should be paid. He had urged her to take up the invitation to a spa treatment. To his surprise, she told him that, if "Madame princess" asked why she had not come along, he should say thank you very much, but she had an important meeting at work that morning. "You can tell her I have a "position" at Metropolitan Life Insurance," Anna said. "You can tell her I've been a clerk for over twenty years, filing individual policy claims for people all over the United States, but for the past months mainly sorting out claims for husbands killed or maimed in the war. And it's going to get worse, much worse."

Bernhard had been surprised at the way Anna had expressed herself. He had detected an undeniable note of bitterness, something unusual for his normally sweet and docile wife. "She must be depressed," he thought to himself, "no wonder, having to deal with those cases every day." They were living in depressing times. He also knew that she wanted to have a child and was disappointed that he did not. He still wanted to wait a few years longer, but then, if he earned enough money at Helena Rubinstein's salon, he thought, he might be willing to rethink their situation. He would not mention those thoughts to Anna yet though.

Tuesday evening, when Bernhard got home, Anna was waiting impatiently, with dinner ready and feeling full of suspense.

"So, how did it go?" she asked, coming to the door with a potholder in her hand when she heard his key in the lock. "I've been feeling remorse or at least regrets that I didn't go with you."

"Well, you should have come!" Bernhard said, handing her his hat, pulling off his coat, and shaking off the snow into the outside hallway.

Anna stood with eyebrows raised over eyes wide open, looking like a personified question mark in the flesh. Then she stepped back to let him come in, waiting for news.

Bernhard smiled and, with a mischievous expression on his face, looked at Anna, raised one hand to flick his dark hair back off his forehead said nothing for a moment. Then, "I wasn't even sure you wanted me to go there."

"Bernhard! Of course, I did, now please tell me what it was like."

"Well, ... what's for supper? Do I smell pea soup? But it isn't Thursday..."

"No, and there aren't any pancakes either, but we do live in the United States and are not obliged to abide by Swedish customs at all times. Come on now, you're stalling..."

"I won't tell until I have a bowl of soup in front of me," Bernhard teased.

Anna hit him on the head with the potholder and went into the kitchen to get two bowls of soup. When he came back in his rolled-up shirtsleeves and slippers, the soup was waiting on the table with some fresh *limpa* bread from the Swedish bakery and a thick slice of cheddar cheese.

"Well, ... you should have gone with me. Not for the spa experience but just to see the interior of the place. We thought it looked classy from the outside? You have to see the inside. No resemblance to our Brooklyn shop, that's for sure! Paintings on the walls, rugs on the floor. More like an art gallery."

Bernhard started eating his soup before he went on, "One rug in the reception lounge was rather strange looking, I would say, some blobs of color connected by lines. The receptionist saw me staring at it as I waited to be escorted to "Madame's" office and pointed to it, saying something like 'Wan Meerow!' Anyway, I supposed I should look more impressed and less confused and said: Oh!"

Anna shrugged and said, "Maybe it was French ... But what was she like... Madame Rubinstein?"

"She looked like she was, ... *jag vet inte...* (I don't know) very smart, sure of herself. Not surprising, I guess, she runs an international business. She was very friendly, but I felt she was really ... sizing me up, you call it. She started telling me about all kinds of plans she had and showed me where I would work. It wasn't a big area and there was no one working there this morning. She talked about healthy hair and scalp and how everything had to fiiit together, the entire fullll body treatment. She was disappointed that you couldn't come, I told her you had an important meeting and she accepted that. She said, though, it was a shame she couldn't show you around because you could have described the rest of the establishment to me. She must have noticed that I didn't know what she meant by that and then explained that 'zeee gentlemen are not admitted into other parts of zeee spa when we are open. You can see the rest of our establishment when you work here, but after hours'. We went back to her office where she went straight to the point and offered me twice what I earn in a good week at our shop in Brooklyn ... on a salary basis! I was shocked, not sure I had understood and just looked at her. She must have thought I was not impressed because then she said, with a big, dark red-lipstick smile and dancing eyes, 'There are the teeeps as well, of course!'" Bernhard chuckled as he finished his soup and reached for a slice of bread.

"So, are you going to work for her?" Anna asked.

"I didn't have much choice," he laughed. "That was what they call the offer you can't turn down. We'll sign a provisional contract Friday, and I'll start in January. She won't be here, but her sister will be in charge and she said she was 'confident it would all work out'. Maybe that's what it takes to be a success in life, or in business at least, confidence. You just have to be willing to take the leap."

.

27

Christmas Eve, 1942

Two weeks later, Bernhard and Anna parked their *lilla* Dodge, - dubbed 'little' by Frank Bjorkman in fun because it was so much smaller than his Hudson - in the street outside the building where their friends Doris and John Gare had an apartment. The car that they had driven to Florida in on their honeymoon was packed full of Christmas presents because they were on their way to the house on Park Place to celebrate Jul Afton (Christmas Eve) with Anna's family. All of her sisters would be there.
They locked the car and went up to the Gares' apartment on the third floor to drop off a bottle of homemade *glögg*, Swedish mulled wine, and to wish their friends a merry Christmas. They did not intend to stay long, but John said they would have to try a glass of his homemade eggnog and drink a toast before they left. What should have taken five minutes took twenty and by the time Anna and Bernhard got back to their car, a side window had been broken and all the presents had vanished. Not only was the robbery swift, but the thief's getaway was perfect. No sign of anyone

in the street, no witnesses anywhere. So, regretting deeply that they had acted foolishly, they drove on and arrived empty handed, except for a big wax candle that had rolled in its wrapping paper under the seat and two bottles of Bernhard's *glögg* that had been placed on the floor in the front so that Anna could make sure they did not break.

Signe's car was parked in front of Bertha and Frank's house. She would be driving back out to Connecticut in the morning to celebrate Christmas Day with Rich and his family. She had been the first to learn to drive and had bought her own car a few years before, surprising and impressing her twin especially. Anna would be at least ten years older when she finally learned to drive a car. Then one of her sisters would teach her, but that would not be Signe or Helen, it would be her little sister Ramona!

After the discussions about the stolen presents had reached an inconclusive conclusion – everyone agreed it was a terrible shame but had differing opinions about whether Anna and Bernhard had been watched as they loaded the car and followed from home or if a local gang had just been lucky – and Frank and Bob helped Bernhard contrive a makeshift replacement for the broken window with an old tarp, everyone had sat down to traditional Swedish Jul fare. Anna and Bernhard exchanged a few glum glances at the table, but soon the merry mood distracted them as well. The indisputable star of the evening was Helen's little girl, Siggi, with her curly blond hair, blue-eyes, and cheerful disposition, who was passed back and forth by Helen's sisters, because everyone wanted to hold her. The twins, Anna and Signe, looked at each other in mutual understanding, their eyes full of longing for their own babies. Signe, like Anna, was growing impatient. Foster Emma was in charge of Helen's boys, who were still living mostly with her. They soon disappeared out into the hall to play on the stairs where they impatiently awaited the presents they would receive later in the evening.

By the end of January of 1943, Anna and Bernhard's daily schedules had changed considerably. While they both could take the subway to Manhattan at the same time in the morning and liked doing that together, Bernhard's evening hours had become quite irregular. The few times they had tried to meet for the homeward trip had failed. He was still establishing his clientele and had to accept late comers who had come for the spa treatments and not originally signed up for hair styling. Clients were enthusiastically encouraged by the receptionists to take advantage of the new opportunity to have their hair done by the "star hair stylist, Mr. Bernárd." He did not complain about last minute clients because he knew that would change as he won over a clientele who would book appointments in advance.

Anna's problem was getting their evening meal ready at the proper time. She did not know when he would arrive. Sometimes he would already be there when she got home, or he would not come until the food was overcooked because of a late client. But that was something she was sure would improve. If not, she was determined to get used to it.

For the time being, they agreed that the excellent pay was worth the inconvenience.

By March, however, they were both beginning to feel less convinced about their new lifestyle. They tried to conceal their doubts, because neither one wanted to complain. Bernhard was beginning to wonder if he was meant to be part of Helena Rubinstein's team. How much easier it had been working with his brothers at the salon in Brooklyn, where they had made decisions together, based on their common interest. Now he had to accept the decisions of the woman running the business and the whims of all the women who were being escorted about the spa in bathrobes while he had no real influence on how things were done. Some of the clients were lovely and gracious people, others were people he could barely stand the company of for the length of time it took to do their hair. It was something he was having difficulty getting accustomed to.

By March, however, they were both beginning to feel less convinced about their new lifestyle. They tried to conceal their doubts, because neither one wanted to complain. Bernhard was beginning to wonder if he was meant to be part of Helena Rubinstein's team. How much easier it had been working with his brothers at the salon in Brooklyn, where they had made decisions together, based on their common interest. Now he had to accept the decisions of the woman running the business and the whims of all the women who were being escorted about the spa in bathrobes while he had no real influence on how things were done. Some of the clients were lovely and gracious people, others were people he could barely stand the company of for the length of time it took to do their hair. It was something he was having difficulty getting accustomed to.

Anna, who was already struggling with shopping, cooking, and household after a full day's work, now had to wash, bleach, starch, and iron a fresh shirt every day for her husband. The shirts Rubinstein required were fancy. Bernhard bought five of them. They had what were called French cuffs that folded back double and were closed with cuff links. Anna had given Bernhard an expensive pair of links for Christmas after hearing how he was expected to dress for work. Now she wished she would never see another one of these shirts again. But it cost "a fortune" to have them done by a laundry service and, besides that, Anna did a better job herself.

By the Time You Are Married

When Anna received a telephone call with exciting news from her sister Signe one evening toward the end of March, she found it hard to react immediately with the pure joy she knew she should be feeling. Signe had called to tell her that she and Rich were expecting a baby in the early fall. Signe noticed the one-second-long delay in Anna's reaction even if her response was then sincerely heartfelt. She said, "So don't despair, Anna. If I can get pregnant, you can, too. After all we're twins!"

They talked for a few more minutes of other things, Signe, telling about the recent snowstorm that had blocked the road to her house for days and Anna, saying how she wished the French had never invented their ridiculous shirt cuffs. She said she was grateful that they no longer put lacey frills on them like at the time of Louis XIV. Then, speaking of France, they hoped the war would be over soon. They had heard depressing stories from that occupied country. Although neither one of them paid close attention to the war news, they agreed with Roosevelt and Churchill that Germany and Japan should surrender unconditionally.

When the two sisters had finished their conversation and hung up, Anna sat thoughtfully next to the phone for a few minutes and then decided she would call and get another appointment with her doctor in the morning.

A week later, Anna was putting on her coat at her doctor's office in downtown Brooklyn.

"As far as I can see, Mrs. Linden, you are perfectly healthy. There's no apparent reason why you cannot get pregnant. My advice to you is, if you can afford it, stop working for a while." He got up from his desk and escorted her to the door of his office, saying in a calm and kindly voice, "It is my experience that that can work wonders."

.

28

April 1943

A Life-Changing Offer

"It seems to me," Bernhard was saying, "the clients at our shop usually want their hair done just before going out for an evening, to dinner or to a movie or a Broadway show... Or some special family event... Friday or Saturday appointments are always booked out well in advance or as standing appointments, so the ladies can be looking their best at the right time, on the weekend. My clients now at Rubinstein's don't want to go out for dinner or a show after a healthy, relaxing, but sometimes exhausting day at the spa. I think that is why my appointments are still so irregular, so unreliable. And hardly anyone comes just to have their hair done!"

It was mid-April 1943, and Anna and Bernhard were finally having an honest and overdue discussion about their situation. The conversation had been triggered by another letter in their mailbox. This time it was from Helena Rubinstein's competitor Elizabeth Arden, not from her personally, but from her general manager at the Fifth Avenue salon, on pink paper with a red border. Bernhard was holding it in his hand, rereading it. It was another invitation to an interview.

"I don't like to... how do you say... change horses in midstream... but...

Anna smiled at him, thinking, "There's my frustrated cowboy husband again..." But she said, "Go for an interview. She might make you an even better offer to lure you away from Madame Rubinstein. Joan told me the two ladies are staging some kind of war of competition for the privilege of smearing expensive creams on our faces. Honestly, you haven't been with Rubinstein long enough to feel like a traitor. And, if you're not completely happy with the way things are going...You have a provisional contract anyway, haven't you?"

"That's right, to be renewed in two weeks," Bernhard said. "So, I have to make up my mind. Another salary increase at a new job would make a difference in our budget. We could really get ahead and then ..."

Anna was looking at him seriously, sitting up very straight and waiting for him to go on. "That's right," she said when he did not, "then we could afford to have a real family. If I could take some time off, I told you what Dr. Johnston said..."

"*Ja, jag vet, men...*, (Yes, I know, but...)" Bernhard frowned. "I was thinking the same thing..., but let's not start counting eggs that aren't chickens..."

"You mean chickens that aren't hatched."

"Exactly. Let me go to the interview first before you quit your job!"

"You know I wouldn't do that!"

"I was only joking!"

"I'm not," Anna shot back, surprising herself.

There was an awkward moment's silence while Bernhard put the letter down and picked up the newspaper. He opened the paper and then put it back down again.

"Anne, my mother was almost the same age as you are now when she had Mimi. She gave her all those names from her favorite romantic French novels, you know: 'Mimi Pamelia Antoinette', because she didn't think she would have any more children. Then she had six more. Hans was born when she was forty-four years old! How old was your mother when she had Mona?"

"She was over forty," Anna answered slowly. "That's why we didn't realize she was going to have a baby when her clothes didn't fit anymore. We were terrible to her. We told her she was getting fat!" She paused, shaking her head in dismay, before she went on, "But I don't want to start having children when I'm forty years old!" Then she got up abruptly and went into the kitchen to finish washing the pots from supper that she had left to soak.

She had hardly got her hands into the soapy water when Bernhard was there behind her. Gently, he turned her around, put his arms around her and said earnestly, "I promise, Honey, we won't have to wait much longer. Whether I take this other job or not, just let me go for the interview. You know two paychecks are better than one." He looked at her, hesitating, and then said, "If we save as much as we can for a few more months ..."

"How many months?" Anna insisted, blinking to keep tears from coming to her eyes. Then the soapy water dripped down her arms into the sleeves of her dress as she could not wait to reach up and wrap her arms around his neck.

"Until the end of summer?" he suggested. "Of course, that means no birthday presents this summer...," he said, teasing her. Both of their birthdays were coming up in June and July.

"No big presents, at least, I agree," she said, laughing. That was, after all, the only remotely positive answer he had ever given her on this topic, but she was determined to hold him to it. Then she left the pots for the morning and grabbed a dish towel to dry her arms as Bernhard turned off the light in the kitchen.

Three weeks later, Bernhard had "taken the leap" again. He had said goodbye to the people at Rubinstein's spa and already started to work at Elizabeth Arden's salon. Although this was also a spa, he knew right away that he was better off here. The hairdressing salon was bigger, busier, and separate from the rest of the establishment. He hit it off with the salon staff from the first day and, since another hairdresser – said to have been "difficult" to work with – had left permanently to work in the Chicago salon only a few days before, Bernhard was booked out almost immediately.

Anna's colleague Joan had given her an old copy of The New Yorker magazine from 1936 that she had read with great interest. She learned and reported to Bernhard that his new boss had been born in Ontario of British immigrant parents and named Florence Nightingale Graham after the famous and courageous English nurse, the "Lady with the Lamp" in the Crimean War. Elizabeth Arden had wanted to become a nurse herself but abandoned that ambition when she realized she could not bear the sight of blood.

Anna laughed at the story about Arden's banker husband who had been told by his wife, "Don't forget this is my business. You only work here." That marriage had unsurprisingly ended in divorce almost ten years ago. Anna would soon find herself buying one of Elizabeth Arden's wartime lipsticks, "Montezuma Red", (packaged in what were said to be recycled bullet shells, to save metal for the war industry and to fit into the uniform pockets of female marine officers). Although such a bright red was not a color Anna would have picked otherwise, she wore it with a navy suit that had red trim.

Some of the people Bernhard had just begun to work

with had family or close connections in Europe. Miss Arden, as she preferred to be called by her staff, had brought over some of her Paris and London employees to work in the United States, as life became increasingly dangerous abroad. She was especially worried about her sister Gladys, who refused to leave her Paris salon, that she had been given ownership of after successfully running it for Elizabeth for years.

Rumors of desperate conditions, atrocities, and rebellion in the Warsaw Ghetto had recently been confirmed in whispers in the Berlin Arden cosmetics business. The awful truth had surreptitiously been passed on to the Paris and London salons and from there to New York. The hairdresser whose place Bernhard had taken was French and had worked in the Paris salon. According to Bernhard's assistant, Monsieur Claude had been constantly distraught, his behavior increasingly erratic, causing numerous assistants to seek other jobs to escape his moodiness. One of the manicurists had refused to work in the same room with him. Everyone was on edge.

Then, when Elizabeth Arden's beloved sister Gladys was arrested in February of 1944 and charged with espionage, the nervous tension in the Fifth Avenue salon reached a breaking point.

But by that time Anna and Bernhard were no longer in New York. Fate had taken them or, more precisely, Elizabeth Arden had sent them back to Florida in November of 1943.

.

29

One morning in October Miss Arden asked Bernhard to come by her office after his last appointment. She had glanced into the salon regularly whenever she was in New York (and not away at one of her many other spas) and asked him if he was happy working for her. A few times she had appeared well before a first morning appointment, making Bernhard wonder if she was checking up on him. Well, she was, but she was checking up on everyone. He always made sure to be there early, liked to be sure everything was ready for the first client and certainly did not want to spoil things with his boss, whom he had in the meantime got to know better. He had heard her switch from her genteel, soft tone to her truly intimidating "boss lady voice" when she was displeased, and he honestly did not know how he would react if she ever talked to him that way.

He did not want to risk anything, especially since Anna had just submitted her resignation at work for the end of the month. Mr. Avery, who was still her boss, had said she could come back any time, after inquiring into her husband's health. She had been surprised that he remembered Bernhard's accident and honorable discharge from the army, since he was an extremely busy man. He had in the meantime been put in charge of several offices at MetLife.

It was almost seven o'clock in the evening when Bernhard's last client finally left with an appreciative smile and a generous tip that she stuffed into his jacket pocket as she turned toward the door. He splashed some water onto his face and wiped it dry with one of the towels stacked on the shelf next to the shampooing sinks. Then he combed his hair, checked in the mirror that his cuffs extended at the proper length from the sleeves of his dark blue jacket and set out toward Miss Arden's office two floors up the stairs, not taking the elevator. He wondered why she wanted to speak to him, in her office no less.

When he got there, the door was open, and he could see that she was not at her desk. So, he knocked on the doorframe, thinking perhaps it had been too long a day for her and she had already gone. But no, a soft voice called out, "Come in, come in, Mr. Bernárd? I'll be with you in a moment. I just have some samples here that I must give my opinion on so they can order the ingredients... some of which are hard to procure in these difficult times..."

He looked into the far corner of the spacious room and discovered her, seated at a table in front of half a dozen pink jars of different sizes and looking extremely professional in a laboratory coverup coat.

"And we do have production deadlines," she continued, smiling, as she got up, removing the lab coat to reveal a flowery, brilliant pink silk dress, and coming toward him.

"Now, Bernard, I have heard some very nice things about you, from clients and from other staff who say you are a pleasure to work with." With her head inclined slightly forward, she looked at him earnestly from under her perfectly shaped eyebrows and said, "I haven't heard that about many of my other hairdressers lately."

Bernhard was extremely pleased but had no idea what to say to that.

"Have a seat, please," she said as she walked around her desk to sit down at the other side. "And I don't think that woman down the street has any idea what she has lost by letting you go!" That was said (referring to Rubinstein) with a triumphant smile, but then she went on, "You know I have spas all over the country…"

"Yes, of course, Miss Arden, and not just all over this country," Bernhard had finally found something he could say.

"That means I have to provide staff for all of these establishments… And that is not always easy to do… Now you say you like it here in New York, but would you consider going somewhere else, where you are needed?"

Bernhard was at a loss as to what to say. He wracked his brain and nodded slowly, saying then, "Well, yes, but I am married, so it would depend to a certain extent…"

"Let me get to the point," she interrupted. "I have a dear client who has already become, shall we say… attached to you as her hairdresser. She is about to leave New York for the season and is going to a lovely place, a brilliantly lovely place where I have just opened a small exclusive spa…," There Elizabeth Arden stopped, shaking her head in disbelief and said, "I've already opened a spa for her and her friends, now they need a hairdressing salon. Some women never get enough, it seems, but… It's such a wonderful place and you can get there in five or six hours by airplane. I don't imagine you have ever been there, you immigrated here from another country not that long ago, I think, but it is so lovely. Could you consider spending the winter months in Florida? In Palm Beach?"

Miss Arden was not a little astounded, almost offended when Bernhard burst out laughing for just a moment.

"We were there," he said, now shaking his head in disbelief as she had a moment before, at the unlikelihood of such a coincidence, "on our honeymoon a few years ago!"

"So, … Did you like it there?" Elizabeth asked, smiling, and surprised at his reaction.

Bernhard thought for a fraction of a moment it might be better not to go overboard in praise of Florida, as that could influence her way of thinking about his salary, but his enthusiasm was not to be suppressed.

"Miss Arden," he said, "as you might know, I'm originally from Sweden. Have you any idea how much we love the sunlight we must do without in my country for many months of the year? It's better even here in New York, but Florida? Florida was wonderful."

She was looking at him intently, with her beautifully shaped eyebrows raised in controlled amusement and a genuine feeling of perhaps actually liking this new employee and his candor. "I was going to offer you a raise, to entice you," she said, "but now... no, I'm joking, of course. We'll talk about that later. I couldn't be more pleased. I take that as a yes, or at least a highly possible yes. Do you agree?"

Bernhard, who could not believe his ears, was nodding in amazement. "I do have to talk about this with my wife, of course. She," he cleared his throat, that was suddenly slightly constricted, "would have to leave her job, but I almost think she won't mind too very much..." Pleased that he had at least done a bit better strategically with that comment, he did not hear Miss Arden's next question. "I'm sorry, what did you just say?

"I was asking about your assistant. What's her name, Annette? Is there any chance she would also be interested? Would you know? I hear you two work very well together."

"Well, you must ask her. But do you realize she is from Denmark? Her name sounds French, but she's Scandinavian too, they don't get that much sun in her country either. So, you never know, chances are..."

Bernhard attributed his long and successful work relationship with his employer to the friendly basis established during this first personal conversation. He would remain in her employment in Palm Beach until his retirement, long after her passing, entrusted with the care of some of her most valued clients, many of whom he genuinely liked, some of whom he did not.

It was not until Bernhard was sitting in the subway on his way home, however, that he remembered the mosquitoes and Anna's sunburn. She had not been quite as convinced that Florida was a kind of paradise on earth, although the mosquitoes had been his problem. Nonetheless, he was certain that his wife would like the vacation from work and maybe, he mused, her greatest wish would be fulfilled.

.

30

Back in Florida

It was the first week in November and Bernhard had just got into his car. He had parked it on Worth Avenue in front of the Palm Beach Elizabeth Arden salon, when he came for a first meeting with his new colleagues. They had arranged for him to come back the next morning for a first client. He had talked with the plumber who had just finished connecting the shampooing sinks in the hairdressing salon in an upstairs part of the building. It was the first week in November and Bernhard had just got into his car. He had parked it on Worth Avenue in front of the Palm Beach Elizabeth Arden salon, when he came for a first meeting with his new colleagues. They had arranged for him to come back the next morning for a first client. He had talked with the plumber who had just finished connecting the shampooing sinks in the hairdressing salon in an upstairs part of the building.

Bernhard hoped against hope that his car would now start and spare him the embarrassment of needing to go back inside and ask for assistance. He knew who he would ask if he had to. Not the plumber who had already left. But he had also just made the acquaintance of a big strong, colored fellow who had introduced himself as Joshua the janitor and smiled broadly when they shook hands. They did not talk long, just exchanged a few words, but Joshua's accent had reminded him of his army pal Joe.

Yes, he would ask Joshua. He had encountered him adjusting the hinges on the iconic bright red door and seemed to be the only man who worked at the shop. Otherwise, he had met friendly but, in his opinion, overdressed women who gushed as they welcomed him and who would be no help whatsoever of the kind he might need.

Fortunately, the little Dodge started on the second try and he could slip away, without attracting too much attention, down past the Everglades Club and back over the bridge to West Palm Beach. As he drove south to Lake Worth he wondered how Joe and Gerhart were doing in England or wherever they had been sent. He felt he should be there himself but did not want to think about it too much. He needed to concentrate on where he and Anna should go on the weekend to look for a better apartment. They could not stay in that "cozy copper-covered cottage" all winter. Nonetheless, they were happy to have found accommodations there on such short notice the evening before when they had arrived exhausted from their long, three-day trip. Anna was probably talking to Mrs. Lewis right now and trying to explain the circumstances of why they had come back.

As he drove on, the sun shone down on him, smiled down on him, he thought, and he smiled back.

"At first she was disappointed," Anna said, "when I told her we couldn't stay here long, just a few days at the cottages. She said, 'Ya'll come all the way down here for a few days? That's not worth the trip!' So, when I said we would be staying for a few months, until end of March or April probably, she just squinted at me, a bit peeved. Then she said, "Oh, that's a different story. 'I'm booked out for Christmas, through Janry and Febry…' But when I told her the gist of the long, complicated story, she smiled and said she was 'real happy' for us. She is the nicest person, Bernhard, guess what she did. She told me to wait a minute and went in her office to get this. Look," Anna held out a slip of paper with something written in pencil on it. "This is the address of someone she knows in Lake Worth who rents out apartments. 'Nice and central', she said. 'Now you just git yourself a bicycle, Annie, with a basket and you can do your shopping at the grocers on Lake Avenue. You won't have to wait till your hubby comes home to do the shopping in his car.'"

Bernhard looked at the address and said, "That sounds like a good idea. And hmm… maybe we'll get two bicycles." The idea flitted across his mind that he might need one by tomorrow if he could not get the car fixed, but he immediately dismissed that as ridiculous, trying to picture himself in suit and tie – and French cuffs – bicycling over the bridge to Palm Beach every morning. He told Anna, they both laughed and decided to set right out to look for a car repair shop.

They were in luck. First of all, the car started on the suspenseful third try. They drove into Lake Worth town and asked a man on a street corner where they could have the car fixed. He directed them two blocks further south where they entrusted the car to a young kid tending the gas pump, who said his dad would take care of it "in a jiffy" when he got back from lunch. "He'll be back in half an hour, folks."

So, they left the car and walked to a little juice bar around the corner on Lake Avenue that the young boy recommended and had big glasses of freshly pressed orange juice. The juice bar was part of the grocery store Mrs. Lewis had mentioned and that Anna remembered shopping at once or twice five years before.

An hour later their car had been checked over. The gas station owner had smiled at Bernhard and said it was a simple matter. No, they did not need a new battery, it was just the battery contact points that needed cleaning. That he did in 15 minutes, then filled the tank with gasoline and added some oil.

When he came over to them where they had waited, sitting on a bench in the shade, he wiped his hands on a rag that wreaked of kerosene and stuffed it halfway back into a pocket of his overalls. Then he smiled and said, "Ya been on a long trip, judging from your license plates."

"That's right," Bernhard said, nodding, "we're from the Empire State."

"The big city?"

"The big city! We both work there but we're happy to be here in Florida for a while now."

"Well, if ya'll are still here abouts when you need that new battery, it's not gonna last forever, ya know… I hope ya come to me! I'd be glad to order it for ya."

Bernhard thanked him and said he certainly would do that. The payment he asked for was so reasonable that Bernhard looked at him in surprise, paid and gave his son, who had stood nearby listening, a generous tip. Then they were off and on their way to look for the address Mrs. Lewis had given them.

"P Street, next to Saint Andrew, just off Lucerne…" Anna read the directions on the piece of paper Mrs. Lewis had given her, as they drove down Lake Avenue past the schoolhouse. "She didn't write down a house number, she said she didn't know that but that we couldn't miss it anyway…"

"Her friend lives next door to a saint?" Bernhard asked.

Anna looked at him and frowned. "It must be a church, silly!"

"I was joking, of course," he said and laughed, delighted

that she had seemed gullible enough to believe he was even more gullible than she was.

They crossed O Street and then turned north on P Street, or Palmway according to the next sign. As they reached Lucerne, after passing two or three pastel-painted little wooden houses smothered in lush green bushes and trees, they could see the church.

"Oh, look! It's tiny, but it's beautiful, Spanish style architecture like in Palm Beach. I guess it's catholic so I'm not supposed to go there as a protestant, as a Lutheran, can I,…" Anna said. "At least that's what they told me when I was confirmed."

"No, look, it's episcopal, that's protestant. Look at the sign. 'All welcome!'"

"Hmm, that sounds inviting. I like churches, they're such peaceful places."

Bernhard parked the car in front of the next house, turning off the engine, saying, "Now we'll know if that guy was right about the battery." Then they went to knock on the door. A smiling woman about Anna's age came bustling to open, accompanied by a young boy, who turned away disappointed. They were not the person he had expected.

When his mother heard that they wanted to inquire about renting an apartment, she asked them to take a seat at the table and chairs in the garden in the shade of an enormous banyan tree while she went to get a jug of iced tea and some glasses. As she went into the house, Anna said in a low voice, "She must be from England. Doesn't she have a lovely accent? I love to hear the way they talk. I'm always imagining that kind of voice when I read Dickens or other English writers' novels."

Bernhard just shrugged. "I'm not good at accents," he said, "but she looks like a nice landlady."

Talking together for almost an hour, Anna and Bernhard learned quite a bit about Mrs. Worsley. She told them her story of immigrating to the United States from England with her husband and two small children six years before, when war seemed imminent, saying how glad they were to have made that decision in view of what was happening in their country now. She said she thought her husband was overreacting at first when he claimed there could be no peace-making with Hitler. But he insisted that they should take his aging uncle's offer, leave London, and come to "paradise to manage my radio shop", as the uncle had put it. Moving to Florida had seemed completely outlandish to her in the beginning, but now she was convinced that they could not have made a better choice. The uncle, she said, was just as pleased as she and her husband were and had put them in charge of some apartments he managed in the area as well.

In exchange, Anna and Bernhard told her about their immigrant family background and why they had come to Florida. Bernhard expressed his enthusiasm about the climate, the warmth, and the sunshine, while Anna demurely smiled and said how she appreciated not having to go to work in an office in the city for the first time in sixteen years. She had never had more than a two-week vacation in her lifetime before.

When a young boy suddenly came crashing into the yard, throwing his bicycle against the hedge, and apologizing in embarrassment when he noticed Mrs. Morley, the screen door opened, and her son came out. "We're going to the beach, Mum. See you later," he said.

"Tea at half six, Harald, remember," she called after him, as he fetched his bike and raced off down the street with his friend.

"It's a wonderful place to raise children," she said, "you don't have any yet, you say, but that can change, can't it?"

Anna nodded and Bernhard smiled.

"But now you'll want to be seeing the only apartment I have that is vacant right now and that I could rent to you. It belongs to a Swedish couple, by the way, a Mr. and Mrs.

Johnson. Just let me get the keys, it's across the street and down one block," she said, as she got up and went into the house.

"We seem to have passed her tenant test, now let's see what the apartment looks like," Bernhard whispered to Anna, as they waited for her to return. "But what did tea at half six mean, I wonder. Seems a little late just before supper, don't you think?"

"Tea, high tea, is their evening meal, Dear. That's British English for 'supper', and the funniest thing is that 'half six' means half past six, I think, at least. One of the girls at the office was originally from England and used to get us laughing with her strange remarks."

The little two-room, sparsely but cleanly furnished apartment was upstairs in a white wooden house on O Street. The outside staircase led to a tiny kitchen and a screened-in porch that let the ocean breeze waft through to the bedroom window when the door was left open. The fronds on tall palm trees swayed next to the porch.

"There are four apartments in the building, two downstairs and two upstairs. I'd prefer the upstairs apartments," Mrs. Worsley said, "because of the breeze. You don't get that downstairs as much."

After looking around for just a few minutes, Anna and Bernhard made up their minds. They decided not to drive around comparing other rentals since they liked the atmosphere of the place and found the price to be reasonable as well.

As they walked back to Mrs. Worsley's house, Anna mentioned to her that she liked the little church on the corner and said she thought it looked somehow inviting.

"It's pretty, isn't it? That's Spanish architecture, a simple example of what's called Mediterranean Revival style," Mrs. Worsley explained. "It suits the climate here. St. Andrew's, the Episcopalian church service is similar to Church of

England, and yes, I would say it certainly is inviting. The minister, Father Frazel, is a fine person. He's a friendly man and a good preacher, too. I don't go to church every Sunday, but when I do, I know I haven't wasted my time."

When they reached the Linden's car, Mrs. Worsley said she could have the apartment ready the next day if they wanted. Since Bernhard would not start working full time until the end of the week, they agreed to come back the next afternoon with their belongings: three suitcases, a duffel bag, a box of kitchen ware and a singer sewing machine. "We don't need a lot of coats and sweaters in Florida," Bernhard had said repeatedly, almost joyfully, as they had packed in Brooklyn a few days before.

31

Valentine's Day, 1944

Anna was sitting at the kitchen table. It was the middle of February, the coldest day they had experienced in Florida thus far. She had just made a pot of coffee and tasted a tiny piece of her own freshly baked *kaffebröd* (coffee bread). She was waiting for Bernhard to come home from work. The week before she had been feeling lonely and useless, wondering if the rest of her life was going to consist of days of waiting for Bernhard and if she should look for a job in town. But today her mood had changed, she had baked and was completely satisfied with the results. It was her second attempt to use the oven of the gas stove after the first time, the month before, had been disastrous. The cake had been burnt on the outside and too moist and unbaked on the inside. Enough to make her think she would never do that again, at least not with this stove.

Today, however, she had been motivated to try again, adjusting the temperature of the oven, and placing the rack lower. That had been a great success. The kitchen was nice and warm now, too, another reason to feel pleased with herself.

On the table in front of her, the local grocery store's free advertisement calendar for the year 1944 showed at the top a brilliantly colorful picture of bright yellow oranges hanging on a lush green branch with a patch of blue sky in the background. It was opened to the month of February, where the 14th was circled in ink, Valentine's Day. The entire week, 7th to the 14th was also underlined.

Apart from a short morning trip to the post office on her bicycle while the dough for her coffee bread was rising, she had not left the apartment. Bernhard had told her he expected to get home earlier today, but it looked as if that was not going to be the case after all. He usually got home by about half past five, and the kitchen clock already said five o'clock. She got up from the table intending to start peeling potatoes for supper when she heard his customary two-note whistle and then his steps as he came up the outside stairs.

She opened the door with a big, dreamy smile as he entered the porch with an equally big smile, reaching out a bright red, heart-shaped box of chocolates to her. She instantly recognized the box from their grocery store and knew why his trip home had taken a tiny bit longer than expected.

"Hmm*! Det luktar gott!* (That smells good!)," Bernhard said, as he put down his satchel, took Anna in his arms and gave her a kiss.

"You wouldn't happen to have a cup of coffee for me there would you? And maybe some…"

Anna proudly presented her coffee cake ring, that she had somehow managed to shape into a heart that was only a little bit lopsided.

As they sat and talked, drinking their coffee, and enjoying the cake, Bernhard noticed a big change in Anna. She had been moody, almost depressed, and now she was cheerful. She laughed and joked. "My heart is full, Bernhard, full of..." she said dramatically, and then pointed to the cake, "sugar, cinnamon and almonds. And your heart is full of... chocolate!"

He laughed too, and thought, "I should bring her chocolates more often. Not just on Valentine's Day." Then he opened the briefcase in which he transported his lunch to work each day and took out a pink box with red trim and "Arden" written in red letters on it. The women he worked with in the shop had put together a selection of lipsticks and nail polish for her, he told Anna.

For Christmas they had given her an assortment of face creams and skin lotions when she came in to meet everyone in December. She had found them all friendly and likable, but most of all she was happy to have finally met Bernhard's assistant. Annette had come down to Florida at Miss Arden's request the week before Christmas.

Anna's opinion of her, when Bernhard asked on the way home, had been: "She's pretty, funny, and smart. I like her best of everyone I met today." To herself she thought, "I'm glad she's your assistant because I felt immediately that I can trust her. I'm not so sure about the other ladies or the glamorous clients..."

When they had finished their coffee, Anna got up to peel the potatoes for supper. Bernhard stood up then, too, and said, "Let's take a walk before you start cooking. I ate so much coffee cake, I don't think I'll get hungry for another couple of hours at least. Nothing beats your fresh *kaffebröd!* Now, just let me change into some other clothes. I've been standing in one place all day and need to move around."

"Fine with me, Bernhard, I haven't moved around much today either. I'll get my shoes on. Do I need my winter jacket? ... It's actually cold today... Imagine that! It can get cold in Florida!"

They walked over the bridge to the beach. When they reached the waterfront, although it would soon be dark, people were still walking along in front of the Casino and looking out at the sea. The high-flying clouds were tinged pink and gold over a gentle surf, as the sun set far away behind them, on the opposite horizon, the Gulf coast of Florida. A cool breeze was picking up. No one was in bathing apparel now, everyone was wearing sweaters or jackets, caps, and scarves.

Anna and Bernhard were reluctant to leave as it got dark. Arm in arm, they stood and watched the fishing boats and cruisers, with their lights flickering over the waves as they crossed on their way to the inlets to the north and south.

On their way home, Bernhard told Anna what the shop news of the day had been. It had been a shock. They had found out why Miss Arden had not come for her planned visit to the Palm Beach salon a few days before. She had not simply been too busy or depressed about her recent divorce as the staff had conjectured and Bernhard had previously related to his wife. The truth was that she had been happy to be divorced from her dubious prince but consumed by worry when she learned that her sister Gladys had been arrested by the Gestapo in Paris. She and Gladys' husband had been desperately trying to use their strong foreign connections, especially those in Berlin, to get her out of prison. That proved a difficult task. In the end, Gladys would spend more than six months in a prison camp before she was released in September.

He had other news, more positive news as well. He had found a potential tennis partner, it seemed. He would find out for sure on the weekend and hoped she did not mind if he went off for a few hours Sunday morning. She told him it was fine with her and that she would attend the church service at St. Andrew's, something she had only done once before.

Last summer, before coming down to Florida for the

winter, Bernhard had taken up a new sport. After years of irregular soccer playing, he had discovered tennis and was thrilled. It was a lot easier to find a singles opponent or three players for doubles than to get two teams of eleven players together for a soccer game.

Once he had taken Anna along to the tennis courts in Brooklyn and put a racquet in her hand, intending to give her a first basic tennis lesson. The project did not end well, however. Anna had not hit the ball more than once or twice with minimal success when an especially hard-hit ball from the next court struck her brutally in the face, giving her a full-fledged black eye and an excuse to never again be coaxed to set foot on a tennis court in her lifetime. Bernhard spent two weeks explaining to the neighbors and family how it had come about, to clear up any false impressions.

When one of the women working at the Palm Beach shop, Irene, heard that Bernhard played tennis, she told her husband, knowing he would be interested to hear about that. Mike then invited Bernhard to join him and two other friends, who had been having a hard time getting a fourth for doubles Sunday mornings at Phipps Park in West Palm Beach. Their problem was soon solved and so was Bernhard's. Two of the men who played together that first Sunday, Mike and a jovial, moustache wearing Russian named Serge would stay in touch with Bernhard for many years and continue to enjoy fighting it out on the tennis courts.

It had not taken long for Bernhard to be certain that he would like to stay in Florida permanently. He was not looking forward to returning to New York in the summer. Anna, on the other hand, was. She missed her family up north. She wanted to see how Signe's little Carrie was doing. In her last letter she had said she might be walking before her first birthday because she was so active, crawling throughout their house in Connecticut.

Anna wore a hat and sunglasses whenever she expected to spend any length of time outside and did not think she would want to live in Florida in the summer heat. She reminded Bernhard about the mosquitoes when he started talking about staying for the summer and that usually helped cool his enthusiasm.

Nonetheless, she was quite happy, too, and getting happier by the day, it seemed to Bernhard. Especially on this Valentine's Day. It was such a contrast to the weeks before. He had no idea why women had these mood swings.

.

32

Woman's Day

One afternoon two weeks later, Anna was on her way over to Mrs. Johnson's to pay the rent when she bumped into her and Mrs. Worsley talking together on the sidewalk in front of the Johnsons' house. Those were her only friends, or at least the only people she knew to talk to in Lake Worth, aside from Mrs. Lewis, the friendly grocer and his wife, or the postman. She had intended to walk over to Mrs. Worsley's after paying her rent because she wanted to ask her a personal question and felt more comfortable talking to her as a person more her age than Mrs. Johnson.

When Mrs. Johnson said hello and spontaneously asked her and Mrs. Worsley to come in for a cup of coffee, "…since we're all here together. If you have time, that is…" Anna could not say no. They went in and sat at the table in Mrs. Johnson's kitchen where she put the coffee on and placed three cups and saucers and a dish of cookies on the table. As the coffee percolated, the three women talked about rationing shortages, the day's prices at the grocers and the foods that were scarce because of the war economy.

"We weren't here for Christmas this year, but I made some spritz when I got back. Made them with margarine this year," said Mrs. Johnson, shaking her head, "since butter was so hard to come by again. Do you bake Swedish cookies, Anna?"

"I usually do, but I didn't make any of my cookies at all this year," answered Anna, "because I couldn't imagine making them with margarine." Then she bit her tongue, realizing that she might just have insulted her landlady. "Somehow I always managed to find butter in Brooklyn," she went on lamely.

When the coffee was ready, the cups were filled and the plate of spritz was passed around. Anna took one and praised it, saying she wished she had tried using margarine. She did not notice the little smile the other two women exchanged while she looked down to pick up her cup.

Mrs. Johnson laughed and said, "I'm afraid they are already slightly stale now, Anna. But I don't have anything else to have with our coffee." Then she paused and reached for a magazine that was lying on a low cupboard counter next to her chair and laid it on the table. "Have you ladies seen the latest Woman's Day magazine? There are some interesting recipes in here in the 'Wartime Cooking' section in the front. I think I'll try one of their recipes with soy grits. Have you ever cooked with soy grits?... And there's a recipe for marmalade. I still have a lot of oranges and lemons from our trees. The two of us can only drink so much orange juice and… I hope you've helped yourself, Anna, like I told you to. I think I'll make some orange jelly and add a little ginger, like they suggest. I've got plenty of pectin, might as well use it. But, what was I asking you, … Oh yes, soy grits. Doesn't sound very appetizing."

Mrs. Worsley said, "Yes, I have tried cooking with soy grits, but we didn't like it very much. I haven't had time to read this month's recipes. Which ones…" They went on talking, but Anna just stared at the picture on the cover and hardly heard what they were saying. She had her own copy of February's edition of Women's Day at home but had put it at the bottom of a stack of other magazines when she found herself wasting too much time looking at that picture. It was a chubby faced little boy, about one year old, wearing a blue sweater and a cap, laughing, and seeming about to reach out for a hug. She had read an article entitled "Do You Want to Borrow One?" illustrated with photos of toddlers whose mothers had placed want ads looking for "foster mothers" so they could go to work.

"*Påtår,* (Some more coffee,) Anna?" Mrs. Johnson asked, waking Anna up to her surroundings.

"*Ja, tack!*" Anna answered, "*men bara fem droppar.*"

Mrs. Worsley looked at the other two, confused for a moment, but then said, "Why, of course, you both speak Swedish, don't you?"

Mrs. Johnson nodded, laughing, "That's just an expression we Swedes use a lot. Just five drops, Anna? I wasn't sure you spoke Swedish. Second generation immigrants often don't want to use a language that makes them feel less American and we haven't talked together enough for me to find out. I was getting a bad conscience about not getting to know you better." She and her husband had been away on a trip to Sweden, to visit a terminally ill relative, and had been unable to return until after Christmas. It had been a risky trip to take on a merchant marine boat and an ordeal that they were thankful to have survived.

"English immigrants don't have any language problems," Mrs. Worsley said. "We have a head start with that, I guess you could say." She dropped another spoonful of sugar into her cup and stirred. She wondered if Mrs. Johnson would ever notice that she did not like coffee, being a devout tea drinker.

Anna smiled at them and said, "My parents spoke Swedish with each other most of the time, but my sisters and I didn't really learn to speak it well at all. We would get together after supper and try to figure out what they were saying at the dinner table if anything seemed interesting to us. My parents went by the principle of 'children are to be seen and not heard' at the table, so we just listened."

When there was a pause in conversation, Mrs. Johnson asked, "How are you making out here, Anna? Do you feel settled after…. How long have you been here now, was it November you got here?"

"Yes, first week in November."

"Have you found everything you needed?"

"Yes, I've done fine. It's not like moving to another country. That must have been hard for my parents and for my husband." She paused for a moment, and said, "I brought my Singer sewing machine with me and was happy to find a little shop on Lake Avenue where you can buy material and thread, so I've done some sewing. Even tried using a pattern for a wraparound skirt, no zipper, that went well enough, considering that I had never sewn anything but tablecloths before…"

"You know, I have never had so much time on my hands. We had only been here two weeks when Mrs. Worsley suggested I get myself a library card, so I did. I'm actually amazed I hadn't thought of it myself yet. It was the best possible idea. I've never been without books. You see, the Brooklyn Public Library was just a five-minute walk away from where I grew up. It's a big, impressive, modern building that just finally reopened with celebrations a few years ago after a long period of rebuilding. But I don't mean to be bragging about our library! What a lovely little library you have here!"

After a pause she went on, "The librarian is a nice woman. I asked her about the history of Lake Worth and she told me something interesting. She said most people in Lake Worth don't realize it, but the town was founded by ex-slaves, a couple called Sam and Fannie James, who had a lot of land and a successful pineapple farm at the turn of the century."

Mrs. Johnson said she had heard something like that but had not believed it because she had also heard that Swedish immigrants had owned land before that, and she did not believe any of that nonsense. "Where were those people now?" she asked.

Anna felt she might be talking too much. She was not sure they would want to hear what the librarian had said about how the town had been segregated and the colored had been sent to "the other side of the tracks." She had spent a lot of time alone and was happy to have other women to talk to. She missed her family. She wanted to say that she loved churches and libraries because they were quiet, peaceful places, both very similar atmospheres of reverence. Respect for God on the one hand and for books on the other. She wanted to say that she also thought she might prefer the small buildings in this town to larger ones in Brooklyn, but she stopped herself and drank a few sips of coffee.

Then, since no one else said anything for a moment, she found the silence embarrassing and went on, "Your library opened a short time ago, too, I hear. The librarian told me it was built just a few years ago and that it was financed by member donations."

"Yes, it was quite a success," Mrs. Worsley said, "we were very proud of our community!"

Passing the plate of cookies around again, Mrs. Johnson asked Anna, "Are you going to look for a job? I'm sure you could get one if you wanted to. There's a new lawyer in town and the doctors always need someone for the phone, you said you did office work, I think."

"Yes, I worked for an insurance company for fifteen years. I could never work on the phone, I tried that for a year, when I was fifteen, my first job was at a switchboard in the New York Telephone Company, but they soon found out that my hearing was not good enough," Anna shook her head and laughed, remembering how frustrating it had been and how glad she had been to leave that job.

"But," she went on, "we'll be going back up north in a few months, so I'm going to wait until next year if we come back to look for a job." Then she sighed, wondering if she should come right out and ask what she wanted to know. "My doctor told me to take a while off," she said. "I was filing young war widows' claims and it was so depressing…"

The other two women listened so attentively, nodding, sympathetically, it gave her the confidence to go on with the question she had wanted to ask Mrs. Worsley.

"We don't have a doctor here. Could you recommend someone?"

Mrs. Johnson looked at Mrs. Worsley and said, "We had a wonderful doctor, Dr. Garcia, he came in the middle of the night two years ago when I thought Arne was having a heart attack – that luckily turned out to be a case of severe indigestion – but last summer he moved back up north where he has family. I think his family was from Puerto Rico originally. Did you folks go to him, Elisabeth?"

Nodding vigorously, Mrs. Worsley said, "Yes, we liked him, too. We haven't found another doctor yet. Haven't needed one, thankfully. A new general practitioner just hung his sign out on South Federal though. I haven't heard anything about him, so I can't recommend him. And there are plenty of doctors in West Palm, of course."

When they left Mrs. Johnson's and stood talking for a few minutes outside, the two younger women came to the conclusion that there was no reason not to use each other's first names. "After all," Elisabeth said, "I think we can take her cue and drop the formalities, don't you, Anne?" Anna agreed and that was the beginning of a friendship that lasted for the rest of their lives. They started meeting regularly to have tea at Elisabeth's or coffee at Anna's and share the latest local or global news – war news at first – from a woman's point of view, one a stiff-upper lipped Londoner and the other a Scandinavian Brooklynite. It was not long before Anna bought a teapot and learned to enjoy a "cuppa" (cup of tea) at least whenever Elisabeth came to visit, since Elisabeth was never going to enjoy coffee.

33

A Shocking Experience

Two days later, Anna was riding her bicycle eastward down Lucerne Avenue, tears of fury streaming down her cheeks. She stopped at the park across from the library and sat on a bench under an immense banyan tree to compose herself, taking deep breaths and looking down at the two empty buttonholes on her blouse. She did not want to run into any of the few people she knew – especially not Mrs. Johnson or Elisabeth Worsley – until she had at least stopped shaking and regained control of her voice.

In the morning she had bicycled over to the other side of the town center after Bernhard left for work to see if she could find the doctor's office her friends had talked about. When she found a house on South Dixie Highway with a signpost in the front yard, saying "Dr. C. E. Brown, MD" and stating his visiting hours, she decided to go right to the door and ask for an appointment. After writing down her name, the receptionist told her the doctor would be arriving soon and that she could be his first patient of the day if she wanted to wait. Anna asked if Dr. Brown did pregnancy tests. When she was told that he did, she decided she might as well stay. She was not going to tell Bernhard about her supposed and much hoped for altered physical state until she was sure, but she was extremely impatient to find out.

When the doctor came blustering in, brusquely shoving a chair to the side with his briefcase, he looked surprised to see her sitting there alone in the tiny waiting room. He nodded to her, lifting his hat, and whispered with the receptionist briefly before he disappeared through a door. Ten minutes later he opened the door and asked her to come into his office.

At closer observation, Anna noticed the white doctor's coat he had in the meantime put on looked less than spotless and even a bit shabby, and his moustache was tobacco stained. But since he was the first doctor she had seen in Florida, that might be, she assumed, like everything else, different than up north. He was wearing a big smile, though, and proceeded to ask the usual questions about the reason for her visit. When she said she just wanted a pregnancy test and had been told he could do one, he started explaining to her how the test was done, saying a bit of her urine would be injected into a frog. She thought to herself, "Oh the poor little frogs, I don't even want to know about that," but said she was ready to supply the necessary sample when he gave her a glass cup and pointed to another door. When she came back, he said he would need to examine her.

"Is that necessary?" she asked, but then sat on the edge of the examination table, thinking he wanted to take her pulse, look in her throat, etc. When he said she would have to undress, she had first hesitated and then refused, saying she only wanted the test. Before she knew it he had roughly torn open her blouse, sending two buttons pinging across the floor. She pushed him away, jumped to her feet and grabbed her pocketbook, heading for the door.

The receptionist looked at her in surprise when Anna burst back into the reception area and asked what she owed for the pregnancy test.

"You can pay when you come back for the results, Mrs. Linden." Then, seeing how upset she was and sensing in dismay what had happened, she frowned and said, "Or you can pay now, and if you leave your telephone number, I'll call and tell you the result in two or three days." Anna agreed gratefully, opened her purse that she had been clutching close to her chest, paid the doctor's standard fee, and left. The receptionist, a middle-aged woman who had been unhappy with her new job for various reasons, made up her mind immediately that it was the last straw. She would look for work elsewhere after collecting her next paycheck. She had known Dr. Brown was unorthodox and impolite, but if what had just happened was what she thought it was, this was simply unacceptable.

Anna never told Bernhard about the incident. She was afraid of how he would react. That evening she complained of a headache when he noticed something was wrong with his recently so cheerful wife. She went to bed early and vowed to keep the secret to herself. She replaced the simple white buttons, but rarely wore the blouse again, because it reminded her of her encounter with Dr. Brown, something she wanted to forget.

On Saturday morning, moments after receiving a call from Dr. Brown's receptionist, Anna had fully recuperated from her shocking and humiliating experience. She felt immediately that she was literally in a reversed state of mind as well as body. Thrilled by the news – the receptionist had not only told her the test result was positive, but also apologized and given her the telephone number of a doctor in West Palm that she could recommend – she went shopping for the makings of a special meal while Bernhard was playing tennis. He was taking part in a round robin and might be gone all day, he had said apologetically, asking if she would mind. She, on this particular Saturday, was fine with that although she would have been disappointed otherwise.

But today she had her own project. She was going to make veal birds according to her own recipe. She did not use a bread stuffing, just pounded the two small but exorbitantly expensive veal slices with seasoned flour, cut them into triangles, filled them with a mixture of butter, margarine and chopped parsley and then sauteed them in olive oil, using a tiny bottle of Marsala to clean the pan for a light gravy. Anna had unexpectedly come across the tiny bottle of cooking wine at the grocers and when she saw veal, an absolute rarity, at the butcher's counter, that had given her the idea. This would be an unforgettable treat. So, she decided to splurge. What had she been saving meat ration points for, if not for this special occasion? They could eat pea soup all next week, cooked with a ham bone that required no points at all. Rice and peas, cucumber salad and then *äpplekaka* (apple cake) for dessert would finish off the menu. She picked a bunch of bright red and pale-yellow hibiscus flowers from the bushes at the bottom of their outdoor staircase and put them in a vase on the table where she had spread out the latest of her sewing achievements, a colorful round tablecloth with matching napkins. The stage was set for her announcement.

In the afternoon, as she was peeling apples for the cake, the phone rang. It was a long-distance call. Her cousin Vivian was coming to visit next month and wondered if Anna could recommend a place to stay. Then she said somewhat mysteriously that she had some news for her. There was a pause in the conversation when Anna heard that and could hardly resist saying that she had some news too, wondering if her news could be the same as Vivian's. She did not say anything, however, since she had promised herself she would tell no one until Bernhard knew. Vivian and her husband Sven would be there visiting with them in soon and there would be plenty of time to talk in person.

An hour later, Anna was just taking her cake out of the oven and enjoying the familiar apple and cinnamon scent in the kitchen, when the phone rang again. Another long-distance call as she could tell by the delayed connection and a series of clicking noises. This time it was her sister-in-law Margaret. After talking about family – Mimi and Harry had been visiting, and everyone missed Anna and Bernhard and wondered when they would be back up north… – and, as usual, recent war reports, both good and bad, Anna could not believe her ears when Margaret said she had some special news for her.

"I just want to warn you that you might not recognize me by the time you get back," Margaret said.

"What? What are you saying?" Anna asked, perplexed.

"Well, my face is already getting rounder and the rest of me will soon too…"

"You mean…?"

"Yes! What else? In a couple of months, it will be undeniable."

"You're expecting?"

"Well, my doctor seems to think so and I'm inclined to agree with him."

"Wonderful!.... And guess what…," Anna paused not to build up suspense but to wrestle a moment longer with her promise to herself to tell Bernhard first, "you won't believe this, but I am too, Margaret! And I only know since yesterday. I haven't even told Bernhard yet!"

"Well, I've known for two months now and just couldn't wait any longer to let you know. But we'd better get off the phone now, this will be too expensive. I should have written you a letter, but I wanted to at least hear the reaction in your voice if I can't see your face, and not have to wait two weeks until you write back or come back. Isn't this wonderful? Just think, we'll soon be pushing baby carriages up and down 3rd Avenue to visit each other, and then in a few years we'll be meeting at playgrounds!"

"You know," Anna said, "there's something else weird about this. We don't get many telephone calls here, but Vivian was just on the phone too, making some mysterious remarks that now are making me think this might be the beginning of ... what...an epidemic in our circles! She didn't really say, but the more I think about it, it seems she was hinting at something. And chances are... I'll know soon, they're coming to visit us in a few weeks."

"Well, it takes more than three to make an epidemic, I guess, but it would be fun bringing up three little ones together."

After they got off the phone, Anna had a few minutes before she had to start cooking the dinner and sat down with her copy of Woman's Day. She turned the pages, read an article about girls having trouble finding young men, entitled "Girls without Dates". The author suggested young women could join the drama club, learn to bowl, or play golf, go to the movies together, but especially write letters to the young men of the town who had gone off to the war. Anna knew she was lucky and felt sorry for so many less fortunate.

No one had to tell her that women without men were at a disadvantage in American society. The standard role models were quite specific. That Swedish "by the time you are married" quote had been automatically and lovingly implanted in her understanding of life at an early age. Most young girls from different backgrounds had received similar messages, explicitly or simply by absorbing them from what their own families were demonstrating, but the war economy was teaching women, by necessity, that they could in many situations take on the head of family position or do jobs they had been previously considered unable to do, at least as long as they were needed.

After the war, women would be expected to return to their former roles, and most did, but some were reluctant to do that. They had learned a lot about their own potential. Soon they would be demanding equal rights that went beyond their hard won right to vote established by

Amendment 19 in 1920. They would be inspired by the civil rights movement, which, according to historical opinion, would itself be set off eleven years later by the actions of a woman who made history by refusing to give up her seat for a white man on a bus in Alabama, Rosa Parks.

But Anna, like many women of her generation, was more than happy with her role. She wanted to be home, raising a family. She was not critical when she saw an advertisement telling her how important it was to make her husband feel like a king by using certain bouillon cubes in her cooking. She made a point of remembering that brand of bouillon. Maybe it really was better than other brands.

She started reading an article encouraging inexperienced seamstresses to try to make a suit, a skirt and jacket, using Butterick patterns. It looked quite complicated, she thought. She knew she would need some new clothes to fit her figure which soon would be changing. But she would need patterns for comfortable dresses and not tailored suits. Clearly she would get plenty of use out of her wraparound skirt, but she could not wear that every day. She went on distractedly flipping the pages, looking at the pictures.

Then she jumped up suddenly, closed her magazine and threw it down when she saw the time. "Oh, my goodness," she thought, "now I'll have to hurry!" The chubby-cheeked little boy on the cover seemed to look up at her and laugh. Anna laughed back.

34

Invitation from a Princess

A few weeks later, in the middle of March, Bernhard came home one evening with a package for Anna. Almost apologetically, he handed it to her and said, "Irene gave me this for you. She said she thought it would fit."

Puzzled, Anna unwrapped the paper and found a long straight skirt, with a kick slit up one side, "slinky" was the word that popped into her mind to describe it. The material was soft, turquoise and pink-paisley patterned silk. "It's lovely," she said, picking it up, "but when would I wear something like this? It would have to be a very special occasion... Besides, I'm not sure I can get into it now and much less in a few weeks. I'm already gaining weight.... Did you tell her we're expecting?"

"No," Bernhard answered, slightly embarrassed. "She has no idea, obviously. No room for a belly there... But one of my clients this week, a new client... I told you about her. She has come in twice. The princess, remember?"

"Of course!"

"Well, Annette heard her invite me to visit her where she

is staying with friends, to come by some evening this week before she goes back to wherever she comes from, Hungary or somewhere…"

"She's going back in the middle of the war?"

"No, I guess not, but she's leaving Palm Beach. And the thing is," he laughed, "Annette chirped in with her funny Danish accent and said – I couldn't believe my ears: 'You can take Anna along too, she would love to see that place, a beautiful house, and meet you, too, Princess Zeletsky. Wouldn't that be possible?' She said that with her sweetest smile. Then Madam Princess said, …graciously, you call it, I guess, not at all annoyed, more like amused, 'Yes, of course! I would love to meet your… wife, is that who Anna is?'"

"You see, I had no influence on the matter. It happened so fast!"

"But where did you get this skirt?" Anna asked, "it's beautiful, but…"

"Before I knew it that woman was gone, we had an invitation for tomorrow evening – just something very caaasuaaal' she said, as she left – and Irene and Annette were standing in front of me with this skirt, holding it up and saying it would fit you for sure, in case this was too short notice."

Anna shook her head for a moment, trying to take it all in.

"They want you to come in in the early afternoon, so I can do your hair and they can get you a facial and a

smiling with her, 'yes madam, and no madam' like they expect me to be. I wanted to play tennis tomorrow after work and now I can't!"

Anna thought it over for a moment, then said, "You can do my hair at home and I don't want a facial, but a manicure would be nice."

"Then come in on the bus tomorrow and bring the clothes to change into. I'll do your hair and they'll do your nails while your hair is drying, okay?"

They agreed. And, after making sure that the skirt fit, Anna started searching for a top to wear with it.

Two days later, it was Saturday afternoon, and Anna and Bernhard were sitting on their porch, laughing about the evening before, which had been an experience they would not forget. By the end of the evening, Anna at least, decided she liked Princess Zeletsky more than she had expected although she was nothing like anyone else she had ever met. As far as they could tell, except for all the servants, maids, cooks, and gardeners, she had been alone in that "lovely house" that turned out to be a proper mansion, built of coral keystone and trimmed with red brick, (like the famous "ham and cheese house").

When they parked their car at the house number on South Ocean Blvd that Irene had written down for Bernhard, a maid let them in at the door. Then she escorted them up two staircases, down hallways, through a luxurious bedroom, and onto a balcony, where their hostess was reclining on a lounge chair, drinking what looked to be a martini, and smoking a cigarette in a long, slim, black cigarette holder that made Anna think of a magic wand. She was not beautiful, but elegant and extremely aware, Anna thought, that the impression she made was the perfect example of a *femme fatale*.

"Oh, there you are! How nice to see people! I am so lonely here," she said, "my friends had an invitation that they could not turn down, something political I suppose, and when they asked if I would mind being alone for a few days, I said of course not. I told them I had been alone in a palace before, for weeks, so why should it bother me to be alone in a mere mansion, for a few days? But to tell the truth, to be perfectly honest, it does!"

She got up gracefully, showing Anna that she was quite tall, dressed in a dark red and gold silk kaftan, black silk, three quarter length slacks, and golden sandals on her feet.

She came toward them, reaching her hand out to Bernhard, who didn't know if he should shake it or kiss it – he took it gently with a bow – and then she surprised Anna with a quick, smiling kiss on both sides of her face.

"You have a lovely wife, Bernaahd. Anna…" she said, assessing Anna with an approving smile and then turning toward him, "but why are you so early? I wasn't expecting you before dark."

Perplexed, Bernhard said, looking at his watch, "But it is 5 o'clock, I believe, just like you suggested, if I remem…"

Their hostess laughed, and said, "Really now, then you are the only punctual guests I have ever met. It must be because of your appointment schedule. They warned me at Arden's not to come more than ten minutes late. In fact, I think I was at least half an hour late Wednesday and you did not turn me away, did you, Dahhling?!"

Anna held a tight grip on her eyebrows that were tugging upward and swallowed a faint vibration in her throat that must not turn into a laugh. She knew that Irene had probably put the appointment into the books with a considerable delay to minimize upsets to the schedule.

"Now what are you drinking? I have a martini here, the gardener made mine, and I dare say I prefer his martinis to any I've had elsewhere. I imagine he can make anything else you might fancy as well."

Bernhard looked at Anna, who was gazing out over the balcony balustrade at the breathtaking view of the ocean and the moon just rising barely discernible on the horizon.

"If the gardener is still here, I guess I'll have to try one of those martinis then," he said, "and my wife would probably prefer iced tea if that's possible, right, Anne?"

"He's here, he's the butler as well, so he lives in, he's here twenty-four hours a day… In fact, he is the real occupant of this mansion, the lord of the house, you could say, twelve months in the year. Funny isn't it?…Really, iced tea, are you sure?" Princess Zeletsky looked at Anna and reached out for the little bell standing on the table next to her chaise longue and gave it an insistent jiggle.

Anna had turned to look at Bernhard, in surprise. She had been looking forward to a martini as well, but then realized her husband was thinking about the baby that was on the way. She was the one who had told him a few days before that pregnant women should not drink alcohol or smoke, that everything could influence the baby's development. So, she smiled at him, sighed, and nodded. "Just water would do fine if you don't have tea, thank you," she said.

Bernhard, who had brought his camera along, looked for a place to put it down. Then he changed his mind and asked if he could take a picture. "It's such an interesting light, and this won't last long, just a few minutes. Would you mind if I took a photograph?"

"No, of course not, Dahhling," and she turned to tell the maid to bring the drinks and to have the cook fry some chicken – the way she did it last week, please" – and make a big salad for us in about an hour to be served on the southwest terrace.

Having made her instructions clear to the maid, their hostess turned and asked, "Where did you want me to stand for your photo?" Then she laughed and her eyes twinkled as she said, "Come, Anna, he wants to take our picture. And, Anna, please call me Marie, I can't stand, I abhor formality!"

So, the two of them had leaned together against the balustrade, smiling, with the moon balancing on the horizon behind them and the cigarette holder gesturing against the night sky and into the future, as Bernhard took pictures that would be put into the family album and arouse curiosity years later.

On the way home, after listening to the princess' amusing, but only barely credible stories of a childhood in Bohemia, Anna had remarked, using an old Swedish saying, "*Fint folk kommar sint!* (Fine people arrive late!) I guess she noticed we're not *fint* folk since we didn't arrive late like everyone else she knows, but she should have realized that anyway."

Bernhard laughed, "You never know with these ladies, they're full of surprises!"

As he maneuvered the car over the bridge and then south on Dixie Highway, he told Anna what he had learned in the past year working for Elizabeth Arden, especially while in Palm Beach. Some of his clients were stiff and unapproachable, even rude, while others were friendly and relaxed. It had nothing to do with the extent of their wealth or fame and that was redefining his conception of *fint* folk.

He would have the opportunity to meet important politicians' wives, even former First Ladies, and many celebrities. Some would be real people and others hopelessly artificial., some would be famous actresses, others were "would-be" actresses. Some told him stories he did not want to hear, while others became friends who confided in him and exchanged opinions with him. A few wanted his advice and acted almost as if he were their minister or their psychotherapist, much to his embarrassment.

He had a few clients who had standing appointments for many years and who occasionally asked him to stop by on the weekend for a "comb out". If the time he suggested seemed inconveniently early, he would remind them that he would be playing tennis that morning. He would explain that he would arrive in his tennis clothes and then joke that they should be glad he was on his way to a match and not on his way home after one. They understood.

Anna was the only woman who, wrinkling her nose and turning her head, could bear to welcome him in the house in such a state. He would be smiling but exhausted, drenched in perspiration and with red clay stains along at least one side of his originally white shorts and shirt. Sometimes but only rarely, he would present green stains, evidence that he and his partner had been invited to play on someone's grass tennis court.

35

Miss Arden Visits Palm Beach Salon

It was mid-April, and the Palm Beach season was coming to an end. That meant it was time for Anna and Bernhard to start getting ready for the trip north. They did not know if they would be spending the next winter in Florida again. Elizabeth Arden's might have other plans for Bernhard, and Anna was looking forward to being near her family in Brooklyn when her baby was born. If they had known that they would be coming back the next winter, they would have reserved the little apartment in Lake Worth.

It had been a happy year. Vivian and Sven had come the weekend before for a visit that flew by. They had rented two more bicycles in town and the couples had taken a bike trip together, the women soon cutting the men loose and letting them race for another hour or two while they turned back to make dinner in Anna's kitchen. Her intuition had proven correct, Vivian was also expecting and was almost two months further along in her pregnancy than Anna. She and Sven had almost canceled the trip for that reason. But, being "tough" as she described herself quite accurately to Anna, who knew it to be not only true but more like an understatement, she had decided it would be more difficult to travel with children and they had better go ahead with the vacation. She and Anna had a good long girl talk while they were alone peeling potatoes and carrots and chopping onions to make stew with the skimpy piece of beef that Anna had been able to buy with her meat ration points. (A couple of "excellent bouillon cubes" would be thrown in to round out the flavor.) She and Vivian were both attuned to the same state of mind of happily expectant mothers-to-be. Neither one of them was thinking about what it would be like if anything went wrong.

After a winter in the sun, Bernhard, if not necessarily Anna, was convinced Florida was the place where he would like to spend the rest of his life. His health had profited from the climate. The clean air and regular exercise had prevented his usual winter cough. In fact, he no longer looked like a Swede. He had not been fair haired since childhood but now, along with his dark hair, he wore a tan that could make some gardeners look pale. Only his intense blue eyes and traces of an accent caused some new acquaintances to look twice and ask where he came from.

On an unusually hot day in the beginning of April, Miss Arden finally came for a visit to the salon to see how the business was shaping up. She liked to keep an eye on things herself and was personally proud of her business successes. When she was expected to come by the staff would be nervous all day until she arrived. She wanted everything to be perfect, the salon had to exude an atmosphere of calm luxury and everyone working for her was to give the impression or illusion of good looks and excellent health.

When she finally arrived, Bernhard had taken off his jacket for a few minutes between clients in the upstairs salon where several hair dryers were running, and the ceiling fans had been unable to maintain anything like a comfortable temperature. He was out on the tiny, shady balcony in his shirt sleeves and did not have time to pull on his jacket when

Annette came and whispered to him that Miss Arden was on her way up the stairs.

Seconds later he heard her say, "Where's our Mr. Bernárd?" He hesitated for a moment but then had to go inside to be at his post. "Here I am, Miss Arden, I was just looking from out here to see if your car had arrived. How are you?"

She was out of breath from the stairs and fanning her face with a lace-bordered hanky. "Oh, there you are! Are you …? My goodness you do look the picture of health... Florida must be good for you. I hardly recognize you."

His dark tan and the brilliant white shirt with the French cuffs made quite an impression, it seemed.

"My, my!" she said, fanning faster with her handkerchief.

"Would you like to step out here on the balcony?" Bernhard asked. "It seems summer is already here, and it gets very warm in the salon with the dryers blowing. It's a bit cooler outside. Have a seat here in the shade while I get you something to drink. Iced tea?"

"Yes, I think I will, that would be nice," she said and dropped down onto a chair in relief.

When he came back with a glass of iced tea that Annette had quickly conjured up in the salon kitchen, Miss Arden had regained her composure. She was talking to the shop manager, who had followed her upstairs and was standing next to her chair and speaking in a low voice.

"How could that happen? Can't her husband…"

Bernhard heard only a few words but knew almost immediately what they were talking about.

"No, it doesn't look good, at all! I warned her… She waited too long. I haven't slept a night since…"

Bernhard handed Miss Arden the glass and got a small table to place next to her chair so that she could put the glass down.

"Thank you, Bernárd," said the manager, "umm…don't you have a client waiting?"

Bernhard started to explain that his next client had

canceled, when Miss Arden shook her head, saying, "No, I don't want to talk about Gladys now. We can talk tonight over dinner, my Dear." Then she waved the manager off, who was a good friend and longtime business associate, but, like all her employees, never forgot who the boss was. She retreated, and left the balcony, looking slightly annoyed but saying, "Of course, *mais oui! À plus tard, chérie!*"

Bernhard and his boss spoke for just a few minutes. She wanted to know what he thought of how the shop was being run in general and if he thought it had potential for a long future. He answered in a strong affirmative. Her one more specific question to him was easily answered. Yes, unsurprisingly, he would be happy to come back to the Palm Beach salon again next year. He would have liked reassurance that he could indeed plan on doing so but, unfortunately, did not get any commitment of that kind. Instead, she explicitly reserved the right to send him to another place, saying he had done so well, she had heard so many positive reports, that she might need him to boost business in one of her other shops. She did say she counted on his working all summer in New York, however, and Bernhard was glad to hear that, knowing it was where Anna wanted to be.

He and Annette accompanied Miss Arden down the narrow stairs to the reception area where his vivacious assistant, who was known for her spontaneous enthusiasms, blurted out that Bernhard's wife was expecting a baby and would be happy to be near her family in Brooklyn for that event.

Miss Arden smiled and said she wished his wife the best. Then she said, "I'd like to give her something. We don't have anything for babies here, but something pretty. I think she gave up her job to come down here, didn't she, Bernárd."

"Yes, that's right, Miss Arden."

She looked around and saw a locked cabinet display with expensive accessories, scarves, gloves, and jewelry.

"There," she said, "Annette, open this for me, I want to look at these things. Maybe there's some little something here that would be appropriate."

Annette went to fetch the key to the cabinet. She came back, looking worried, with a ring of half a dozen keys, each one numbered for a different display case in the shop. She had taken off her eyeglasses before Miss Arden arrived and put them away in a drawer upstairs, knowing her boss did not like to see staff wearing glasses in her salons. That did not fit into the illusion of perfect health.

Miss Arden stood impatiently next to her as she struggled to find the proper key without being able to read the tiny labels. She placed a random key in the lock and was, of course, disappointed. Standing behind them, Bernhard, who noticed what was happening, came to her rescue.

"Oh, that's the lock that sticks, I believe. Irene had trouble with it the other day. Let me try." Annette gratefully gave him the keys. He immediately read the labels, picked the right key, and opened the door with a slight jiggle.

"Thank you, now let me look at that blue scarf," Miss Arden said. After holding it up to the light and checking the price tag, she shrugged and then said, "That will do fine. Get Irene to wrap it up nicely and take it home to your wife, Bernárd. I really must leave now. I have a massage appointment at the Breakers and my chauffeur is waiting at the door... Things are going very well here, I can see. The future looks rosy for this salon. Irene knows not to take any more appointments for next week, just about everyone here has already gone back up north." She smiled and waved as she headed for the red door.

36

On Their Way North

A week later, it was early Wednesday morning. The car was packed and waiting out in front of the Johnsons' house on Palmway. Anna and Bernhard had said goodbye to their landlords and Bernhard was standing next to the car, looking at the map he had unfolded and spread open on the hood. It was the same map they had used on their honeymoon trip to Florida six years ago. He was contemplating a different route for at least part of their journey to perhaps take advantage of an opportunity to see some places they had never been before. While weighing the attraction of Davy Crocket and the Cumberland Gap against that of Abraham Lincoln sitting high on his monumental chair in Washington, D.C., he began to realize the additional wear and tear on his car that the trip further west could entail. His car was not new. Driving via Washington would not require taking much of a detour, it was practically on their way.

Getting impatient, he folded the map again, eager to get

on the road and wishing Anna would finish saying goodbye to Elisabeth soon. He had helped his wife carry a large carton full of leftover kitchen supplies and two small potted plants of dill and chives down the street to Elisabeth's house and then had gone right back to the car, feeling uneasy and reluctant to leave it unlocked and fully packed for more than 5 minutes. But a repeat of that painful experience when their Christmas packages were stolen from the car two years before was so improbable in the quiet little town of Lake Worth that he had ended up laughing at himself. Nonetheless, such experiences do form lasting memories and it had been a lesson.

When Anna came hurrying back, looking apologetic, she was holding a small package wrapped in brown paper and a square, blue plastic box.

"What have you got there?" Bernhard asked.

"Elisabeth said this is for you, for the road. The box here is full of her shortcakes. They are delicious! I had some last week. They're for the road, too, but they are for me!" she teased, laughing. She gave Bernhard the little package which he opened immediately, as he walked around to the driver's side of the car, uttering a confused but then satisfied "Umm... aha!" He took a funny looking little black thing out of a box, that was labeled HULL CAR COMPASS, for Chevy, Ford, or Dodge.

"She said Harald, her husband, not her son, had ordered it for his car months ago and then thought his order had not gone through when it took so long, so he ordered another one that came last week and now this one came as well... You know, anyway, he doesn't need it and Elisabeth said, 'Just in case you get lost... on the wrong road or something, at least you can keep on going north. And then be sure to come South next fall!' Wasn't that nice of her?"

"You can always tell where north is by looking at the sun, you know."

"And if the sun isn't shining, at night, for instance?"

"I can always find the north star."

"Not if it's cloudy!"

"Well, at night this thing would have to have a light…"

"Oh, for goodness sake, Bernhard!"

Bernhard was already sitting at the wheel, grinning at her. "Come on," he said, "Get in. We have a long trip ahead. Give me one of those shortcakes! You can find a place for this gadget. You're the co-pilot."

"Sometimes I still cannot tell when you are joking," Anna said, smiling at him affectionately, as she settled into her side, the passenger side, of the wide seat, that was piled high between them with things to eat and drink. "And no, you are right. I am the co-pilot, so no cake now. That will be later with coffee. Where's the thermos? You'll have to wait until… Where's the map?"

He handed her the map and then, off they drove, up the coast, Route 1 north to Ft. Pierce, Daytona Beach, St. Augustine, Jacksonville, passing a place called Cape Canaveral that meant nothing special to them or anyone else yet for that matter.

They spent the night in a little motel south of Savannah, Georgia, called, strangely enough, My Old Kentucky Home. Out in front there was an enormous tree hung with Spanish moss and stretching its long arms in the circular entrance driveway, beckoning to them to come in. They could not resist having supper at a nearby restaurant they had passed by that looked like a stranded boat with bull's eye windows. They agreed that although they had driven north all day, Georgia felt more southern than Florida. They ate fresh shrimp, clam cakes, speck trout and flounder with baked potatoes, coleslaw, and hush puppies that they dipped in honey. Coconut custard pie went with their menu or they would not have said yes, but they enjoyed that as well and vowed on their way back to the car not to eat again until they reached New York.

By the Time You Are Married

The next day, ready to continue their journey north, they did not mind that the motel offered no breakfast, just coffee or tea. They were encouraged to fill their thermos at the reception desk when they paid. They did that and then got off to an early start. On the road, they soon finished the shortcakes with their coffee, and, at lunch time, they munched on a boxful of Ritz crackers. There was nothing wrong with their appetites as they ate bananas and apples and drank the orange juice that they had bought at South of the Border just before leaving Florida.

Anna did not have much to do as co-pilot or navigator, they did not need the compass to follow route 1 northward, so, when she was not doing crossword puzzles, she just looked out the window and sometimes sang. Bernhard had installed a car radio before they drove down to Florida, but the reception was not good. Each time a song or music they liked came on, they lost the station. But that was usually enough to set Anna off singing if it was one of her favorites. She had been writing down lyrics to songs she liked for years, but that notebook was packed away in one of the boxes on the back seat, so she did a lot of humming. She had no trouble carrying on when Dinah Shore's voice faded in the middle of The Blues in the Night even if her mama had never told her about "sweet talk" or warned that "a man was a two-faced… a worrisome thing that will lead you to sing the blues in the night…" She had seen what happened to her sister and knew what it was all about.

Perhaps her most favorite song was the "September Song" since Bing Crosby had recorded it. She did not need her notebook for that. So, when they caught only the tail end of that one, Bernhard switched off the radio and said "Come on, Anne, you sing "It's a long, long time…"

A minute or two later, as she was singing and he was thinking what a sad song it was, actually – not healthy and carefree for his baby in Anna's belly, he saw something on his side of the road ahead that he could not quite make out.

As soon as he realized what it was, a dead cow that had probably been hit by a car, he decided he had to keep Anna from seeing it. She was looking out the passenger side window as she sang, and he was determined to keep her looking in that direction. He started pointing into the woods, saying, "Look, Anne! Did you see that? It might be a ... wild turkey. Look!"

Anna stopped singing and strained her eyes but could not for the life of her make out anything between the trees. When she started to turn back toward him at the worst possible moment, he continued the charade, pointing and saying, "I think there are more of them. Look!"

Finally, safely past the dead cow, even enjoying the success of his little charade, he said, "Well, it's too late now. I'm not going to stop the car and go back. It was so easy to see. You should have gone hunting with me as a boy in the woods at three in the morning. I had to learn how to see in the dark to see the big wild bird up in the tree and bring it down with my rifle. We didn't have flashlights, you know."

Anna just looked at her husband, perplexed. He had, after all, wanted her to sing, and then interrupted her, rudely, she thought. She did not understand his behavior sometimes. That she had to admit.

"But...," she said, her head cocked slightly to one side, "do you really think there could be one of those wild turkeys here? We are still in the south. Sweden is so much farther north..."

"Yes, you are right, Anne," he said, smiling, "It was more like wishful thinking, I guess. Go on singing, please."

She frowned and said, "I think I'll try to finish that crossword puzzle now, maybe later."

Bernhard, raising his bushy eyebrows just slightly, glanced at his wife, who was already getting her puzzle book and a pencil out of the bag at her feet and, pointedly, not looking at him. Then he put the radio back on, listened to yet another report about how many tons of bombs had been dropped on Germany and parts of occupied Europe. He could not help but think of his boot camp buddies, Gerhart and Joe, hoping they were all right. He had not heard a word from either one of them since he had responded, with Anna's help, to Joe's letter the year before.

Letting his thoughts wander, he recalled the people he had talked to on that motorcycle trip to Germany with his school friend Kalle ten years ago. He wondered how those carefree young German fellows in the *kneipe* were faring. They had not seemed to be any different than he and Kalle were, until that one guy started talking about Hitler. Bernhard shook his head in disgust at the destruction and the particular horrors of this war. He had heard things he could not believe were true and wished he could conceal from Anna.

As the radio station reception faded away, he fiddled with the tuning knob and found another one up the road a bit. Then, after once again hearing how long a way it was to Tipperary, and more about bluebirds flying over the White Cliffs of Dover, he decided that was enough wartime radio for a while. He turned it off and then tried unsuccessfully to whistle an old tune he knew Anna liked, "My Cutie's Due at Two to Two". Admittedly that was a hard tune to whistle, but he struggled on with it until Anna started laughing. They both remembered how, ten years before, when Bernhard came back from his Sweden trip and came to visit at the Bjorkman's house, Signe had embarrassed Anna by telling him her twin sister had been dancing and singing that song all day long. Anna had not spoken to Signe for the rest of the day.

37

Through the Carolinas to Virginia

Anna and Bernhard had hoped to travel through South and North Carolina, taking the route they had used on the way south in the Fall in reverse, and making headway well into Virginia by nightfall. However, a change in the weather, heavy rain and numerous detours slowed them down. It had taken twice as long as expected to reach the North Carolina border. Every time they stopped for gas, Bernhard walked around the car, checking the tires, but today after two lengthy road construction delays, he started asking the gas station attendants for advice on the road conditions going north. While still in South Carolina no one had had any helpful information for him, but in Fayetteville, North Carolina, the young fellow who came to fill the tank said Bernhard should go in and talk to Flurd, his boss, when he asked him about the roads ahead. Anna and Bernhard looked at each other, thinking it was a strange name.

When Bernhard came back from the office, Anna said the boy had tried to tell her something she could not understand.

He came back over and said to Bernhard, "Cheg y' erl, sir?"

Bernhard looked at Anna to see if she understood, but she looked as mystified as he was.

"With a big grin, the boy went and got a can of oil from the garage and held it up to them.

"Oh yes, okay. Thank you!" Bernhard said, embarrassed, thinking he should have understood, but sure the oil level was okay. It had been checked just that morning. When he came back from paying for the gas, the boy confirmed what he had expected and stood smiling until Bernhard gave him some of the change he had just received.

Back in the car, Bernhard told Anna the boy's boss, Flurd, "or whatever his name was", had driven up to Richmond a week ago and said they should get off Route 1 and switch to 301 for their trip to Washington. He thought he had understood him all right. So, as they pulled out onto the highway again, they decided to take 301. Anna got the map out and folded it to a more manageable shape to look for the 301 connection.

She looked at the receipt before she put it away. It was hard to read, but she could make out the header "Floyd Boydson's Tune Ups, Fayetteville, N.C.". Anna laughed, and said to her husband, "Well, Boynad, Flurd was Floyd. We just got gas at Flurd… um… Birdsongs Tune Ups! Isn't it funny? In New York they turn the 'er' to 'oy', you know how Mimi's Harry says New Joysey and so on, and maybe here they do the exact opposite. Or the poor kid has a speech problem of some kind."

"What? What are you saying?" Bernhard asked, confused and impatient to get moving. "Get a look at that map, the man said at the next big junction 301 should join Route 1 and…."

By evening they had made it to Emporia, just into Virginia. The advice had been good as far as road construction was concerned, but the rain had been relentless. They found a motel called "Sleepy Hollow", got a room, finished off what was left of the Ritz crackers with some juice from a cooler in the office and collapsed into bed as if they had run a marathon. They had not left their car for more than 15 minutes the whole day.

The next morning, they awoke hungry for breakfast and refreshed from a long, exhausted night's sleep. They had forgotten to set the alarm clock, so it was already later than intended, but one look out the window extinguished in every sense of the word any desire to get on the road again. It was still raining, not bucketing down like the night before, but still a steady, if gentle, downpour. On the desk Anna found an advertisement for a restaurant nearby that boasted of "Virginia's best breakfast". Reading about the pancakes served with butter, bacon, and real maple sirup, she got so hungry she could hardly wait. Bernhard was in the bathroom.

"Hurry, Dear, I am starving, aren't you?"

"Well, maybe I could skip shaving for one day, what do you think?" He stuck his head out the door.

Anna looked and then, without a moment's hesitation, said, "No, don't think so. You don't want to arrive in our nation's capital looking like the future Rip Van Winkle!"

"Who? What's that?"

"I'll tell you all about that over a delicious breakfast and a hot cup of heavenly coffee at Bella's Best. It's just down the road."

"Would you like some more coffee? Can I fill up your cups?" the friendly but otherwise preoccupied looking waitress asked, as she appeared next to their table with a full pot of coffee.

She had been standing at the window looking out at the rain splashing in puddles in the parking lot, while they ate their breakfast. But Bernhard had just asked Anna, "*Ingår påtår, tror du?*" Wondering if she thought a second cup of coffee was included, or if they should order another cup. So, it was as if their waitress had understood what he said.

"Oh yes, please," both Anna and Bernhard responded gratefully with big smiles. They were the only guests in the restaurant and had been hoping the rain would stop while they ate, reluctant to get back into the car where the windshield wipers would go on sloshing and slicing their view of the road ahead the way they had most of the day before.

"It's been like this all week," the waitress said, "I don't get many customers now anyway, all the guys that worked out at the mill, including my husband, are off as potential cannon fodder. Downright depressing! But if at least the rain would stop, then someone might come in for some of our home cooking." She had filled both cups and took a good look at her customers. "Don't imagine you're gonna be here at suppertime, but we make some really fine *Lasagna Neapolitana*."

Anna and Bernhard shook their heads sympathetically and listened to her as she told them how hard it was to keep the business going, just getting the supplies for her kitchen was hard enough without having to worry about her husband out getting killed somewhere in Italy – his last letter had come from there – while she was cooking spaghettis and Bolognese sauce.

"Are you Bella, then?" Anna asked.

"Bella's my husband's momma, her real name is Isabella. Someone called her Bella, said 'Bella's the best!' and it stuck. She's had this restaurant for twenty years. Before she came over from Naples with her parents and then down here with her husband from New Jersey, people around here didn't know what Italian cooking was. We've been running this restaurant together now since my husband's been away. If we're busy, Bella comes in, but that doesn't happen much lately. I can make out here most days alone. As long as one of us is there for the kids when they come home from school, or here, if we are busy…"

Back in the car and pleased to see that the rain was letting up, Bernhard was glad to be making progress and started off again, whistling the tune of "You Are My Sunshine". It was not long, however, until they had to stop to get gas, so while the tank was being filled just south of Petersburg, Anna showed Bernhard the towns that they would be going through on Route 301 toward Richmond. Seeing that Routes 1 and 301 joined up very soon in Petersburg, they decided they would follow Route 1 again from there to Washington, D.C., because it looked like the straighter route to the nation's capital.

When the rain finally stopped and the sky cleared after Richmond, it put Bernhard into a cheerful mood. At first he tried to find some good music on the radio. But since there were too many radio stations vying for attention and causing interference, he switched it off and asked Anna to tell him more of the funny stories from that book she said she had read in her last year at school. She had already told him where their Sleepy Hollow Motel had got its name from and what she remembered about Rip Van Winkle and his twenty-year old beard while they were eating breakfast. Bernhard had laughed when she said the American Revolution had taken place while Rip Van Winkle slept. When Rip woke up and stumbled into town, everything had changed. He hardly recognized anyone, including his family, and no one recognized him. He was completely unaware of what had happened in the meantime and when asked who he was, he had professed to be a loyal British subject. That, of course, was a dangerous thing to do at the time.

Now, as they drove along, she did not remember much more about those stories, except for one about a headless horseman chasing someone by the unforgettable name of Ichabod Crane. She told Bernhard she knew that the author was from New York, and his strange stories were probably required reading in public schools in New York. The writer's name, however, had been lost in the back recesses of her brain in the sixteen years since she left school.

Then, after a moment's silence, she asked, "Did I ever

tell you why I quit school?"

"No. You know I quit as soon as I could. Now, of course, I wish I hadn't, but I didn't like school. I bet you liked going to school, so why did you quit?"

Anna told Bernhard the whole story, about how her father had asked her to do an errand for him. He wanted her to walk to the Bell Telephone Company's Brooklyn Office and pay the telephone bill. He gave her a ten-dollar bill and she set out with the money in her hand. By the time she reached the branch office, she realized she had lost the money, dropped it somewhere along the way. She went back, looked everywhere, in the gutters, on the pavement where she had stood watching an ice delivery man who joked with her, along the stretch of flooded sidewalk where a fire hydrant had burst and was still gushing water, but it was hopeless. She knew that ten dollars was a lot of money. Anyone who found it would have felt lucky and put it in his pocket. That was the way the saying went: "Finders keepers, Losers weepers!"

So, Anna wept all the way home. By the time she got there, she had figured out how to ward off her father's anger. She confessed immediately, apologizing and saying she would quit school and go to work to repay the loss. Her father accepted her offer with no hesitation. When her mother heard what had happened she protested but was eventually silenced when he kept insisting that, "the girls will just get married anyway so what is the point of an education? She can read and write."

Bernhard did not really see things much differently, but said he was sorry to hear her story. "How long did it take you to earn ten dollars?" he asked. "Not long, I'm sure. That wasn't fair."

Anna said nothing for a few minutes, then she sighed, and said, resolutely, "If our baby is a girl, I want her to get all the education she can!"

By the Time You Are Married

The weather was beautiful, a lovely day for an afternoon walk in the capital. After Fredericksburg it would only be about forty miles to Washington. When they got through a series of confusingly twisted road construction detours they found themselves on a straight two-lane highway that stretched out in front of them like an unfurled roll of ribbon all the way to the horizon. It went up and down big and little hills, cutting its way straight through seemingly endless woods, and showing a border of rich red earth on each side. The sun stood high directly above and they had the road to themselves, which was enjoyable after all the traffic and detours. Enjoyable that was, until Bernhard started to worry.

"Honey, are you sure we're still on that detour? When was the last time we saw a Route 1 sign?"

Anna shrugged, and said, "I've been asking myself the same thing, but it's so beautiful here, I didn't want to ruin it…. To be honest, I don't remember when that was, but turning back now would be so frustrating. Maybe we should drive a little further, there might be a crossing with a sign soon."

"It doesn't look like it," Bernhard remarked glumly, as he scrutinized the road ahead. It dipped a few times but continued unwaveringly straight toward the horizon.

"At least I don't think we're going south, but I don't know," he went on, looking up at the sky. Then, grumbling, he said, "I bet we would have been better off staying on 301."

Anna frowned but said nothing.

Then, as she rummaged through the bag at her feet, he looked out his side window. All there was to be seen was trees and more trees. "I don't see any wild turkeys either…," he joked half-heartedly.

"Well, now," Anna said with a big smile and a slight but distinct note of triumph in her voice, "I can tell you, captain, when the sun is directly overhead and your *nordstjärnen* (North Star) is invisible, the best thing for an experienced co-pilot to have at her disposal is a ... compass!" and presented the gadget with a dramatic gesture.

"Well, I'll be darned! I forgot about that thing," Bernhard said, as he pulled the car to a stop at the side of the road. Together they unpacked the compass and figured out that they had been traveling due west for almost half an hour. The map showed no big towns or crossings ahead for the road they assumed they were on, so they turned around and drove back to the last detour.

38

Washington, D.C.

They had lost a considerable amount of time in the morning with their extended detour but as they drove past Mt. Vernon, through Alexandria and the last stretch along the Potomac River to Arlington they realized they were lucky with the weather. They planned to take their chances and leave finding a hotel room for later in order to enjoy as many hours of daylight as possible. They had eaten a big breakfast and could skip lunch, so they planned to stop for a coffee somewhere after driving around for a while. There was a small insert map of Washington, D.C. included in their Eastern Coastal States map that gave them a general idea of where they wanted to go.

Their route led them first past the enormous, recently completed Pentagon building, where an abundance of flags was flying and military vehicles of all sizes and varieties filled the streets, and then past Arlington National Cemetery, which had been established after the Civil War and extended many times as the country participated in World Wars I and II and brought home more than half a million dead soldiers to be buried and honored.

As they crossed Arlington Memorial Bridge, Bernhard said, "Let's go see if the President is home. Okay? Do you think you can direct me to the White House?"

"Do you want to knock on FDR's door?" Anna laughed. "I think I can get us there, but we would need an invitation! The President I want to visit is always home. Look, he must be in there." She motioned to the Lincoln Memorial that they were just driving past, slowly in the heavy traffic. "I want to see Abraham Lincoln sitting on his chair. Let's try to just get a look at the White House, since we don't plan to go inside," she giggled, "and then come back here and find a place to park the car nearby, maybe have a coffee. Then we can have a walk from the Lincoln Memorial to the Washington Monument and on to the Capitol building."

She paused and then said, "Hmm, maybe that's a bit too far for one afternoon. In fact, I can see that it's much too far... Oh look, we're heading toward a section called Foggy Bottom, sounds like a funny place, but we can go straight here on 23rd Street and after about five or six blocks if we turn right that should bring us to the White House."

That, then, was what they did. Finding their way was not easy, however. It was a busy city, and even if they were used to traffic in New York, this was a totally different place. They eventually got where they wanted to go, but there was nowhere to park near the White House. So, they continued along as slowly as they could, ignoring the horn-blowing and angry gestures of other drivers. It became obvious that they could not stop even for a moment to take a quick photograph, especially since the camera was packed away under all their belongings and would have taken a while to retrieve.

As they drove on, hoping to find their way back to the Lincoln Memorial, they wondered if it was true that the flag they saw flying above the White House signaled that Roosevelt was present. When Bernhard asked Anna if she thought he would run for a fourth term in office, she said she did not know but, if he did, he probably would win. Americans would not throw him out if the war was not yet over. Bernhard said he hoped FDR would be appreciated for his New Deal the way Lincoln was for ending slavery.

An hour later they had parked their Dodge in a guarded parking lot, had a coffee and a piece of apple pie in a small cafeteria and set out to walk to the Lincoln Memorial. When Bernhard asked why Lincoln meant so much to her, Anna had told him that the only history lessons she could remember were those about Honest Abe. He had made such an impression on her that she had learned the Gettysburg Address by heart, although it had not been required by her teacher. She had been inspired not only by the words and the simple eloquence of the facsimile document that was printed in her history book, but also by the handwriting of the president. It had been clear, steady, and graceful without unnecessary embellishments.

When they reached the Memorial, after a longer walk than anticipated, they climbed the steps up to the statue of Lincoln in his chair. A sign at the top supplied interesting facts about Lincoln's presidency and pointed out, among other things, that the number of steps, exactly 87, reflected the famous "Four score and seven years ago...", the first words of the Gettysburg Address, which had represented the years at that time since the founding of the nation. Bernhard asked Anna if she could still quote the rest of the text.

She tried, "...our fathers brought forth upon this continent a new nation, conceived in liberty and dedication to the proposition that all men are created equal...Now we are engaged in a great civil war..." She was unable to go any further, but they found the entire Gettysburg Address carved into the wall inside the Memorial building and read it together. Back outside, Bernhard took a photograph of Anna standing at the base of the statue and smiling broadly.

By the Time You Are Married

For the rest of her life Anna read everything she could find about her favorite president and at some point started calling herself a "student of Lincoln".

They walked to the Washington Monument but declined to enter it saying it was impressive enough to walk down the Mall toward it and then stand outside and crane their necks looking up. They sat on a bench and watched the long shadow stretch toward the Capitol until they were ready to go back to their car. It was getting dark.

They were exhausted from all the walking and when they reached the cafeteria where they had had their coffee in the afternoon, they noticed that it was still open. There was a sign in the window, advertising a soup and sandwich menu. They did not need any more encouragement than that and went inside. There were no other customers, but the woman who had served their coffee was still there. She said they did not close for another half hour at seven o'clock and yes, of course, there was plenty of soup, tomato or chicken noodle, whichever they wanted. "I can make you some baloney sandwiches, no grilled cheese since I've already cleaned the grill. The soup is still hot, so tell me what you want, make up your minds quick before I take my apron off and start clearing the cash register."

39

The Capitol

The next morning, just after seven am, Anna and Bernhard were back in the cafeteria. Bernhard was standing in line with a tray to order two plates of scrambled eggs, bacon, and toast, while Anna was making sure no one took the table they had been lucky to get. It had turned out to be an extremely popular breakfast venue. Businessmen and government employees sat drinking coffee, eating platefuls of food, and poring over the latest copies of their newspapers.

When Bernhard came with the tray, Anna got up to get coffee from a dispenser. He pulled his chair back and found a copy of the Washington Post that someone had left on the seat. As he sat down he looked at a headline on the front page, "Hitler and Mussolini meet in Salzburg". Muttering a Swedish expression of disgust and condemnation, "*förbaskada!*" he slapped the paper down on another empty chair at the table before Anna arrived with the coffee. He smiled stiffly up at her, determined to be cheerful, but she had seen what he did with the paper and was curious…

"Was that today's paper? Anything of interest?" she asked.

"Yes, but it looked dirty, you know grease spots... Doesn't this look good?" He stabbed the eggs with his fork as she buttered her toast and they started eating.

"Hmm, yes, this is good! The eggs are light and fluffy." Anna answered. She looked around at the other people seated all around them and leaned forward to whisper, "I wonder if there are any important politicians here now."

"If FDR was here," Bernhard said, "I'd recognize him, I've seen him in the papers and the newsreels at the movies. And Mayor LaGuardia, but I don't think I'd know anyone else."

Anna looked at Bernhard. "What would LaGuardia be doing here today?"

She wondered what he was trying to hide from her and did not think it was grease spots on a newspaper. Then she realized it was not the first time he had hidden a newspaper from her recently or turned off the radio when the war news was reported, which was almost constantly.

When they finished breakfast, they took the tray with their empty dishes and placed it on a rack near the door. Anna went over to the line of people still waiting for food and tried to peek between them into the kitchen, but soon came back when a man who was annoyed and evidently thought she wanted to butt in told her, "You have to go to the end of the line like everybody else, Lady".

Bernhard was watching, ready to intervene, but Anna shrugged it off, saying something about the man just having a bad day and that he had a New York accent.

Then she said, "I can't see our friend Rosie anywhere. Maybe she works afternoons, or she's off for the weekend. I would have liked to thank her, but we'd better get going."

Last night, after preparing their soup and sandwiches, the woman who had seemed so gruff at first had asked them where they were from. When she heard they had spent all winter in Florida and were on the way back to New York for the summer, she told them she hoped they knew how lucky they were. They had talked for a few minutes until a man came in and asked for a cup of coffee. Bernhard had asked her about the flag over the White House and learned that it flew there every day, no matter where the President was.

Later, when they were paying the bill, she asked where they were staying. Bernhard said they were looking for a hotel nearby that was not too expensive. She reached into a drawer under the cash register and, after rummaging around a bit, found and handed them a card. "This is a nice little guest house. Just around the block. Fair prices, nice and clean. Lots of people who stay there, work during the week and go home for the weekend. It's Friday night, so they should have vacancies." She smiled and said, "Tell them I recommended their place to you. I'm Rosie."

They had followed her advice, walked around the block, and found the guest house with a neon sign burning dimly over the entrance ("Turn Inn"). They got a room and slept well after perusing a map and a pamphlet telling them what not to miss while in the nation's capital that the man at the reception desk had given them. After Bernhard mentioned who had sent them there, he also gave them a bus schedule and a discount coupon for the parking lot, so they were able to leave the car overnight at a reduced twenty-four-hour rate. As he gave them the key to their room, he said, "Rosie makes a good breakfast, too."

They went to the car to put their overnight bag back in the trunk and check to make sure that they still had the morning's parking covered. Then they set out once again, turning left on Constitution Avenue this time to walk toward the Capitol. Bernhard took his camera and Anna took his big umbrella. She had a feeling that the weather might be changing.

One thing quickly became clear as they approached the National Mall. Weekends meant tourists and there were already more about than the day before. It was cloudy but not raining when they reached the Capitol and walked up a pathway through the trees toward the steps that led to the entrance of the impressive building. The sun peeked over the dome between gathering clouds as they climbed the steps. Inside, they stood silently for a while in awe at the grandeur of the place.

There were signs that directed them to the Crypt, which was at the center of the architecture of the building, under the dome, just as the Capitol had been designed as the center of the city. Anna had read aloud about that to Bernhard in their hotel room the evening before and was looking forward to seeing it. With other tourists, a family, and some soldiers on leave with their girlfriends or wives, she and Bernhard followed the signs and entered the strange chamber that was called the Crypt. A guide was lecturing to a group of young students, so Anna took Bernhard's hand and whispered, "Let's listen to him."

They heard about the thirteen statues, one from each of the original states in the union and about the many columns in the middle of the room, that support the entire structure of the building. After a while, as more people came, they went upstairs to the Rotunda, hoping it was not yet as crowded, to look up at the dome high above the hall. They had read about the painting in the top of the dome called "The Apotheosis of Washington", a glorification that they say President Washington would never have approved of. In his will he had explicitly rejected the suggestion that he be buried in the Capitol building as many of his admirers had wanted and his final wishes were respected.

The painting was enormous, and they stared up at it for a few minutes, trying to figure out what they were seeing. Prominent historical persons and events were portrayed along with Greek gods and, in the center, surrounded by thirteen women who represent the original thirteen states, sat George Washington.

As the school class came into the Rotunda with their guide, Anna and Bernhard decided to move on. Going back down the stairs they encountered another big group of students. A whole school class of teenagers was coming up, following another guide, who was having difficulty reigning in some of the boys. He managed to clear room on the stairs for them and shook his head apologetically as they passed by.

When they went from there to the House of Representatives, the larger of the two Houses of Congress, Bernhard read one of the signs posted outside while Anna sat on a bench resting for a few minutes. After a moment, he went over and sat down next to her, saying, "Well, if I wanted to, I could run for congressman in Bay Ridge, Brooklyn, in three years."

"Would you want to do that?" Anna asked.

He laughed and said, "No, of course not, but I could, theoretically, at least. It says on that sign over there that you can run for congress if you have been a citizen for seven years. I never thought about that before. You have to be twenty-five years old, too. But that requirement I filled a long time ago."

"That means I could run too, Bernhard. I wonder how many women are in the congress."

After a tiny, barely noticeable hesitation, he said, "Of course, honey, you could run, too."

Anna smirked at her husband. "I would not want to," she said. "But I'm sure plenty of highly qualified women would."

They looked inside at the long rows of empty seats and tried to imagine what it would be like if Congress were in session. Recently there had been reports in the news on debates about a bill to provide unemployment and education benefits for soldiers coming home from the war. The so-called GI Bill was also supposed to help soldiers' families to buy homes and set up businesses.

By the Time You Are Married

When they went to the Senate, they were surprised to find that there was official business taking place, so they went to sit in the gallery for a while and watched as the few Senators present discussed procedural questions. It was not a topic that interested Anna and Bernhard, but before they left they found another sign from which they learned that Anna was eligible to run for the Senate, but that Bernhard would have to wait a few years. They both laughed and decided they had had enough of government and Washington D.C. for the day and that it might be time to get back on the road north.

Standing in the entrance area of the Capitol building, they could see people shaking out umbrellas as they came in. It was not raining heavily, but steadily, so the weather made the decision easy for them. They did not want to walk all the way back to the car in the rain. Anna opened her bag and took out the bus schedule while Bernhard stored his camera securely in its carrycase and hitched it over his shoulder. They asked a police guard about the closest bus stop and then set right out, huddled together under Bernhard's big black umbrella to find it.

40

Back in Brooklyn

It was well after midnight when they arrived in Brooklyn and parked the car in the street outside their Bay Ridge apartment building. For Bernhard, the most exhausting part of their trip had been the very last stretch. Pleased that they had reached the Staten Island Ferry to 69th Street just in time for the last crossing to Brooklyn, they had driven on board and then watched as half a dozen other cars drove on and parked close behind them. Then the ferry should have left the harbor at 10pm, but, except for one sudden jolt when the engines started and then went right off again, nothing else happened for half an hour until an announcement came over loudspeakers saying there was a mechanical problem. Passengers were informed that repairs had to be carried out before they could set sail and that that could take a couple of hours. In the cars behind them some drivers became angry. They got out of their cars and demanded furiously to be allowed to reverse back down the runway. They were told that was impossible and soon quieted down. Bernhard was equally impatient and wanted to leave the ferry to drive over to the 59th Street ferry only fifteen or twenty minutes away. He went to have a look. He soon came back, cussing softly, to tell Anna he could see why the irate drivers had eventually given up. The boat was about yard away from the dock with its ramp jammed at an angle, probably caused when the boat had lurched unexpectedly.

"Well then, there's no use in getting upset," Anna said. "After all, our long trip is over, we're safe and sound and almost home." Having said that, she leaned over the pile of belongings between them on the front seat and put her head on Bernhard's shoulder. Soon she went to sleep, or should we say back to sleep. She had been sleeping before they reached the ferry port, knowing he would not need any navigation support driving through Staten Island. So, along with everyone else on the ferry, they waited until the engines finally started up and they chugged off, crossing the Verrazzano Narrows toward Bay Ridge, Brooklyn.

Bernhard gazed sleepily at the Statue of Liberty in the distance. The lights in the crown were flashing "dot-dot-dot-dash", a morse code V for Victory in Europe. He thought about how he had arrived in New York eighteen years before, unable to speak English, about how he had learned the language and earned his citizenship. Anna snored faintly into his right ear, as he sat in the driver's seat, feeling not only exhaustion but, at the same time, also a deep sense of satisfaction, an awareness that he was on his way to realizing his own personal version of the American Dream.

Home at last, they started emptying the car and lugging their things up the two flights of stairs. Anna carried their small overnight bag, her handbag, and a paper bag containing a tiny cactus plant that she had rescued from the kitchen window moments before they left Lake Worth. Upstairs in their apartment everything looked fine, as if they had never been gone, Bernhard said. Then, as he went out the door, "You sit down, Anne, you've carried enough. I'll get the rest of our things."

He quickly emptied the car, locked it, and put everything in the lobby to carry up in a few, well organized trips. Then he noticed the dumbwaiter cabinet next to the staircase and thought there might be a better way to transport their things. Smiling at his own ingenuity he summoned the dumbwaiter and packed it with the heaviest items and sent it on its way. Unfortunately, the little service elevator merely groaned after moving a few feet upward and then fell crashing into the basement below the lobby. The noise awakened the janitor, who came out, very alarmed and in his pajamas. When he saw what had happened, he chided Bernhard, "This dumbwaiter is not designed to carry heavy items up! The trash goes down all right, but the garbage cans that go back up are empty. Please don't try that again, Mr. Linden!"

Bernhard apologized politely and even managed to smile through gritted teeth as he turned to go down the stairs to the basement to retrieve the things, their heaviest things, the sewing machine, a cast iron frying pan and a box containing two or three books that Anna had taken along to read in Florida and wanted to pass on to her sisters. So now these things needed to be carried up not two but three flights of stairs. He hoped that the Singer sewing machine was not broken. It looked all right as far as he could see and certainly was sturdily made and safely packed in its portable case. Nonetheless, he worried because he knew Anna wanted to start sewing things for the baby. He said nothing to her about the little incident and would keep his fingers crossed for the time being.

When he was finished and closed the apartment door for the night, Anna had already unpacked half of the luggage. He got ready for bed and then wondered what was taking Anna so long. He watched her walk back and forth from the living room to the bedroom a couple of times and then asked her what she was doing.

"I'm trying to figure out where we should put the crib," she said.

"The what?" he asked.

"The baby's bed. We call that a 'crib'. What do you call it in Swedish?"

"*Sängen, barnsängen, tror jag,*" (Bed, child's bed, I guess) Bernhard said, distractedly, "but, Honey, it's almost two o'clock in the morning!"

"Oh, of course, Dear. I guess there's plenty of time. We have to buy the crib and I have to start sewing the bed clothes. They're easy to sew on my Singer, lots of straight seams. Don't know what colors though. Blue and pink are out of the question since we don't know…"

Bernhard winced at the mention of the sewing machine, but said, sighing, "I think we have plenty of time to do all those things. Come to bed now."

Almost two months later, everyone was talking about D-Day. The news started coming in a few days after Bernhard's birthday, reporting how British, American, and Canadian forces had landed on the beaches of Normandy. So much had gone wrong with the complicated military strategy for so-called operation Neptune. First, the weather had forced a one-day postponement, then Allied bombers had been unable to do any substantial damage to the defense wall along Normandy's coast. Horrific fighting went on for almost a week and took a brutal toll on soldiers' lives – more than 4,400 Allied troops died on D-Day alone, something Dwight D. Eisenhauer would never in his lifetime mention without tears in his eyes they say – before the five beaches were securely linked under Allied command on June 12th. The tremendous and costly effort would be considered by history to have been the "beginning of the end of World War II".

When Bernhard came home from work one evening

another month later, he was full of the latest news about the war. He had been talking to two men on the subway who agreed with him that it was beginning to sound more positive. There were new rumors about resistance in Berlin, about an attempt to assassinate Hitler.

He found Anna sitting in the living room, next to the telephone, sewing a lace hem on a tiny pillowcase, by hand. She looked slightly perturbed for some reason and he had a pang of bad conscience, wondering if the sewing machine had given up, although he knew she had been using it just days before.

"You're sewing by hand? Why aren't you using the machine?" he asked, as he gave his wife a peck on the cheek.

"Hello, Dear," Anna said, "No, this lace is much too delicate. I wouldn't dare use the machine on this. It would snag."

Bernhard put the newspaper on the couch next to Anna and went to the kitchen to get himself a drink. He peeked into the pot where something was simmering on the stove.

"Oh, I've just been talking to Vivian," Anna called out to him. "They have a healthy little girl, born last night. I am so happy for them!" Then, after a short pause, she went on, "They've named her Christine."

"Did you say 'Christine'?" Bernhard asked, as he came back from the kitchen.

"Yes."

"Oh…. But that's…"

"I know. Funny, isn't it? I never discussed names with Vivian. To think we picked the same name for our baby… if it's a girl!"

"Maybe it will be a boy. Anyway, there is plenty of time to pick another name, isn't there. We could still use that as a middle name, couldn't we?"

"Of course, I just wish I hadn't been imagining little Christine for a month now. Silly, isn't it? But, as you say, there's plenty of time and the main thing is that Vivian and her baby are both fine." Anna got up and went to the kitchen to see how the potato soup was faring. She wanted to drop two small sausages into it to round it out a bit.

Bernhard followed her into the kitchen to show her an article in the newspaper's evening edition entitled "Light at the End of the Tunnel?" Soon he would be wishing he had not mentioned hopeful news that would almost immediately be squelched.

The next day the world learned that Graf Claus von Stauffenberg had already been executed, just hours after a failed attempt to overthrow the government in Berlin. It was the beginning of a brutal purge of courageous German patriots who had plotted to free the country and Europe from the Nazis' stranglehold.

That was not the only reversal of good news into bad. A short time later, Anna and Bernhard received a cheerful announcement saying that Vivian had given birth to little Christine, only to be shocked two weeks later by the devastating news that this healthy baby, had died in her crib for no apparent reason. The strange diagnosis, explaining nothing at all, was termed "sudden crib death".

41

October 1944

As Bernhard went through the door to the entrance of Shore Road Hospital, in his haste, he almost tripped over the slightly raised threshold. He was the first visitor to go up to the reception desk that morning and had never in his lifetime experienced such extreme mixed emotions. He had just the night before become the proud father of a little girl whose birth had almost cost the life of her mother, his dear wife Anna. At ten o'clock in the evening, Dr. Johnston had finally come out into the hall where Bernhard had been sitting on a bench and waiting since early afternoon with a bouquet of wilting flowers. A nurse had tried to persuade him to go to the cafeteria for a bite to eat, but he had been unwilling to leave his post. She had come back later with a cup of coffee for him from the staff kitchen. Anna's sister Helen had come and kept him company for a while in the early afternoon and almost driven him crazy with her repeated efforts to reassure him. "Don't worry, she'll be fine, you'll see," she had said too many times, it seemed to him. Nonetheless, he had felt deserted and frustrated after she left to catch a train back to Park Slope where Bertha and Frank were taking care of her little three-year old Siggi.

He had been about to despair when the doctor had at long last come wearily up to him and said in a rasping, hoarse voice, "Congratulations, Mr. Linden, your little daughter is healthy... But your wife, I'm afraid...." He had paused, and then said hesitatingly, echoing Helen's words in Bernhard's head, "Don't worry, she'll be fine. But she's in no condition to see you or accept your flowers right now..." He turned to the nurse who had come out with him and gestured to her to get a vase to put Bernhard's flowers in. "It will be hours before she comes out of the narcosis..." In a shaky voice he went on, "I think I told you it was a breech birth, I don't know if you know what that is," he looked at Bernhard, who shook his head, "well, that is always difficult... But to tell you the truth, Mr. Linden, in my opinion, your wife..." He shook his head as he turned to go, saying Bernhard should come by his office in the morning when he came to the hospital to visit Anna and then he would explain what had happened.

It was eight o'clock in the morning. The reception desk was just opening when Bernhard approached and asked where he would find Mrs. Anna Linden. The gray-haired lady behind the desk had just arrived as well and not yet taken off her coat. When she did, she consulted her directory of new admissions for what seemed to him a long and tedious moment and then asked, "Mr. Linden?" When he nodded impatiently, she said, "Congratulations! I see a new member of your family was born yesterday!"

Then, with a big smile, she directed Bernhard to the maternity ward, saying, "Your wife is upstairs in room 211."

Bernhard took two steps at a time, climbing the stairs. As he was about to knock on the door, a nurse came toward him and asked which patient he wanted to visit.

When he told her, she looked at the charts on the door and said that it would be better for him to come back in the afternoon. Nonetheless, seeing his disappointment, she went in and came back to say he should not stay too long, not more than ten minutes.

He found Anna asleep in the bed next to the window, where sunlight was streaming in through the venetian blinds, casting stripes of light and shadow across her bed's white covers. Two other women in the room were sitting up and talking in hushed voices. One of them smiled and motioned to him with one finger in front of her lips. "Shhh! Don't wake her," she said, shaking her head. "They just wheeled her in here about an hour ago."

So, he stood silently, holding his breath, and looked at Anna. She looked so transparent that he wanted to touch her to be sure she was real and ... alive! He did not touch her, however, because he could see the covers rise and fall with her breath and did not want to wake her. For a moment he chided himself, *"Det är dum, fånig!"* (That's stupid, silly!") for even thinking she could be dead. What would she be doing in this maternity ward if she were dead? Women did not die having children here in America the way he had heard of often in the old country, or did they? He frowned as he threw Anna a kiss and turned to go, intending to go directly downstairs to find out where Dr. Johnston's office was when the woman who had smiled as he came in got up from her bed, wrapping her robe tightly around her and slipping her feet into a pair of slippers.

"Have you seen your baby?... Do you want me to show you where the newborns are? I'm going there now anyway to see my little boy. They won't be bringing them to us for another hour or so."

Bernhard, who might have forgotten that there was someone else here that he wanted to see besides his wife, looked at her in surprise and then said, nodding, "Oh, yes, thank you, that would be nice of you."

He followed her down the hall to a big window. There, behind the window, he saw a dozen bassinets with, as far as he could tell, identical babies sleeping in half of them. The only difference was the blue or pink ribbon on the side of each tiny bed. It was daunting. As far as he could tell none of the babies looked anything like Anna.

"That's your little one, if I'm not mistaken, a girl, right?" asked the woman, pointing to a bassinet in the second row. "That's my little boy and Mrs. Higgins' little girl, all with our room number, 211, on the foot end."

Bernhard just stared in inexplicable astonishment as the bundle that must be his daughter stretched a tiny arm and fist.

"It's hard to see them from here. We don't get a good look until they bring them for feeding. That will be in about an hour. I imagine you won't see her properly until you take her and your wife home."

"Ja, so," said Bernhard, nodding helplessly. He stood next to the woman for a few minutes, each of them looking at their respective babies. There was not much to be seen, just two or three inches below a cap revealing a miniature nose and cheeks, certainly no resemblance to anyone in the family.

"How do they tell them apart?" Bernhard asked. "They all look alike!"

She laughed and said, "Not up close, they don't. And they wear little bracelets with their surnames on them." She smiled and looked at her watch before she turned to walk back to the room.

"Thank you very much!" he called after her.

"You're welcome! And congratulations!"

"The same to you!" Bernhard said. He looked at his own watch and decided to go and look for Dr. Johnston's office, planning to come back up to see if Anna was awake after that. Feeling a new kind of pride and looking curiously forward to what the future might bring, he went down the stairs. He had no idea that he was in for a surprise that morning and that it would not be a pleasant one.

Downstairs he once again approached the reception

desk behind which the gray-haired woman was now standing and talking with two nurses. One was whispering to her while the other stood to one side, quietly crying. Bernhard hesitated, not wanting to be impolite, but when the receptionist turned and saw him she asked if he had not found his wife's room.

"No," he answered, "I mean yes, but she was sleeping, and I didn't want to wake her... Now I'm looking for her doctor's office. He wanted me to come by this morning."

She looked at him distractedly as the two nurses walked down the hall and asked which doctor he wanted to see. When he said, "Dr. Johnston" she looked startled and hurried after the nurses, saying, "Wait here, please."

The older of the two nurses came back with her and said, "Mr. Linden, would you please come with me."

Bernhard followed her down the hall to a door with a sign on it that read: "Dr. Johnston, M.D., Obstetrics and Gynecology." She opened it and they both went in. Then she closed that door and went past the waiting room to another door, which she opened without knocking, and which lead into Dr. Johnston's office. She motioned to a chair and surprised Bernhard by going over to sit behind the doctor's desk.

"Please sit down, Mr. Linden," she said as she picked up the folder that was lying in the middle of the desk on the ink pad and opened it. She took out a document for a moment and studied it while Bernhard waited. He saw the stripes on her nurse's cap and the "Supervising Nurse M. Gates" badge on her uniform pocket.

Then he was shocked when she looked up at him and said grimly, "I don't know if you have heard, but Doctor Johnston died last night, or... early this morning."

Stunned, Bernhard did not know what to say. He just stared at her, thinking he might not have understood.

But she took a deep breath and went on to say sadly, "We are devastated. He had a heart attack. His wife called the hospital at three a.m. when he didn't come home last night. And the night emergency team found him sitting here, slouched over his desk. They couldn't do anything to save him. It was too late."

Bernhard shook his head slowly, murmuring that he was sorry. He was horrified, but all he could think about was that he did not know how to express proper condolences in English. He had not experienced the death of anyone he knew in America, the last death having been that of his mother before he left Sweden. He could have responded appropriately in Swedish, but, of course, that was no help.

"Let me say that I don't want to make any connection here with Dr. Johnston's death. It's such a shame, because he was retiring at the end of this year," She looked at Bernhard intensely, "but your little daughter's birth was an extremely difficult one."

"He tried to tell me something about that last night, but I didn't understand what...," Bernhard mumbled.

"It was a breech birth. That means the baby was so positioned as to be born feet first and could not be turned. That can be fatal for both mother and child. Cesarean operation – making an incision into the abdomen and removing the baby – is being used more safely nowadays, but it's still a matter of last resort. Since Dr. Johnston's colleague was not available, he was on his own last night and decided against a cesarean. Unfortunately, it was even more difficult than anticipated."

Bernhard squirmed uncomfortably in his seat, "Do you mean that Dr. Johnston's death was…"

"No, I don't mean anything of the kind." She interrupted him sharply. "Of course not, it is just very unfortunate!"

After a pause, she went on, "Your wife and your baby daughter are going to be fine, Mr. Linden. We will keep them here for as long as is necessary. It's amazing how fast young mothers recuperate when they get their babies in their arms. No pain is forgotten as swiftly as the pain of giving birth. But Dr. Johnston made a note here to tell you that your wife might not survive another breech birth if she were to become pregnant again. There will be internal scarring that would cause difficulties for any birth."

Bernard listened somberly, frowning. He knew that would be a disappointment for Anna, but he, himself, had no desire to have a big family. Where he grew up, big families were not rare but often meant poverty. Now he was mainly worried that he might not be able to take his little family with him to Florida in two weeks as planned. The Palm Beach salon was expecting him to be there for the start of the winter season.

"Is she going to be well enough to travel in November?" he asked… "and the baby?"

"Travel? Well, we shall see, Mr. Linden. Short trips… For the time being, she will need plenty of rest. Don't rush her. The baby will be fine. Do you have any other questions?" Then, when he could not come up with any, at least none that she could answer for him, she stood up from Dr. Johnston's chair, indicating that she had finished.

"If you do think of anything, the nurses on the ward and Dr. Blake, our other obstetrician, will be glad to help you in any way that they can." Then, walking toward the door, she said with an almost rueful smile, "Your little girl will always want to stand on her own two feet. That's my prognosis."

42

For the next week, Bernhard came to see Anna late every afternoon or early evening on his way home from work. Bertha and Frank also came to the hospital to visit with their daughter and to see the baby. Helen came by again for a short visit before having to return to Connecticut on the weekend.

Anna made a surprisingly quick recovery. Nurse Bates had been right about that.

There was only one day when Anna seemed less than cheerful when Bernhard arrived a little earlier. That was the second day after the birth. She was sitting up in her bed, her hands clenched to fists, looking extremely upset, in fact furious. He did not remember ever having seen her such a state.

As he walked down the hall, one of the nurses at the ward station told him he was just in time to get a closer look at his daughter and he was looking forward to that. Until then the baby had been in her basinet on the other side of the window, too far away for him to see properly, and already bedded for the night.

"What's the matter, Anne?" he asked, realizing that she could, of course, still be in pain, but thinking she looked more angry than suffering.

Anna looked at him in wide-eyed exasperation and said something he could not understand.

"How could anyone think I wouldn't know my own baby?"

Bernhard frowned, confused, but before he could say anything in response, the door opened and a nurse bustled in, carrying a screaming baby. "I'm so sorry, Mrs. Linden. These things do happen, but, of course, you are right. That's why we put the little bracelets on their arms the moment the newborns arrive in the nursery. Nurse Greene hasn't been working here very long."

Anna's indignation disintegrated, as she reached out her arms for the baby they had decided to name Mimi Christine. The nurse left, only to reappear a moment later with another crying baby on her arm for one of the other women and a bottle of baby formula.

Bernhard went up to Anna, almost feeling like he should tiptoe and looking awestruck.

"If you go and wash your hands at the sink in the corner, you can hold her," she said, now smiling proudly at him. When he came back, she showed him the tiny, beaded bracelet on the baby's wrist, with the letters:

"l*i* n* d* e* n – g*i*r*l"

printed on the beads and said, "I didn't realize she was wearing this identification bracelet. It's under her little sleeve most of the time. But I don't need this to recognize our little Mimi Christine…. Isn't she beautiful?"

Shaking her head in indignant annoyance, she said, "They brought me someone else's baby! How could that happen? And then that nurse tried to convince me that I was wrong! Here, hold her for a moment while I get ready to feed her."

Bernhard drew back, thinking she did not look very pretty, red-faced and screaming. He said, "But she doesn't want me to hold her. She's crying!"

"She's hungry," Anna said and reached the bundled baby over to him. "Hold her like this… Be sure to always support her head… I'll just be a minute." As he took the baby, reluctantly, trying to gently rock it back and forth – he remembered dimly how his mother and sisters had done with his six years younger brother Hans to quiet him – Anna started opening the buttons of her nightgown's bodice. Bernhard did not know where to look in this situation and offered his extremely upset little daughter one finger by touching her hand. The tiny fist opened and immediately clutched his finger tightly, making him laugh in surprise. But, since she went on screaming, he soon handed her back to her mother.

Then the nurse came in bringing another baby for one of the other mothers and said, "I'm afraid you'll have to leave now, Mr. Linden. You can wait out in the hall, or maybe have a coffee down in the cafeteria, and then come back in half an hour. Fathers can't be here while the babies are being fed."

So, Bernhard had followed her advice. After his coffee and a soggy pastry in the cafeteria, he had gone back upstairs to sit and talk with Anna. Then, on his way out, he had gone by the nursery window and stopped to look at his little daughter, who was sleeping peacefully in her basinet. "I guess I'll never have a son," he thought to himself, "and I won't be teaching a little girl how to hunt wild turkeys, will I?! But there will be other things to teach her in Florida, to swim and maybe play tennis. But then she might be as disinterested in sports as Anna.

The other evenings with Anna at the hospital had been less eventful because he usually arrived too late to see his daughter in action. One evening he brought his sister Mimi along to meet the latest member of the Linden clan. She and Harry had driven the long trip down from the farm in

Rochester despite an early snowstorm. Harry did not come to the hospital, but Mimi was delighted to see her little namesake, even if only through the nursery window.

"I now have two new nieces!" she said proudly, "It's been over ten years since Svea and August had their little girl. There don't seem to be any brothers and sisters for her on the way either," she commented. "What a shame that there aren't any little boys yet to carry on the Lindín name! But that can of course change!" she said beaming at Anna, who smiled and blushed.

"We're staying with Hans and Margaret," she went on, "where I can spend more time getting to know Janice, too. She's three months old and crawling about now, you know. But I wanted to see little Mimi before you all go back to Florida. When will you be leaving?"

That question touched directly on the main topic of most of Bernhard and Anna's recent conversations. Bernhard was expected to be in Florida by mid-November and they both were worried that it would be too early for a new mother and a tiny infant to take such a long trip in the car. He needed to tell Miss Arden when he could go down to the Palm Beach salon but knew, if that was too long off, he risked losing the job there, something he did not want to let happen. The sun was shining in Florida and winter was already beginning in New York. "Florida is the healthiest place to bring up children," he argued when he explained his viewpoint to Anna.

She, on the other hand, was reluctant to leave her family and friends in Brooklyn when she was just starting out as a young mother. "I'm not a pioneer, Bernhard!" she said during one of their discussions. That made him laugh, but he realized she was serious about not traveling south.

The day after that discussion, Anna's parents called on the phone to ask Bernhard how she was doing. During that conversation, Frank mentioned that they now had efficient heating in the Connecticut house and would be going there more often. He said they were thinking of giving up the house in Brooklyn because it was too much work to keep both. That information gave Bernhard another argument for his "Healthy Life in Florida" campaign, almost a trump in his hand because Anna's parents would not be nearby much of the time that winter if they were out in Connecticut.

Nonetheless, a week after he had brought Anna and Mimi Christine home to the Brooklyn apartment, he still did not know what to do. Perhaps for the first time in his life, he was feeling nervous. Anna was not getting much sleep at night – nor for that matter was Bernhard, although he did eventually learn to roll over and go back to sleep – so, she was exhausted. When the pully on the line that she used to hang out the wash from the kitchen window broke, she could not keep up with the laundry. In desperation she joined a diaper service that her friend upstairs used for her one-year-old baby boy. Marian had recommended it to her, saying, "They invented this for women working in the war industry and we might as well take advantage of it, too, Anne."

The stacks of clean diapers lifted Anna's spirits, and soon she was trying to make use of the many too many diapers provided. They could be used as dust cloths, she discovered, dish towels, and even as a head scarf to keep her hair out of her eyes.

A few days after the first diaper delivery, Bernhard had an appointment to talk with his boss, Elizabeth Arden herself, about the winter season in Palm Beach. He had already told the New York salon manager that he was not sure he could start the job in Florida on the planned date in November and might need to be staying on in New York. But now Miss Arden was in the city for a few days and wanted to speak with him. Climbing the stairs to her office, he felt heavy hearted. The timing was all wrong and it was about to ruin his dream for the future. He bit his lip as he approached the door and then gave himself a three second pep talk. This was the job he wanted, he just had to think positively. Determined to do so, he knocked on the door.

Miss Arden was sitting at her desk. She looked up from her paperwork and said, smiling, "Hello, Mr. Bernard. I must congratulate you! I hear you are the proud father of a little girl. What have you named her?" He sensed immediately it somehow was not going to be as difficult as he had feared.

43

A Bumpy Journey

A month later, at about half past eight in the morning, Bernhard was in Lake Worth, talking to Elisabeth Worsely about the crib and the changing table she had been able to find for him in a second-hand furniture shop in town. They had been in almost perfect condition and would only require a bit of paint on one side of the little bed that could be turned toward the wall anyway. The mattress was brand new. Elisabeth had covered it with a moisture repellant sheet that Anna had purchased in Brooklyn and included in the box of baby bed linen she gave Bernhard to take with him in the car when he drove south in November. Bernhard had picked up the two pieces of furniture at the shop the evening before and then hauled them up the stairs to the little apartment where the J. B. Lindens were going to spend another Florida winter. Elisabeth was advising him as to where to put the bed, saying the baby should sleep in the corner where there would be no draught, but plenty of fresh air. Bernhard felt relieved that everything was ready after all, at last minute, and he could pick up his wife and baby daughter at the airport in the evening and not have to make any excuses.

It was Miss Arden who had solved the problem of how to get Bernhard and his family to Florida without delaying the Palm Beach salon's winter season opening. She had told him to "get on with it", to drive down as soon as possible, and gave him a bonus and Anna a voucher for a flight with Eastern Airlines whenever she wanted to go. She assured him that her Manhattan shop manager would see to it that Anna and her baby would be picked up and transported to Newark Airport on the chosen date. She gave her word that they would be treated "like royalty".

And so, while Bernhard was getting everything ready in Lake Worth for his little family's arrival, Anna was sitting on an Eastern Air Lines plane, underway to the Lantana landing strip six miles south of West Palm Beach with her baby asleep on her lap. The tiny airport was being used for private and commercial transport since Eastern's bigger Morrison Field airport, which would later become Palm Beach International, had been converted into an Army Air Base following the Pearl Harbor attack. When the United States joined in the European war effort, the West Palm Beach air base became an important military transport and training hub. Soon it would be considered the leading Winter Port of Embarkation for all major war fronts.

Bernhard had been skeptical about asking Anna to fly to Florida with the baby. After all, she had never been on an airplane before. Neither had he, for that matter, nor anyone else he knew, except his boss, Elizabeth Arden. He did not think his wife was timid, but this might require something akin to courage. And had she not only recently made it clear that she was, as she put it, "not a pioneer"?

Anna had been astounded at first, if not shocked, and hesitated when he told her the idea. She said she would rather travel by train. However, when Bernhard recounted all the arguments Miss Arden had used to support her idea, that it was no longer a novel means of transportation, that

Anna could get to Florida in one day by flying, and that she herself was sick of traveling to Europe by boat because it was so "time consuming", her final point seemed to convince Anna. Miss Arden had said they would win this war thanks to airplanes. Bernhard was not sure what that claim was based on but passed it on to Anna as part of his case.

Looking out the window of the plane at Newark Airport, Anna watched the propellers start turning faster and faster until they became invisible. She asked herself if she was in her right mind. What was she doing here? Taking her baby on an airplane was a ridiculous idea. She looked down at her Mimi Christine, sleeping peacefully on her lap. As the plane started moving, backing out of the gate, Anna was suddenly aware that it was too late to change her mind. Obviously.

She was afraid she might start crying, when a smiling, young woman wearing a smart Eastern Air uniform appeared at her side.

"Is everything all right, Mrs. Linden? I'm Amanda, your stewardess on this flight to Miami. We will be taking off in just a few minutes, as soon as we reach the runway. Is your seatbelt buckled under that little darling? My, she is getting her wings early!"

Anna just nodded, thinking, "Yes, much too early…", but then looked up and managed a smile. "Thank you," she said.

"I have to go to my seat now, too. I'll come back and check on you when we reach our cruising altitude. It could be a little bumpy until we get up there. But don't worry, just relax and let me know if you need anything."

Anna smiled, took a deep breath, and said thank you again. She felt exhausted after the last few days' preparations for the trip and having to get up at three in the morning to be ready when the limousine came to pick her up and drive her and Mimi Christine to the airport. She would take that woman's advice. What had she called herself, a stewardess? She would try to relax, she told herself. And she would think positively.

Across the aisle two older men in uniform sat talking in voices that were muffled by the sound of the plane's engines. She heard one of them say something about a "Commando" and thought they might be going to the newly constructed Pentagon that she and Bernhard had driven past on their trip north in the summer. She thought about the war going on far across the ocean in Europe, where German planes were dropping bombs on people hiding in houses in England and France. And allied planes were dropping bombs on people hiding in houses in Germany and France. Why couldn't wars be prevented, she wondered, would mankind never learn?.

In her handbag she had a letter that had come for Bernhard the day before, with a return address to Gerhart Schroder in Pennsylvania. That was the young fellow Bernhard had felt sorry for in training if she remembered correctly. So, he must be back from the war. She wondered where the other fellow, Joe, was now and if he was safe. She had not opened the letter, it was not addressed to her, so she did not know that it would tell Bernhard how Gerhart had been honorably discharged after being wounded in France in June and sent home with a Purple Heart and the use of only one of his legs. It also relayed the even sadder message about Joe's death in action in Italy, in the summer. According to a Fifth Army 45th Division report, more than half Joe's platoon had died in combat in an ill-fated struggle to liberate Rome.

Anna was already falling asleep when the stewardess came back with two pillows. One for her and one for the baby, "If you want to put her on the vacant seat next to you. Then you both might be more comfortable." Anna was grateful for the suggestion and together they got Mimi

Christine, who did not wake up, settled onto the other seat on one of the pillows. Anna stretched drowsily and rested her head on the other pillow, that she had placed so that she could lean onto it against the window. She heard the men across the aisle who were discussing the differences between the Curtiss Commando and the Douglas DC-3. Barely awake she now figured out that they were discussing types of airplanes, one of which was the kind they were flying in. It did not really interest her which one was which, as long as it stayed up in the air until it was supposed to land... Soon mother and child were both fast asleep.

A rather rough landing in Washington, D.C. half an hour later woke Anna and her baby. Mimi Christine's cries brought the stewardess to their side before the plane had come to a full stop. She apologized for the rude awakening, asking Anna if she would like some coffee and a snack, and if she should warm one of the bottles her colleague had put in the refrigerator for Anna as she boarded the plane. Anna said yes, please, but that she would wait with her coffee until her baby, who sobbed and hiccoughed dramatically to emphasize her own point of view, had calmed down. A few minutes later, the bottle had done the trick and the baby was sleeping peacefully again. Then, when a good number of passengers had left the plane and new passengers were boarding, the stewardess came back with a tray. On it there was a square shaped cup that would not tip over easily and a small, square bowl of donut hearts. She pulled down a table flap from the back of the seat next to Anna to place it on.

"Where is our next stop and how many stops will we be making?" Anna asked her when she came back to take the tray. She wondered if it was going to be as unnerving an experience the next time. Mimi Christine had gone back to sleep in her arms after her bottle, but if the next landing was as rough as the last, Anna thought she should perhaps keep her on her lap and not put her on the seat again.

"Don't worry, Mrs. Linden, we usually touch down much more smoothly than that. Of course, I can't promise you a smooth landing, it depends on the weather and other factors. Our next stop is in Charlotte, North Carolina. There could be a bit of turbulence… Now, are you going with us all the way to Miami?"

"No, I'm flying to West Palm Beach."

"Then we still have Richmond, Virginia, and then Atlanta, Georgia – where we have a two-hour layover, unfortunately," she said, cheerfully grimacing, "then Tallahassee, with another layover, and after that it's West Palm Beach. A long trip but at least you won't have to change planes."

The other stewardess called and motioned to her from the front of the plane and she hurried off, saying lunch would be served after the Charlotte stop.

Anna was still tired and thought she should try to sleep again while her baby was sleeping. It was Mimi Christine's best morning nap time, and she should take advantage of that. Gently, she placed her on the pillow again and dozed off within minutes, leaning against the window. This time Anna slept so soundly that she did not even notice the bouncing and swooping of the aircraft through high clouds.

She woke up to hear the captain announcing over the intercom that the plane would be landing in Charlotte in a few minutes and saying that passengers should remain seated with their seat belts fastened. He apologized for the rough flight and said that considerable sidewinds could make the landing difficult as well. "Nothing we can't handle, though, ladies and gentlemen! We're not taking enemy anti-aircraft fire, at least." Those joking remarks were meant to reassure the passengers, some of whom laughed, but they did not have that effect on Anna.

Already worried, as she stretched her arms and turned in her seat, she looked down toward the seat next to her and her heart stopped. The seat was empty. Her baby was gone!

Had Stewardess Amanda taken her for a walk while she was sleeping?

Anna looked around her in shock. People were talking in the rows in front and in back of her. Some were getting things from the overhead bins. The middle-aged couple who had taken the seats across the aisle that were vacated when the two military men disembarked in Washington were not looking in her direction, but out the window and trying to make out what they could see on the ground. When Anna looked at the floor, she saw the pillow lying there but no sign of her daughter. Terrified, she panicked and screamed, "Where is my baby?"

Passengers turned to look, and one of the stewardesses started coming down the aisle toward Anna, telling everyone to sit down and buckle their seat belts. Anna stood up, crying out almost hysterically, "My baby is gone!"

Before the stewardess could reach Anna's row, however, the middle-aged man to her left leaned across the aisle and pointed under her seat.

"No, no, no! Don't worry, Ma'am" he said, trying to calm Anna but at the same time looking quite amused, "He's fine. Let him sleep. I was wondering when you would wake up and notice. When he would start crying... He must have landed like Aladdin on his magic carpet. Softly. Didn't even wake up! He's been down there for at least five minutes."

Anna looked at him in horror. Then somehow, as the plane lurched about, she got down on her knees in the cramped space between seats, still extremely upset but strangely also aware of being ridiculously annoyed that that man had assumed her little girl was a boy.

But then she could see her. There she was, her Mimi Christine, in her quilted, pink sleeping bag, tucked under the seat, under the passenger parachute and lying on the floor, still asleep. The stewardess, whose name badge said "Nancy" also got down on her knees in the aisle, and she and Anna managed to retrieve the infant from her unlikely nest, unharmed but now awake and protesting the disturbance indignantly.

Just seconds before the plane careened down onto the landing strip in Charlotte, the stewardess fell haphazardly into a vacant seat a row ahead of Anna and sat down, struggling to fasten her seat belt. "Is she all right?" she asked, looking back apologetically. "We weren't expecting quite that much turbulence, or we would have asked you to keep her on your lap. I'll warm another bottle for her as soon as I can."

As if from a distance, between Mimi Christine's cries, Anna heard the voice of the stewardess and that of the woman sitting to her left, who was saying to her husband, "That's a girl, Henry, boys don't wear pink! And why didn't you tell me if you saw what happened?" Then his answer, "You know I'm color blind. And I didn't see the pillow lift off of the seat, like it must have done. I just saw the bundle roll off the pillow and under the seat. It was probably safer under there. What could we have done, anyway, while we were bouncing around like we were on a rollercoaster? He's...she's going to be fine."

The rest of the flight despite four more stopovers was uneventful by comparison. Both stewardesses, Amanda and Nancy, paid an unusual amount of attention to the mother and her six-week-old baby from then on. Other passengers came by to ask what had happened and express their astonishment when they heard the story. During the layover in Charlotte, the captain came to inquire about his youngest passenger and make sure that she was unharmed. He said there were no more storms to be expected further south and that Anna could continue to put her baby on the seat next to her. Anna smiled wanly, said nothing, but decided she was most certainly not going to follow his advice.

When the plane finally arrived at Lantana Airport and

the captain came to the exit to say goodbye to the passengers who were disembarking, he personally offered to help Anna carry her hand baggage and the baby down the rollaway staircase. Stewardess Nancy spoke up and said, "We'll take care of that, sir!" She was already holding the case with now empty baby bottles and the baby's blanket, while Amanda had taken the hand luggage. But Anna was not entrusting her baby to anyone and held her on her hip as she carefully descended the stairs, her other hand on the railing. Someone clapped when the captain told Anna that she and her baby had passed the qualified fliers' talent test with "flying colors" by not getting air sick despite half a dozen stopovers. Anna, feeling weary, found the fuss embarrassing and just wanted to get home to Bernhard. Nonetheless, she was grateful for all the help she could get.

The sun had just gone down. A few high clouds glowed golden pink above as dusk settled in. Although it was much cooler than when she had left Florida in the summer, it was much warmer than in Brooklyn, and a balmy breeze caused the tall palm trees on the other side of the security fence to sway gracefully. When Anna reached the bottom of the stairs and looked toward the almost ramshackle provisional terminal building, she heard a familiar two-tone whistle and noticed a lone figure standing apart, behind the fence next to the gate and waving a fedora. In the dim light she could recognize Bernhard, even sensing the broad smile on his face that she could not yet see. The two stewardesses accompanying her, asked who would be picking her up as they walked with her across the field. Anna smiled serenely and, looking toward the fence, said proudly, "My husband. He's over there."

*Here is a glimpse of what the reader can expect in
By the Time You Are Married, Volume III:*

Ten years later, when they are boarding a plane that will take them back to New York after a trip to visit with relatives in Sweden, Anna will tell her daughter about that first plane trip. Mimi Christine will laugh, imagining how it must have been. Then, as they sit on that plane, Anna will tell her about other early experiences her daughter has had before she was old enough to remember them. How, once when she was not yet able to walk, after her nap, she had climbed from her crib through the open window, out onto the fire escape of their Brooklyn apartment. Half-way up the treacherous metal steps on her way to visit her playmate upstairs, she was miraculously rescued by a fireman who lived across the street. He had just happened to look out his window, noticed the strange sight, ran to pull down the escape ladder, and climbed to the rescue.

After recounting several such personal anecdotes to her daughter, Anna will say something a child cannot understand. She will say, "Life can be a bumpy journey" without knowing how very true that will be for the rest of her own life. A few years later her sister-in-law Mimi will come to live with her and Bernhard in their house in Florida. Bernhard's unquestioned loyalty to his sister will cause a challenging situation which will go on for many years until Anna becomes a widow and asks her sister-in-law to find another place to live.

Anna was reluctant to move south to Florida and away from her family, but her parents and her sisters will follow her and Bernhard there not long afterward. Her father,

By the Time You Are Married

Frank, always eager to find new interests, will start painting in Florida. He paints landscapes and sells them like hotcakes at South Florida art festivals. Living for many years in that subtropical environment, his favorite motifs are not the palm trees or the luscious, colorful vegetation all around him, but the birch trees and the snow-covered landscapes he remembers from his childhood in Sweden.

ABOUT THE AUTHOR

Susan Emde was born in Brooklyn, New York but grew up in South Florida. She studied at Florida State University before going to Europe to study French and German at Université de Lausanne and Universität Heidelberg where she received teacher's diplomas for both languages. She taught and worked as a freelance translator in Germany until she moved to Majorca in 2002 where she and her husband spend the summer. They spend as much time as possible in the winter in Florida. She has three children and five grandchildren.

Made in the USA
Columbia, SC
08 December 2021